# Tahoe Destiny

**Books by J.L. Crafts**

**Will Toal Novels**
RailRoaded
Silver City Reckoning
Clear Cut Justice
Range War
Tahoe Destiny

**Coming Soon!**
**Will Toal Novels**
Break Out

**For more information
visit:** www.SpeakingVolumes.us

# Tahoe Destiny

## J.L. Crafts

SPEAKING VOLUMES, LLC
NAPLES, FLORIDA
2025

Tahoe Destiny

Copyright © 2021 by J.L. Crafts

All rights reserved. No part of this book may be reproduced or transmitted in any form or by any means without written permission.

ISBN 979-8-89022-260-2

This book and all the books in the Will Toal Series
are dedicated to the memory of William Jeffrey Crafts
October 28, 2003, to December 2, 2020

# Acknowledgments

*Thanks must always begin with to my wife of four decades, Colleen. More and more the time to write seems to impinge on other events in our lives. Colleen runs 'front' to protect time for me to work on that which I have come to love. She is always the first reader, first advisor. Nothing I do could be accomplished without her in my life.*

*Heartfelt thanks go out again to my editor, Diane Davis-White. Having worked with her now on multiple books, I cannot imagine getting a manuscript ready for publication without her. Professionalism and experience abound are delivered with gentle yet firm suggestions. She makes what might be tedious enjoyable.*

*I must also thank Dale Paris, our close friend and farrier for years. Though not an investigator in real life, he is the closest thing to a horse whisperer I've ever witnessed. Fabulous with our horses, he has reviewed all things equine in my books. His advice and approval are much appreciated. I've never seen him wear a bowler hat. But he does make showcase hand-manufactured knives which he sells at shows throughout the west.*

*To all my friends and family who volunteered their names. I hope I have done your characters justice.*

*To my first readers, Wayne Purcell, Dan Frisch, Linda Crafts, I cannot thank you enough. Your input and suggestions make a huge difference.*

*I again must thank Jim and Nancy Harrell for their contributions in creating a map of the not so fictional Carson Valley and Lake Tahoe to give the reader a glimpse of Will Toal's world.*

*The seminal battle over control of Lake Tahoe's crystal waters raged from 1865 to 1915. Only a mistake made in 1844 saved the Lady of the Lake and her remarkably pure water.*

*While many of the events and several of the people you will find in my tale did walk through history, I have compressed that true historical timeline and interplay of the personalities dramatically to fit the story here. My aim is to highlight the fascinating events over a three to four decade period that shaped the destiny of Lake Tahoe. For those concerned about my twists and turns of the historical timeline, I do my best to unravel the literary fancy in my Fact from Fiction section at the end of the book. I hope any historians who read the book will forgive the contrivances and enjoy the story which is mine and pure fiction.*

*J.L. Crafts*

*"Tahoe is surely not one but many. As I curve around its heads and bays and look far out on its level sky fairly tinted and fading in pensive air, I am reminded of all the mountain lakes I ever knew, as if this were a kind of water heaven to which they all had come."*

—*John Muir in a letter to his friend Jeanne Carr posted from Tahoe City in November 1872*

Duane Bliss railroad pier to SS Tahoe out on Lake Tahoe circa 1900

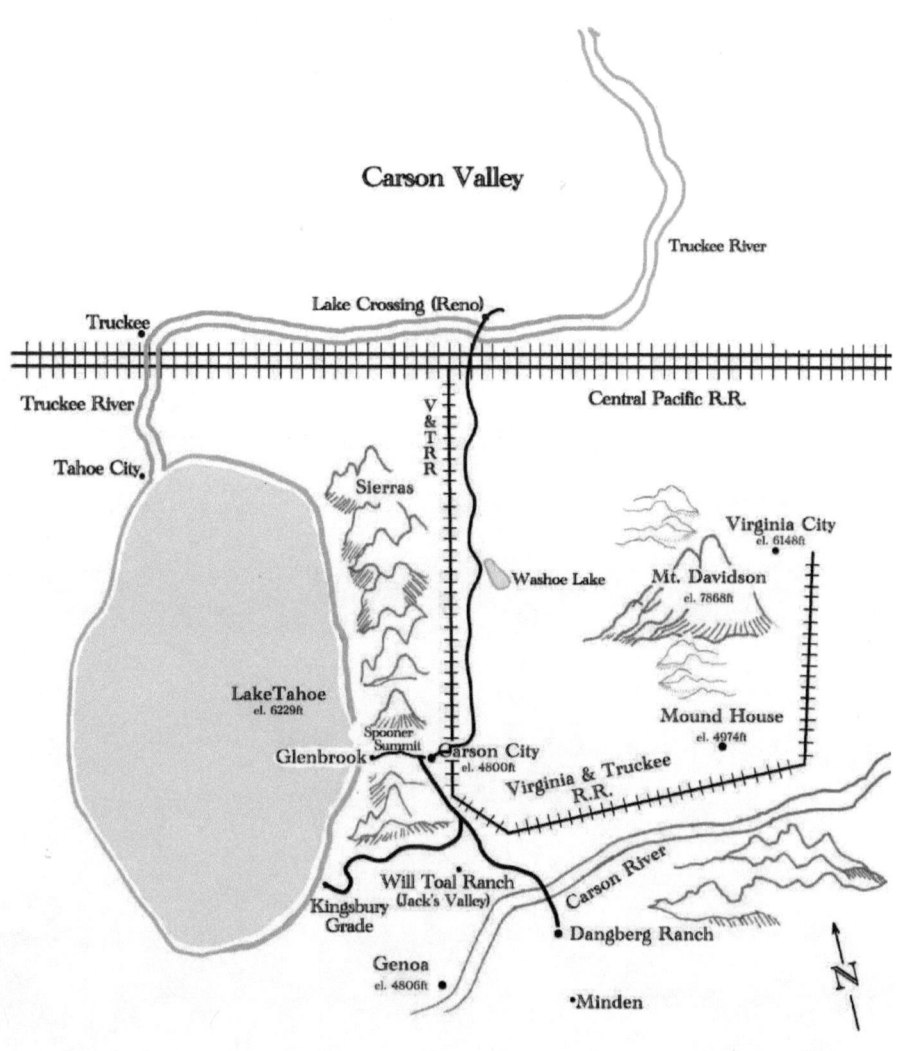

# Prologue

*October 1849*
*Monterey, CA*

A musty smell of men and emotion floated across the poorly ventilated hall. The California Constitutional Convention had progressed little despite nearly two months of debate. A lingering hot spell boiled both air temperature and passions. Respectful discourse had exited the packed room. A din of baser dialogue, accusatory and angry, had taken its place. The noise of the collected delegates was boundless. Parliamentary propriety hung in a delicate balance. Tempers were taught. And now this. The question blanketing a two month standoff was whether the territory should enter the union as a slave state or non-slave state. The powers in Washington were equally divided as to how this new territory known as Alta California should be admitted. The territory encompassed all lands recently won in the Mexican American War. Here in Monterey a motion had just been made that California enter the union as a slave state. That call was in direct and immediate response to a prior motion that California enter as a non-slave state. Chaos had ensued.

A gunshot stopped everyone in their tracks. The report of the weapon boomed repeatedly between the walls of Colton Hall. Everyone quieted. Knowing the volatility of emotions behind the topic, a few ducked thinking the shot was leveled at someone. The smell of gun smoke wafted to the ceiling.

The crowded conference room spread and gave way around a single man holding a gun pointed to the ceiling. It was John C. Freemont. He looked directly to the dais at Bvt. Brig. General Bennett C. Riley who had convened the entire convention at his own instigation.

"General Riley. May it please this convention. We have been arguing over slave versus non-slave for two months since September. We've made little progress. I would offer a solution. It is a compromise that will make no one in these halls happy. But I hope it might lead to an agreement all delegates here in Monterey can abide by. The aim is to have California admitted to the United States of America. We make no progress and compromise is needed."

General Riley stood. He and Freemont had clashed repeatedly over the authority, location, invitees, and scope of the convention. Freemont believed he had the rightful authority from the United States Government to preside. Riley disagreed. That Freemont was making his current point by way of formal plea signaled an intent at a broader appeal despite issues of authority.

'Lt. Freemont, you have the floor albeit obtained via an unorthodox request. Can we now have your weapon returned to its holster?"

"By all means. But I must make a demand before I present my motion."

Riley now looked puzzled. "And that would be?"

"That we table the two motions just made and move to my proposal first."

"Is there a second to the motion just now made to table those offerings?"

Freemont subtly kicked the shin of his compatriot standing next to him. "Second."

Riley then called the question. However, in a display that his own patience had waned with the endless argument over the slavery issue, he called the question skipping over asking in the positive and moved directly to the negative. "Those opposed to hearing a potential resolution to the issues before this convention before we continue the bottomless argument over the two earlier motions?" Silence. Riley's breach of the standard rules of order probably caught most in the hall off guard. There had been so much rancor, such emotions, Riley had used the newfound quiet created by Freemont's gunshot to his advantage.

"I will take that as a vote we should all listen to Lt. Freemont. Sir, you have the floor."

Freemont moved to the dais. He turned to the entire gathering, collected his energies and began.

"Gentlemen, we have argued over the issue of slavery for almost two months now. Arguments have been raised to slice our proposed new state in half forming a north portion and a south portion. Some would have our new state split by the same Mason Dixon Line that now divides the rest of the country. Those favoring the northern states to the east have suggested that our new state should encompass the entirety of Alta California recently obtained as fruits of our country's battle with the neighbor to the south which would have this new state extend all the way to the Rockies. Nothing has been offered to resolve the polar differences that confront us."

From the middle of the crowd standing before him, "There's nothing polar about this room right now. I'm hot. The room's hot. Hot as hell." A few chuckles followed.

Freemont did not hesitate, "Hot is why we have to act. The polar I'm talking about refers to the distance between the two sides in our midst. Why do we have to take up the same confrontation that is leading our country back east down a ruinous path? We have gold, San Francisco, along with the pueblos of Los Angeles and San Diego. Our roads stretch over a coastline as pristine as any on earth. We have a central valley the middle of which is carved by the San Joaquin River. That valley and its water could become one of the biggest agricultural farms the world has seen. And we have weather like nowhere else. Why do we need to carve it up? Why do we need to make it any bigger than necessary?"

There was a faint murmur. Freemont, pleased the rancor had stopped, took it as measured momentary harmony. He pushed forward.

"Gentlemen, here is my idea boiled down in its most fundamental simplicity: Let us keep California long and lean. Let us not slice it horizontally in half but let us keep the state only wide enough to maintain the uniformity of our geography and weather. Let us establish a border just east of the Sierras. Let us leave the barren wastes of the Great Basin in Utah and Colorado to others. In this way we do not comply with the wishes of those in the eastern north to expand California to the Rockies. But in this way, we also do not split our state in half to comply with those in the eastern south who want us to become a slave state. Our state does not have the soil, geography, or climate to benefit from slavery anyway. Let us put these insoluble differences aside and push them back east where they originated. Let us create a magical state homogeneous in its climate, its region, its people."

The murmur grew. The sound of multiple conversations increased.

Then someone yelled, "Huzzah! California long and lean! From the Sierras to the sea, from Mexico to Oregon!" A roar throughout the crowd broke out.

Freemont turned to look at Gen. Riley. Riley nodded admiringly. He was forced to acknowledge the import of what had just happened, a result from someone who had heretofore been personally adversarial on all issues related to the convention. He rose and leaned in to speak to Freemont over the din.

"Why to the east of the Sierras? Why not set the border on the west side of the range? If we don't want the Rockies, why do we want the Sierras?"

"We need to include the mountains too. The state should run to the 120$^{th}$ Longitude."

"Why so? Why to that specific point at the eastern border?"

Freemont virtually glared at the general, "Because I want Tahoe. There is no jewel on this earth to compare."

Knowing Freemont had laid eyes on the lake of which he spoke during his expedition with Kit Carson and Joe Walker, Riley smiled, "Then let us make sure the eastern border runs along the 120$^{th}$ Longitude."

## Chapter One

*August 1877*
*Tahoe City, California*

Walter Prichard stood on top of his creation, a pile of rocks and wood blocking the Truckee River as it exited the azure waters of Lake Tahoe—the Lady of the Lake as many like to think of her.

A man of slight build, Walter had used his brain in life, rarely his muscles. His unschooled intellect could see things before they were built. Despite the lack of formal education, he'd become recognized as a man who could get things built. He would usually just construct whatever he had been asked to design after he saw it in his head and drew his client a sketch.

He was on his morning inspection to check on the flow out of the lake. That flow had to pass over the top of his construct and continue down the Truckee river, the Lady's gift to those downstream.

It was a beautiful mountain morning. The early cool temperature here at higher elevations was now starting its migration from brisk beginning to warm summer day. Walter reached down and unbuttoned his thin woolen jacket. Thick enough to warm on a chilly summer morning, this same jacket would be nothing but an undergarment of his long fur coat had this been his daily check in January. But here in August, the prospects of coming warmth were good.

Tahoe was huge, twenty-two miles long and eleven miles wide. No one knew how deep she was. They just knew she was deep. And cold. The crystalline waters of the Lady were fed by alpine streams and snow melt. A deep royal almost teal blue early in the day when she was calm and her waters flat, the Lady turned a dark midnight blue when the late day breezes picked up. Rising winds each afternoon whipped her placid morning surface into fluid peaks and valleys of angry narrow chop, topped with white crests where the waves broke.

With the approach of darkness, only the largest of vessels could navigate the Lady's waters. Small boats would be swamped and torn asunder by the inordinately short-spaced waves breaching over a bow lowered in a trough as the stern was lifted. With the tail raised, the fast-breaking crests were spaced so close that the next wave would crash into the vulnerable bow sending the vessel nose down into the Lady's grasp. Those unfortunate unsuspecting few caught in the Lady's chop and brought down never returned to shore. They did not last long in the blue waters. Too cold. Even the strongest body numbed, stiffened and in a matter of several minutes, sank. The Lady never gave up her dead. Her waters were so cold the dead simply descended and never rose.

But Walter stood above the waters. Seven feet above to be exact. The pile of rocks and wood beneath him was a dam. It spanned the Truckee at the north end of the Lake. This end of the river was the only outlet for Tahoe. A.W. Von Schmidt had paid Walter to build the dam. But Leland Stanford and Mark Hopkins, both of whom made millions with the construction of the Central Pacific Railroad, now controlled it. Simple though it was, the dam had taken Walter almost five years to build. This pile of rocks and wood was his baby.

Allexey W. Von Schmidt, a surveyor and entrepreneur from Russia, had years ago convinced the city of San Francisco to make a reservoir out of Lake Tahoe. The city needed fresh water for its goldfield-fed growing population. Von Schmidt had convinced the city fathers to dam the Truckee and raise the level of Tahoe by five feet. He had bought property around the mouth of the Truckee as part of his concept. He still owned that property. The plan was to divert the extra water through a series of tunnels and pipelines all the way to San Francisco

Bay and across to the city. He had been well financed. But he ran into a massive conflict with Stanford and Hopkins who were much better funded. Far better.

Von Schmidt estimated that the new body of water five feet deep created atop the natural level of Lady Tahoe would exceed seven hundred forty-thousand-acre feet of water. He was right. Walter's new dam had created a massive reservoir of crisp clean water that rested on top of the original level of the lake.

However, though it took five years to finish the dam, Von Schmidt had never been allowed to build his tunnels or pipelines. Stanford and Hopkins with their government connections had beaten him. Using their associations, both business and political, the railroad barons had threatened to build another barrier a matter of yards from Von Schmidt's. Von Schmidt was forced to abandon his efforts for the entire project, conceding control the fluid blockade he built to Stanford and Hopkins before the second dam was built. But word was, Von Schmidt had recently returned to again try and convince the city of San Francisco to fund the pipeline.

Walter shook his head. A crucial problem confronted all those involved in trying to alter Tahoe's natural bearing. The lady was not completely in California and not completely in Nevada. About a third of the lake fell within the borders of Nevada, a mistake made by John C. Freemont who first looked out over Tahoe's waters in 1844 on his well-known Kit Carson guided expedition west. He appeared to keep the wondrous Lady of the Lake a secret as he did little to describe this treasure in his famous diary of the expedition written along with his wife Jessie Benton Freemont. But when Freemont later acted as temporary territorial governor in 1849 at the California Constitutional Convention, he wanted to make sure Tahoe was completely located within California's borders.

Walter chuckled to himself. Though acting with the best of intentions following the California Constitutional Convention, in setting the eastern border of the state, Freemont relied on his outdated and inaccurate maps from 1844. In a mistake that would incite argument for decades, Freemont unintentionally carved Tahoe in half. Walter shook his head at the confrontations and fights that had resulted. They never seemed to end.

With almost half of the reservoir surface water created by the Donner Boom and Lumber's dam located in Nevada, a veritable war broke out as to who had rights to the water. The combatants included the city of San Francisco, beachfront owners along Tahoe's shores whose properties had been flooded, the state of California, the State of Nevada, milling and power interests further down the Truckee and, of course, the Central Pacific Railroad. The war still raged.

As of the moment, the owners of the Central Pacific Railroad controlled Walter's dam through their lumber company. Leland Stanford and Mark Hopkins had personally petitioned the State of California Legislature for that control. California felt authorized to grant the petition as the flow of the Truckee originated at a point where it was completely in their state. However, after moving north to the Donner Pass, the river made a right turn and headed east to Nevada. The railroad required lumber for the tenders behind a score of locomotives the CPRR ran from Sacramento to St. Louis. Chunks of split timbers were needed to fire the railroad's steam engines. The wood for those engines was to come from forests around Tahoe sent as logs down the Truckee to the CPRR's sawmills.

The barons had waged a good battle in the California legislature. Walter thought only someone like an ex-governor with Stanford's political pedigree could have pulled off such a coup. The back-room politics put Stanford and the railroad at direct odds with Von Schmidt and the state of Nevada. But he also knew that the Legislature granted a license for *use* of the water *flow* down the Truckee. The Donner Boom and Lumber Co. did not *own* the water.

Walter gazed up at the peaks of the Sierras all around him. The mountains surrounding Lady Tahoe spawned pine trees, and lots of them. After their political victory, the Donner Boom and Lumber Co. started lumbering trees all around the north side of Tahoe. The logs were then floated down the Truckee to their lumber mills near Donner Pass where the river met CPRR's main transcontinental line. The logs were milled, cut and loaded in the engine tenders for the trips east and west. The CPRR needed to control the dam in order to control the flow of its logs to their locomotives. To do that, they needed to control the water.

Following completion of the dam, Walter had remained the chief supervisor of its operations. He'd come to love living up here in the pristine mountains watching the progress of the crystal-clear water flow over his creation. He was now employed by the Donner Boom and Lumber Co.

Walter wondered if Von Schmidt could once again re-generate any interest to divert the Truckee. San Francisco certainly needed the water. How famous he would be some day if San Francisco eventually reaped the benefit to draw their city water supply from this pristine source? His name would live for decades. But Von Schmidt had been battling the CPRR robber barons for over seven years. Von Schmidt's chances were probably no better now than before the Water Act was passed in 1870. He had initially been backed with finances in excess of over twenty million dollars. It was a prodigious sum. But word was he'd run out of money fighting the barons. If he had returned to try and revitalize his vision, the City of San Francisco could grant him new funds. However, any such plan would again pit Von Schmidt and the City against

Walter's employers. Battling the seemingly bottomless coffers of the CPRR would probably bring them only further frustration.

Standing here at the middle of his dam in the warm July sun, Walter tried to put away thoughts of political and financial battles. He had other concerns. The Lady and her extra five feet of water stood calm on one side. Large trout easily visible in the clear waters swam in place, habitually feeding on the current up to the dam before it crested the overflow at the west side of the river. But there was only a trickle making its way over the dam. There had been two years of drought. This past winter's snowfall was the lightest any of the Oldtimers had ever seen. There just wasn't enough snow melt to feed the flow of the Truckee. Ranchers and farmers down slope in Nevada were angry. The sawmills downstream that used the normal flow to power both the movement of logs and milling machinery were angry. The CPRR was angry as there was barely enough water to float their logs which kept getting caught among the now exposed rocks.

All the focus was on Walter. Locals blamed him for what they thought was a restriction of the normal flow. Folks in Nevada argued that California was stealing their water. Nevada newspapers had dubbed Von Schmidt's project to divert Tahoe's water the *Tunnel of Doom*. They challenged the existence of the dam itself asserting that if removed, the Truckee would still flow at its normal rate. Walter scoffed at the idea. The five extra feet of water above 6,232 feet in elevation was stored, like a bank. If there had been no dam, there would be no bank. Whether dammed or not, the drought of the last couple of years would not feed a flow out of the Lady's rim even if that rim had remained unchanged.

Walter heard the rifle shot. He didn't have time to feel the pain exploding in his chest. He fell forward over the side of his legacy, his pile of wood and rocks. He splashed among the large trout no longer interested in feeding. They scattered with the impact to the surface as if to scurry away from further impending danger. A pool of ink dark fluid began to spread from Walter's body marring the remarkable colors of the Lady's teal blue waters. Ripples broadened outward to the shores on both sides of the Truckee, ripples that would spread even further to both California and Nevada.

# Chapter Two

*August 1877*
*Jack's Valley, NV*

The animal trembled, legs shaking as it reached down into one of the many small rivulets that cut through the grasslands. Sharply carved sides of the small streams jabbed straight sided into what usually was soft dark dirt. But the dirt was not moist. It was not dark. The rivulet was dry, full of nothing but dust.

With the utmost effort, the steer spread its front legs to drop its head and nose below the normal level of the turf. The beast lowered all the way to the base of the natural sluice in anticipation of a watery reward. Its brain, though markedly limited, kept accurate memories of kin, herd, food, and water but not much else. It had come here pushed by a stored recollection that it would find something to drink. Survival was simple and water was necessary for survival. But the effort was for naught. The animal's head lifted out of the empty streambed. With a heave of resignation from its lungs, a bovine version of a sigh, its legs gave way. It buckled onto its side in acceptance of its fate.

Will Toal watched from atop his gray mustang Powder, as the steer collapsed. That was his beef. He now counted nine steers that had collapsed in the last few days. It was only August. He gazed up, lifting his hat off his head to wipe away a bead of sweat from his brow. Still early morning and already getting hot again. Would it not end? Nine steers, he had to do something.

He and Powder stood in the middle of his ranch of three thousand acres. Will had headed west from New Mexico along with his hands on his way to California searching for ranchland. He stopped here because of the water and grass. His property reached to the eastern base of the Sierras. The crest of those massive mountains rose like a gray stone wall from the western border of his homestead. The contrast of the green knee-high grasses running up against the base of the gray monoliths all beneath an endless blue sky gave him pause to end his migration west.

It was a perfect place to raise beef cattle and horses. Most months of the year the stately peaks were crowned with caps of white snow. However, this year succor from the heights was in short supply. Just like last year. In fact, what little snow that had fallen in the elevations this last winter melted off before April. Snowmelt from the adjacent Sierras is what kept his personal Eden green. But not now.

The heat and lack of rain would likely continue for at least another month. Too many of his stock looked much like the one here collapsed before him. Will and the hands had pumped as much water from the only well back in the compound and tried to distribute it via wagons. But it was not enough. And the well was showing signs of petering out. That had never come close to happening in the nine years he'd ranched here in the valley. He had to do something or he'd lose his whole herd.

He had an idea.

*****

Will rode slowly over the bleached grasses. The sight of his cattle suffering seared questions of the future in his thoughts. His family depended on the money that beef brought. Everywhere he looked, waves of heat wafted up from sections where the grass no longer survived. What had been green soggy marshland over most months of the year now pushed back the sun's rays in pulsating bursts. In normal years, the carpet of grass turned the heat into the succor for his stock. But that also required water, something in short supply these days. He was not sure his idea would work, but he could not sit by and watch a slow decimation of his herd. It was time to act.

He pulled up in front of the main house. The quadrangle that served as the headquarters of his ranch had four buildings on its borders. The four-room main house on one side, the barn on another. As a special house for his ramrod, vaquero Juan Medina and his wife Maria, occupied another side. The last side was occupied by a bunkhouse for the rest of his crew. Will dismounted and tied Powder loosely to the hitching rail outside the main house.

"Beth, are you anywhere nearby? Got something I'd like to talk to you about."

A long-legged blonde with the deepest blue eyes he'd ever seen stepped into the doorway. Her lengthy tresses were grouped in a loose ponytail but light strands of fine hair floated around her face looking to escape confinement. In the ever-present winds, those strands provided a constant motion about her face. She wiped her hands on the apron worn as standard apparel within the house. She wouldn't think so right now, but to Will she looked spectacular. Beth was his wife.

"Yes, I am near. Any reason you can't come inside and see for yourself rather than bellow from the outside like a cave man?"

"Right now, I'd like to take you to my cave and act like a Neanderthal."

"You *are* a Neanderthal." The comment was delivered with a wry smile. Challenge accepted.

"Ah, and you wouldn't mind hunkering down in some cave?"

"Depends on the cave man." No expression, but sarcasm dripped from her retort.

"A cave could be nice and cool right now."

"Yeah, but your accommodations are not inside some rock, they are out here on a blistering plain."

"Maybe, I should go look for a rock house." Will knew he usually lost these light-hearted exchanges, but he loved them anyway. His wife was a master of words. Will was a master of horses, cows, and men.

"You'll need to grow a beard and peel off your shirt. Maybe the rest of your body would get to look like your red neck."

The doorway to the house was recessed under a wide ramada. It faced east because the winds raking down the eastern Sierras routinely raced across his property to the desert basin east beyond the Carson Valley. His ranch was in Jack's Valley, a smaller section tucked right at the base of the Sierras in between the mountains and the much larger Carson Valley. Further east of that valley were the cities of Mound House, the cutoff to Virginia City, and then Dayton. Beyond Dayton was the great basin that stretched all the way to Utah.

It was hot enough here; he could not imagine what it was like out in the basin. But that massive hot desert sucked the cooler air of the mountains steadily to the east. The cool breezes of the mountains were sucked east by the desert heat and picked up speed after hitting the level plain of the valleys. It was often difficult to stand up straight in the force of the daily blast of air. Thus, the door to the ranch house faced the east side of the structure in the lee from the constant gusts.

Will decided to concede the verbal contest. He usually did. "Come sit on the bench here on the porch. We need to talk."

The fact that Beth refrained from any further quip told Will she had picked up on the seriousness of his tone.

"Sounds important."

"It could be very important," said Will.

"What is it?"

"Saw another steer collapse. No water in the small creeks to the west. That's nine in the last few days. We have to do something before the whole herd is dead."

Beth paused. "You have an idea?"

"Yep."

"And that is?"

"Move 'em before they can't be moved."

"Move 'em where?"

This was the part where Will needed her advice. Though not a ranch hand, Beth was excellent at assessing and processing information to a solution. He never hesitated to consult her on big decisions.

"Move 'em to your ranch, on the Truckee."

Will could see Beth was taken aback. While the topic of property at the Truckee might be innocuous on the surface, it dove deep into a problematic period in their relationship which had prevented Will from proposing for several years. She proceeded with care.

"Will, it's not mine, it's yours. You know full well that I gave you twenty-five percent in the sale to Mr. Henry Millard."

"Yes, I know, but I've always treated it in my mind as if it is still yours. It came from your prior marriage. If we decide to do what I have in mind, I suspect the grasses will be damaged for years. I don't want to take this step without making sure you agree. But the beef need the water from the Truckee river. Juan was up at that ranch and says the Truckee is quite low, but it's flowing. We're goin' dry here. We have to move the herd before they can't move at all."

Beth tucked her hands around Will's arm as they sat down on the porch bench. She smiled. "Sounds like there will be another decision made on this bench. Seems like most of our major choices are made while we sit here."

"Other than making babies. Those come from further inside." Will smiled.

"Still thinking like a cave man." She grinned.

"Always."

"I appreciate your considering my interests regarding the Truckee ranch. But it's part of the whole operation now. We already have cattle at the ranch section on the Truckee. Why the concern about moving the herd up there now? I think you know I would always follow your lead when it comes to management of the ranch. I would have one question though."

"Only one?" Another grin.

Ignoring the bait this time she continued, "The land along the Truckee is more mountainous. There is less grass. Will it support the herd?"

Here was another example of how well Beth processed information leading to a decision. It was exactly why he would run these kinds of issues by her.

"Oh, I'm sure it'll support our herd. We only need to keep them there until November. The winter rains should start by then. But that isn't my full idea. That's why I wanted to make sure this is going to be okay with you."

Beth did not speak. She knew and respected her husband and could tell he'd given this some thought. Best to hear him out. Will started in a serious tone.

"Since the day we met in the confrontation with that man Reynolds . . ."

Beth interrupted this historically important factor in their original introduction with something of a forced yet playful inquiry. "The one you shot to protect my honor?"

Will nodded. "Yes, the one I shot to protect your honor. That list has grown quite a bit since then." This was offered with a rueful smile.

"Always appreciated. Much the better that I have survived and given you three children."

"I'm tryin' to talk about cattle and you keep bringing me back to cave man thoughts."

"I'm sorry. I'll try not to tempt you further." The teasing sarcasm in this comment was unmistakable.

"Seriously," said Will. "I've always felt the Truckee property was still yours in a way. You came into title when your Mormon husband died. You are the real link to that part of the ranch. It only took a crack to the back of my head for me to have any claim to it."

Beth looked out over the quadrangle compound to the fields beyond. It took some time for her to respond. She then turned back to Will.

"How strange it is that so many of the paths our lives have taken are rooted in that decision." Beth was not smiling now. Not at all.

Will knew Beth now referred to the dark time between them. She had indeed hit him with her handgun in an instantaneous decision she claimed was done to protect Will from an outlaw Beth had inadvertently brought between them. In that momentary decision Beth hoped she could draw the man away from harming Will. She'd left Will unconscious on the ground that day. Will had seen it differently and it took him almost four years before he'd fully forgiven Beth.

"It was a pivotal part of what has become you and me. But it's in the past." He squeezed her hands tucked between his arm and chest to affirm the fact all prior disapproval was distant history. Beth dropped her head onto Will's shoulder in silent indication of her appreciation this was behind them. While they both loved their regular lighthearted banter, the most touching communication between them was often nonverbal.

"But I think we need to move more than just our herd."

"Now I am confused. Are you talking about the horses or more than that? What other cattle would you need to move?"

"Your Truckee property was pivotal in the events leading to the creation of the Cattlemen's Association here in Carson Valley. The Johnson and Dangberg families—along with others— have been involved from the start. You sold that Truckee piece to Henry Millard. Actually, your ex-husband, Josiah Purcell, did. The piece you gave me led to my personal arrangement with Henry and the Millard Luce Cattle Co. That later led to all the Valley's ranchers joining the Association so we could sell beef through Mr. Millard's brokers when Fort Churchill closed and our market evaporated. Now I think that same Truckee property will be the key to saving the Association and all our neighbors."

"I think I see where you are going now."

Will had been looking out to the compound but now turned to Beth, "We need to move all the herds from the valley up to the Truckee. All the ranchers are in the same position as we are. The Carson River is dry and has been for months. That river supplies all the Carson Valley ranches."

"But Will, you are probably talking about ten thousand head of cattle."

"No, not that many. But there's a lot no doubt. Maybe six to seven thousand. We'd be moving them to the Truckee ranch which is about fifteen hundred acres. It would support that large a herd for only a few months, maybe three, four at the most. But those grasses and the water in the Truckee would keep the beef alive until the winter rains or we can sell, whichever comes first. But the grass on the north ranch would be done. And it could be done for several years, depending on this season's rainfall. That's why I want your approval before I do anything."

Beth paused, "Like I said earlier, I've never questioned your decisions with the stock. You know best. If you think it's important to our position here in the Valley to take all that stock north, then I understand. How do you plan on moving them?"

Will grinned, "A good ole cattle drive."

# Chapter Three

*August 1877*
*San Francisco, CA.*

Heat emanated from his body in a sticky scent of defeat. Solitary, Allexey W. Von Schmidt stood amidst a disappointing silence. Frustrated, he looked back and forth across the supervisors arrayed in the city council chambers before him. The lack of any direct response to his vehement argument that the city of San Francisco needed to address its lack of decent water supply spoke volumes. He tried to shake off the reality that the last chance of seeing his vision come to fruition was about to perish right before him.

The crumble of a project so vital to the future survival of the city made him burn. To make matters worse, the room was also hot, though not because of the weather outside. A gloom of marine fog from the ocean to the west was sucked across the city by the heat of the Sacramento and Salinas Valleys to the east this time of year. Outside there was no sun. The heat in the chamber came from the tension among the collected bodies aligned in their oppositions within a room having no windows and few doors. Each man had come dressed in woolen finery. The city fathers now felt the friction of the moment.

Precise and focused, Allexey had come to this country like many in search of gold. He had been trained as an engineer in the demanding schools of eastern Germany. He soon realized that his training was more valuable than panning for metal. Tall and slender, he commanded any room with his aristocratic bearing and intellect. Any room but this one. He had been the darling of San Francisco's monied elite not long ago. But he had fallen out of favor. People had lost money in his project with the Placiaritas dam. Then his first plan to bring water from Lake Tahoe failed. More money was lost. This city required water. His engineering being could see it. Why could the city fathers not see the same dire need? He needed to convince them. But his prior failures made the present argument an uphill battle.

Von Schmidt had planned this day. He had convinced this same council in 1865 that the city needed an additional source of water. They had backed his plan to tap the expanse of Lake Tahoe and its pristine liquid. He'd built a dam as the first step in generating the water to send to the coast. But politics and the Central Pacific Railroad blocked him. They turned this council against him. He had postured the current politics with the obvious need for the fundamental fluid leading to his presentation of today. Here again he had tried to convince this group of leading citizens that Tahoe was their answer to future water needs. But it had not gone well.

The councilmen were positioned on a raised bank of seats behind a wooden semi-circle that functioned as one giant desk with sections for each. Burnished burl wood carvings brandished designs and state images along the facia. Those images and scenes of California and San Francisco were obviously meant to impress those who stood below to address the council. The woodworking was exquisite. Von Schmidt felt on one hand like he was in some auditorium with the landed and important gazing down upon him. On the other hand, he felt like he was in trial attempting to defend himself. The setting was intended to create both reactions.

The men behind the circled desk looked everywhere but directly at him. Some shifted in their seats, while others busied themselves lighting a cigar to cover their lack of response. A few looked at the mayor seated in the center of the semi-circle.

"Gentlemen, your silence is telling." Von Schmidt delivered his comment with a taste of disgust, disappointment.

Mayor Andrew J. Bryant finally responded, "Mr. Von Schmidt, you know very well from our private discussions that the city is locked in the throes of an economic depression. We do not have the money you suggest. There is no way we can ask the people of this city to support a bond issue of ten million dollars. Not now."

"Mr. Mayor, more than ever this council understands San Francisco's need for more water. The Spring Valley Water Company has done its best to drain the watersheds north of the city, but it is running out of additional flows despite this council's extensive grants of eminent domain."

Supervisor Jonathan Edwards then interjected, "And don't we have you, Mr. Schmidt, to thank for our beloved Spring Valley Water Co. along with its monopolistic control fueled by graft and corruption? Water has become the next gold field. It has fueled fortunes and speculation like silver in Nevada."

"You are correct, sir. Back in 1865 I did plan and begin the construction of the Placiaritas Dam. That dam has given the city of San Francisco its only reliable source of water. But the dam did not create the corruption surrounding its creation, people did." He burned even hotter at the accusation just lofted in his direction. In his anger he now insulted them. "Spring Valley is a monopoly which benefits only a few here in the city. I am not one of them, though some of those few beneficiaries do sit on this council." Von Schmidt knew that if his plan were not already dead, the volley just fired would push it closer to its impending demise.

But Von Schmidt didn't stop there. He was on the precipice of winning or losing. Might as well lay it on the line. Insult rarely led to agreement.

In a more conciliatory and strategic tone he continued.

"The reason Spring Valley functions as a monopoly is because this council allows it to. If you will consider my plan to bring water from Tahoe, then San Francisco reaps two benefits. First, there is an almost bottomless supply of water. Second, there will be desperately needed competition for Spring Valley."

Mayor Bryant then spoke, "But did you not tell me some time ago that you planned for your Lake Tahoe and San Francisco Water Company to buy out Spring Valley? If your company rose again from the ashes like a phoenix, would you not try to buy Spring Valley again? Would we not be facing another monopoly, only bigger and more powerful?"

Von Schmidt was determined to meet the challenge, "This council could issue city charter regulations to control the rates charged. You have seen the railroad robber barons obtain control of Tahoe and the Truckee with their Water Act of 1870. You have seen William Ralston and his Bank of California purchase the Spring Valley company and then run grandiose stock speculation schemes so unsuccessful it led to the imminent demise of his Bank. Gentlemen, are you not tired of being controlled rather than control?"

Supervisor Edwards nodded, "Sir, you are correct. The speculation scheme involving Spring Valley led to the Bank of California's collapse only to be propped up by William Sharon of Virginia City fame. The collapse and Sharon's takeover of all Ralston's assets is rumored to be the real reason why Ralston two years ago took his swim in the San Francisco Bay from which he never returned."

Von Schmidt now chuckled, "So, the person who currently controls your city's water supply, albeit insufficient, is the ultimate stock speculator and robber baron, Mr. Sharon, who's notoriety for shady business deals spans the country. It seems to me you have traded the railroad robber barons for the silver mine robber barons. Are you comfortable with that?" He had called them out.

Again, an uncomfortable silence.

Once more, it was mayor Bryant who tried to fill the void. Von Schmidt could see Bryant was simply protecting some of his compatriots who were in league with the referenced Spring Valley investors while at the same time doing his best to bring a most uncomfortable meeting to a close.

"Mr. Von Schmidt, I think it would be wise for this council to discuss your proposal further. We will meet in executive session to decide what we believe is best for our city. I will be in touch."

Von Schmidt remained upright for several moments looking at each of the supervisors individually. With no small amount of resignation, he then sat and started to collect his papers. The supervisors began to file out of the chamber. He watched them go. He had the sense that any chance of reviving his plan to bring Tahoe's water to San Francisco had just walked out of the room with them.

*****

"I thought that went well."

Von Schmidt looked at his assistant, Jonas Greerson, and with significant incredulity said, "Were you actually watching or sleeping? That could not have gone worse."

"But they said they would consider your proposal."

"They said they do not want another monopoly to replace the one who is passing money under the table to more than half of the men sitting up there on the dais."

Greerson, a young engineer with dark slicked back hair had worn his best suit and shined his shoes until they sparkled. He looked upon

Von Schmidt as something idyllic. Von Schmidt had built the anxious fledgling's hopes of working on what he had said would be the most prodigious water project ever contemplated. Some had even said it would be the most stupendous water works enterprise ever undertaken on the American continent. But Greerson was now being told the chances of that occurring using proper channels were next to hopeless. He did not want to let go of his hope.

The inexperienced youth had been walking just forward of Von Schmidt. He stopped and turned. "It cannot be that bad."

"Oh, my young Greerson, it is probably even worse than I have described. You have no idea how the real world works here in this era of exponential expansion. Those who have money will do almost anything to protect it."

"Does William Sharon really own the Spring Valley Water Company?"

"Yes, he obtained it when he bailed banker Ralston out as the supervisor said. Sharon is now reaping untold profits while he virtually rapes the watershed north in San Mateo County. And those supervisors let him do it. You know why?"

Greerson sheepishly said, "Because the city needs the water?"

"No. Even though the city desperately needs the water, the real reason is that Sharon is regularly passing funds to many on that council. And those payments as we shall call them are in addition to the payments Stanford is paying to the same bunch."

"Why is Stanford passing money?"

"Both of those villains have their own separate schemes to protect."

"Do they work together?"

Von Schmidt shook his head, "Stanford does not want to lose control of the Truckee dam because he needs to keep the flow of logs heading down to his sawmills. Sharon wants to protect his Spring Valley monopoly."

Greerson looked dejected. The significance of what Von Schmidt was saying now hit home.

Von Schmidt waited and thought. "Greerson, maybe it is time we come to grips with the reality of the situation. The council is in the back pocket of Sharon and probably also Leland Stanford. Stanford and the mayor are known to be quite close. We need to take a different course."

"Then what are you going to do?"

"We are going to unseat the good Mr. Stanford from control of the dam I built."

"And how are you going to do that?"

"I am not going to do anything at the moment. You are," said Von Schmidt.

Completely taken aback, Greerson could not hide his lack of comprehension. "What am I going to do?"

"You are going to contact a man I know. You are going to tell him to hire the men we talked about. That man is going to unseat the Donner Lumber and Boom Company from control of the Truckee Dam. If necessary, he is going to do it by force."

Unquestionably flustered, Greerson asked, "How is that going to help?"

"I have tried to present logical strategies and solutions for the monumental water needs San Francisco has and will have into the future. The city council knows my concepts are well founded. But I am blocked by other interests who do not have the city as their first concern. I've tried proper channels, now we'll use the same methods the robber barons would use if the roles were reversed. We'll use force to show they cannot competently secure the water flow and therefore their license should be revoked. At the same time, we will show that Spring Valley's monopoly must end."

## Chapter Four

*August 1877*
*Toal Ranch, Jack's Valley, NV*

"Ma, we get to go on a cattle drive!"

Luke and Sean Toal, twins aged eight, ran in the house barely squeezing through the door on their joint beeline to their mother.

The adolescent exuberance was something Beth could almost reach out and grab. Instead, she had two over-active eight-year-old boys hanging on her skirts jumping up and down at different intervals.

"Stop you two! You're pulling on my dress. It'll come off!"

"Might be interesting."

Their father stood in the doorway with a wry smile watching the outpouring.

"Only you would be amused," came her tepid response.

Beth looked down at her boys, hesitating to crush the joy she saw in their faces. She looked back to Will. "You did this. Are you sure it's a good idea they ride on a cattle drive?"

"I am the guilty party," said Will as he walked into the room and put his arms around his concerned wife. "They are almost nine."

"That is not exactly justification for going on a cattle drive."

Will shrugged. "We will put them in the back. They can push the slow steers and drink dust. It'll do 'em good to start like every other hand on their first drive. All new hands work drag. They won't get hurt working drag."

"I don't know Will." Beth's maternal instincts were on full display in the look on her face.

Will knew that when it came to the twins, those instincts and any confidence in the security of their home had been shattered several years ago. Will had killed a man about to shoot Beth. Later, that dead man's kin rode onto the ranch bent on revenge and kidnapped the boys. It took a week to recover them. Beth had been manic in her protection ever since.

"And what about Juliette? She's two. Are you going to saddle her up too?"

Will smiled down at the blue eyes he loved so much. "Might. Could give her a rope and tell her to swing it."

His gibe netted him a light slap on his chest.

Will then held Beth at arms-length, "You have to come too. The idea is that we all head up to the Truckee. Could be there for a month or so. Wouldn't want to be up there with only a bunch of ranch hands."

"And exactly how am I going to carry an entire temporary household forty miles?"

"The wagon. It'll be just like old times when you used to bring the boys out to the ranch each week. But this time it will be you and Jules in the wagon not the twins."

Beth looked down at the boys. The joy in their faces struck deep chords. Will counted on the fact that Beth would not want to be the one to crush those looks. Beth returned her gaze to Will. As if she was accepting something of a challenge, she said, "I suppose it would be good if I came and kept an eye on you all. However, I am not sure keeping Juliette Toal still on a wagon bench all the way to the Truckee is in the realm of possibility."

Ignoring the problem presented as if it had been established, he said, "There. Settled."

Will looked down at the boys and winked. "We're goin' and you two will get your first real taste of cowboyin'. Now go tell Juan to help you work your horses. You have to get your mounts ready." The boys immediately ran out yelling for Juan.

"They are excited." Beth clutched Will again enjoying the closeness.

"They should be. It's only a short drive. Probably will take two days, three at the most. They'll get to ride, rope and chase steers by day and sleep under the stars by night. It won't be Texas to Abilene, but they'll get a good taste."

"When are you planning on starting this expedition?"

"I am going to ride over to Henry Dangberg's and the stop in and talk to the Johnson's. If they agree to come along, I figure it will take two to three days to gather each of our herds in the short pens so we can coordinate a start and push them together."

"And your route?"

"Right up the road from Carson City to Reno. We'll drive them right through the middle of town, right up main street. That'll get those legislators' attention that they need to deal with the water from Tahoe."

"And from there?"

"Straight up the road by Washoe Lake, which is pretty much dry right now, and cross the Truckee outside of Reno. Then head to the ranch."

"Cross the Truckee?"

Will nodded, "Juan was just up there and says its flowing but real low. Shouldn't be any problem walking the herd right through it. From what he said, it'll only be ankle deep. We won't have to swim 'em."

"Got it all figured out don't you."

"Not all. There's always something that upsets the tea kettle. It'll be done only when we get the herd north of the Truckee to some water and grass worth grazing."

Beth kissed Will gently on the cheek. "Say hi to Mrs. Dangberg and Sue Johnson for me."

"I will. I'll be back for supper."

"You better be back for supper." An impish smile accompanied the command.

"Sounds like an invitation." Will returned with an equally impish smile.

"Be back and we'll see."

*****

Powder stepped through strands of brown dried grass. Will looked at the field he'd crossed. Henry Dangberg's grasses were in no better shape than his own. A tall sky opened in blue oven heat. Will could not remember a summer like this one. It was even worse than last year and he thought that was bad. Not a cloud anywhere. No respite from the sun's rays. The normal moist scent of the grasses was gone. Life smelled like dirt and dust. There was an impending sense of death that came with that smell. Everything was burnt.

Will pulled up to the Dangberg residence. The house, though modest, was bigger than most ranch homes here in the valley. It did not have the look of a log cabin or an adobe as most did. It looked like it belonged on a grassy knoll back in his native Georgia. The home's white clapboard sides made it look stately, almost out of place. And the Dangberg's had planted trees that had probably a ten-year head start over those Will and Beth had planted back home. These Cottonwoods were large enough to provide some welcome shade. It drove the thought about his own home. *It'll be nice when our trees get big enough to shade the buildings around the quadrangle back home.*

"Will Toal. Nice to see you. Jump down and come in and have something cold to drink. It's much too hot out here." Will smiled at the welcoming face of Margaret Dangberg. The Illinois native was quite a bit younger than her German born husband. But it seemed to all a good match.

"Mrs. Dangberg, a cold drink sounds wonderful."

Margaret held the door until Will came up to the porch. He then grabbed the upper reaches of the door and beckoned her to lead the way. He had been to the house several times before. The home had a sitting room just off the entrance. That sitting room was large enough for several couches and chairs, though the room still maintained a feeling of comfort and efficiency. Everything about Henry Dangberg was efficient. His stock, his agricultural fields, his ranch hands were all handled with the utmost efficiency.

"And what brings you here to visit? Knowing you to be a young man of focus, I am sure it is not to simply talk. Had that been the case you would have brought your lovely wife, Beth."

Will grinned, "You know me all too well. Yes, I need to speak to Mr. Dangberg about our collective herds. Water is dryin' up."

"It is so hot again this summer. And we had no snow. The Carson River is our main source of water for the stock and it's been dry for weeks. I see the concern in Henry's face each day. I hope you come with an idea. You've shown all of us here in the Valley to be quite resourceful. Let me get him."

Will admired the stateliness of the lady. She had a carriage about her. Henry Dangberg was such a leader here in the southern end of Carson Valley. Lucky man to have a wife like that.

He walked to the fireplace and regarded the painting over the mantle. It was a winter landscape with copious amounts of white snow. But the trees were different. He couldn't place the location. It was not like any place he'd ever seen. Margaret walked back into the room with a glass of clear fluid.

"Sorry we don't have any ice left. That was gone some time ago. But we try to keep the water from the well cool down in the root cellar. Henry was in his office. He'll be right along. Please sit."

Will turned to the painting again. He asked, "What is the location in the painting?"

"It's Minden." The words came from Henry Dangberg who had just entered the room. "It's Minden, Germany. Not the Minden here in the south of Carson Valley. It is where I was born. That painting was one of the few things I brought with me from the old country. I thought it would remind me of home. I keep it there to do just that."

"Looks cold. But we could use some of that snow about now. Looks like they get a lot of it in Germany."

"It can be bitter cold in the middle of winter. People must plan for food and stock to make it through winter to spring. But that need for planning makes us Germans attentive to detail. It can mean survival. We are a precise people."

"Henry Millard always uses that same word *precise*. He's German too is he not?"

"Yes, from my short conversations with Mr. Millard, we have similar roots. That he was German was one of the reasons I tended to agree with your suggestion to start the Cattlemen's Association and sell our beef to him."

Dangberg then sat across from Will. "Margaret tells me you want to talk about the herds."

"Mr. Dangberg . . . "

"Will, call me Henry."

"Ok, I will try. The simple idea is that our herds are dying from lack of water. We need to move them."

"Where? My water sources are drying up too, but where are we going to take them?"

"My idea is to drive the herds from all those in the Association up to the old Purcell Ranch while they can still walk."

"That ranch was your wife's if I remember right."

"True. While its title rests with Henry Millard and myself, I've asked Beth about this and she agrees."

"And water?"

"The Truckee flows right through the ranch. My ramrod, Juan, was just up there late last week and says the river is low but still flowing."

"You want to take all the herds in the South Carson?"

"Yep. They will die if we don't."

"Will, that is an amazing thought. You could just take your own herd up and survive. Can I ask why you are thinking to take the rest of us?"

"If only my spread survives, then the Association dies. Our strength is in our numbers. Since starting the Association after the Railroad tried to run us off, the process of selling the beef in Reno to Millard for shipment to San Francisco makes us a huge factor in that market. If the ranches fail, maybe they look somewhere else to supply beef and my ranch becomes too small by itself to justify the network currently in place. I think there is risk to run it alone. Anyway, I figure we are all in this together and have been since the start. No time to change now."

Dangberg shook his head. "Just like when the railroad came after us, you're thinking about the whole, not just yourself. My hat's off to you Will."

"Like I said, I figure we're all in it together. We live or die as a market together."

"Is there enough grass for all the herds combined?"

"Yes, but for only a limited time. It will keep them all until November for sure and maybe to December if we need to." Rains should start and the rivers should flow back home here after that."

"It will damage your grass at your northern ranch with all that beef."

"Yes, it will. I've told Beth I would bet the grass would be hard pressed to return for a year or two. But in moving the herds north our basic supply survives. Our place in Millard's network survives."

"How do you plan on getting them up there?"

"Drive 'em. Take that huge herd right through Carson City. Right in front of the State Capital building."

Dangberg now laughed out loud. "I definitely want to be there for that. There are several of our local representatives who need to be reminded who their most important constituents are."

"Might be some help at that."

"When are you thinking of starting the drive."

Will hesitated, "This is a tough part. We need to start in no more than three days. My beef might not be able to take a walk even if it's only fifty miles if we wait any longer."

Dangberg thought a moment, "I agree. I agree with the entire idea. So, how to we set this in motion?"

"I was going to head over to talk to Martin Johnson and the others right now."

"I'll come along. Let me get my horse. I'll tell my hands to begin gathering our stock and be ready to move in three days. Might as well get things started."

"I'll be outside when you're ready to go."

# Chapter Five

*August 1877*
*Sacramento, CA*

"Freemont was an idiot!"

The comment came from Leland Stanford, railroad baron and ex-governor of California. He sat in a broad armchair off to the side of a massive desk. The office and desk rested amid the three-story Stanford Mansion in Sacramento located at the corner of N street and 8$^{th}$ street. Sitting across from him was his longtime friend and fellow investor, Mark Hopkins.

"Nice that Governor William Irwin lets you use your own office," smirked Hopkins.

"Yes, I've let every governor since my term ended back in '63 use the mansion for formal functions. Doesn't bother me. Jane and I spend most of our time in the house on Knob Hill or the Palo Alto estate with its racing stables. It comes in handy to have a place in the capital, but we're not here that often. Speaking of Knob Hill, how is your monstrous mansion coming along?"

Hopkins reclined in a fully customed tailored suit under his waist length gray beard. He chuckled. "That small abode is no more a palace than the monstrous mansion of your own on the same Hill."

Stanford chortled, "Yes my friend, we have done well haven't we when we can flit away a million dollars in today's money on our small wee homes?"

"Your small wee home has 25 bedrooms," imped Hopkins. "And at one-hundred-twenty-five-feet-square at its base, it is reputed to be the largest personal residence in California."

Not shrinking from the almost childish exchange, Stanford retorted, "Your small wee home has four stories, and I'm told it has 35 living suites not counting bathrooms, walk in closets and special areas for unwed ladies. I hear those special rooms are done in the purest of white."

Stanford was a laconic man, devoid of expression to a fault with all others. In fact, visiting dignitaries had told stories of being granted the vaunted audience with the baron only to find him virtually non-communicative. But not with his friend Hopkins. These two men had done business together for over twenty-five years. Stanford looked almost fondly at the man before him. These two had remained close.

Not so with Corliss Huntington and to some extent, Charles Crocker. Stanford and Huntington were known to have had legendary fights. Hopkins had always supported Stanford. Crocker had generally supported Huntington. No love loss there.

Stanford tried to return the conversation to the-business-at-hand.

"I believe you heard the report that Walter Prichard was shot as he stood on our Truckee Dam. Walter was the only decent thing that came out of the battle with Von Schmidt." Stanford delivered his comment with no effort at concealing his contempt for Von Schmidt.

"Yes, I saw the report. Walter was a good man. That someone would do such a thing is abominable. The report said he was shot from some distance, probably a rifle. How cowardly."

Stanford shifted his position in his chair to light a cheroot. "And that is not all the bad news."

"Now what?"

After getting the cheroot fully lit, Stanford dropped the expended match in a silver tray atop a small table next to his comfortable chair. His relaxed motions conveyed this process had been done many times before.

"I've heard word from San Francisco that Von Schmidt has returned from his celebrated state line survey. Apparently, he has nothing better to do now but try and re-visit old projects. My sources tell me he is once again attempting to get funding for another run at building a pipeline of Tahoe water to San Francisco."

"Not again. I thought this would end with the Water Act," said an exasperated Hopkins.

"I thought so too. After the act was passed in 1870 Von Schmidt tucked tail and took on a contract to confirm California's eastern border. He's spent over two years doing that. As an aside, my informers tell me Von Schmidt couldn't even do that well and there is some question as to his methods and results. Either way, he's trying to get the city council to re-start the pipeline project."

"Is he going to try and reassert control over the dam he built? Could he be behind the shooting?"

Stanford shrugged, "Don't know. He bought several tracks of land adjacent to the Truckee River in his first run at the project. He still owns them. He could attempt to assert water rights from those properties. His aim obviously remains to divert water from the Truckee to San Francisco."

Hopkins now rose and began to pace. "Will the man never cease?"

Stanford brooded aloud, "We keep running into trouble protecting our rights to the Truckee. And Freemont, his blunder at setting the eastern border of California is the root of it all. No one has complete control over Lake Tahoe, neither California nor Nevada. Von Schmidt wants his pipeline. But we need that flow out of Tahoe down the Truckee to float our lumber to the Donner Boom and Lumber Company you and I established."

Hopkins agreed, "We have been fighting Von Schmidt for control over that dam since 1870. It's time we bring this to an end."

"Mark, and how would you propose to do that?"

Hopkins waited, collecting his thoughts. "I think we go about it from two different directions. One, we look to take the fight away from him using our political clout again. But with the shooting of Walter Prichard, maybe he's getting set to take the dam by force. If so, then we are going to have to hire some men with special talents to protect the dam."

"Let's take them one at a time. What political steps do you envision?"

"We should go back to the Legislature and ask for confirmation of our right to the Truckee waters. You should pull some strings with Governor Irwin. Also, maybe you should speak to the Mayor of San Francisco to try and head off any movement by the city council to go forward with this again."

Stanford was now the one who paused in thought. He looked away from Hopkins but then returned having germinated another idea. "I could speak to a few friends in the state senate to see if I can generate some interest to introduce an appropriate motion. We won't need to create new legislation. All we need is affirmation of our 1870 rights. That shouldn't take long."

"Irwin should listen. He owes us some favors."

"No, that won't be a problem. And I will talk to the Mayor. I'll have Jane invite he and his wife to dinner. Better to have that conversation when no one else is around."

Hopkins returned to his seat and appeared more relaxed now that a plan had formed. "That should work."

"But you mentioned men with *special* talents." Stanford's tone covering the word special made sure it was used with a myriad of meanings. "And exactly how would they use those talents?"

Hopkins responded with obvious feigned innocence, "Well, we would need men who can competently protect our employees. These men need to be good with the appropriate weapons. The flow over the dam cannot be interrupted."

"I suppose you are right." As he spoke, Stanford flicked off another length of ash from his cheroot to his tray.

Hopkins continued, "We cannot let it be known our employees on site are vulnerable. We'll never get anyone to work the dam again. Oh, another thing, I think we need to hire someone to identify who killed Walter Prichard. We cannot rely on some local sheriff."

Stanford raised his hand holding the cheroot in the direction of Hopkins as if the small burning object contained an idea. "We could hire that man Crocker used to pursue the right of way issue along the Truckee we had during railroad construction. I think his name was Dale Paris. I believe he works out of Reno, right there in the same area."

"I'm headed east to Colorado and then southwest to Arizona on an extended trip to inspect the progress we are making with the Southern Pacific rail lines. I can stop in Reno and speak to this Paris man."

Stanford nodded. "That will work."

Hopkins persisted, "Leland, we have been at this for seven years now. The Legislature gave us the rights to the Truckee in 1870. You and I were tasked by the CPRR to start a company to log timber for use in the locomotives as fuel to heat the steam engines. We started the Donner Boom and Lumber Company to do just that. Here we sit still talking about a potential interruption of the water flow that could immediately halt our ability to send logs down from the mountains to our sawmills. If we have no logs riding down the Truckee, I don't think it takes much to imagine the disaster that such a loss would have on our ability to fuel our locomotives."

"You are right there. As you know, we are looking at purchasing coal fields in Colorado and Wyoming. While we temporarily prevailed with the passage of the Water Act, the Act did not give us any ownership rights to the water itself. We have only rights to protect and control the flow. Our situation has never been solid. Coal mined from property we own will be a much more permanent solution. But the conversion to coal fuel is at least a couple of years off, maybe as many as five."

"All the more reason we have to protect our rights on the Truckee. We cannot stop our trains from running. It's as simple as that."

"No, you are right, we thought we had won the battle in 1870 with the passage of the Water Act. But we seem to be bogged down with no further control than we had seven years ago."

"Then we are agreed?"

"First, one more question: you mentioned men. Do you know of such men?"

Hopkins looked away then returned his gaze to Stanford. "Leland, I do not dine with men of this ilk if that is your question. I don't even know of any. But I know someone who does."

Stanford smiled, "Ah Mr. Hopkins, you are a man of many hidden talents. The less I know about these talents of yours, the better."

"How would you suggest we then proceed?"

Stanford considered, then answered, "I'll talk to Governor Irwin tomorrow. Afterwards I must return to San Francisco. I have board meetings for Wells Fargo and Pacific Life. While I'm doing that, you can talk to Dale Paris and work on securing the men with *special* talents."

"I will begin my search tomorrow for those men. I will keep you posted though I will use some appropriate diversion in the wires so it is not obvious."

"I agree we must push this issue. We need certainty of fuel supply until coal is brought online."

"By the way, how is our little bank doing?"

"From what I can see, quite well. Mark, who would have thought that when we started the Pacific Union Express it would ultimately merge with Wells Fargo. We started the Pacific Express to channel all the funds generated from the Central Pacific Railroad project. Now, you and I along with Collis and Charles have a controlling interest in one of the top five banks in California."

"Turned out to be a very strategic investment. Lucrative too."

"But I am most interested in my little Pacific Life venture."

Hopkins stood, "I never would have thought you could make any money in life insurance. There aren't enough men with money who think their lives are worth enough to pay some premium on a long-term policy."

"But Mark, there are plenty of wives who think their husbands are. In fact, your beautiful wife Mary has approached me to buy a policy on yourself."

Hopkins smiled, "That sounds almost ominous. I must speak to her about that. Maybe I should watch myself as I travel to Colorado and Arizona to inspect the new rail lines."

"I doubt your lovely bride would ever do anything untoward. But maybe you should have someone taste your food first for a while." The comment was delivered with a hearty chuckle.

# Chapter Six

*August 1877*
*Toal Ranch, Jack's Valley, NV*

The sun had not yet fully risen but the heat was already lifting off the ground underfoot. This time of the morning only fine glimmers of light streaked through the gaps in the low mountains on the eastern horizon as the source of light started to rise above the valley's rim. Those beams would bake those below with full force in less than two hours. Will marveled at the fact it was so hot though the bare sizzle of the yellow orb's rays had yet to be brandished. Mounted, he looked along the frypan of a road. The hardpacked dirt probably never had a chance to cool overnight from the prior day's boiling temperatures. The oven was already burning and the sun wasn't even up.

The herds had collected just before dawn. It was a sight. The road to Carson City was only a short mile or two from his ranch in Jack's Valley. From his vantage on a slight rise, the road looked like a living brown arm, the muscles of which were constantly twitching with the motion of cattle. And the dust, the dust rose like a dirty geyser on either side of the snaking brown movement.

Will tapped his gray mustang, Powder, on the neck. "Poor Luke and Sean. They will get their dose of dirty air today. And their mother insisted on driving the wagon right behind them. Her way of keeping an eye on her little ones. But she's drinking dust just as bad. Should probably go check on them."

*****

Dust was everywhere. A bone-colored cloud of fine dirt particles hung twenty feet tall already and the drive had just started. Will pulled up his bandana.

Every herd was made up of leaders and followers. At the rear of every herd were those steers that needed to be constantly pushed. Without much recent water, the animals here at the rear were even more lethargic than their basic nature.

Luke and Sean were atop their horses swinging ropes and doing their best to look like old experienced hands. While only youngsters, they both had voices that boomed out of their small frames carrying far and away over the din. Will had no trouble finding his sons in the cloud of dust. He rode up between the two after trotting past Beth and Juliette in the wagon. He had stopped to make sure Beth still wanted to hang here to the rear.

"Boys don't try to push them too hard. We don't want to start them running."

"Pa, these cows are so slow." Sean slapped a particularly lingering steer on its backside with an extended loop of his lariat.

"Sean be careful you don't hook a set of horns. You shouldn't use your lariat. Just make noise. If you do use your rope, keep the loop short."

"Ah Dad, I'm not goin' to hook anything I don't plan to hook." Sean had long since become the better roper of the two and regularly practiced swinging loops with his left-handed delivery.

"Yeah, Pa. These cows are really slow. It's hard to make 'em go." Luke chimed in his agreement.

Will smiled. "Someday you'll see a stampede and after that you'll be really happy to see steers just walk."

Sean looked away from the stubborn steer. "I'd like to see a stampede."

Will shook his head, "No you wouldn't."

"It'd be fun to run with the cows," said Luke. "Better than slapping these lazy things on their butts."

"They are not cows, they are steers. If you are going to do any wrangling you should get your names right."

Sean, never one to let a conversation end quick, asked, "Do you think we'll ever see a stampede?"

"Nah, better you don't," said Will. "If these guys ever start running you know what to do don't you?"

Both boys just looked at Will. Good time for instruction.

"If they start runnin' away to the front, just stay here. Let them go. If you're ever in the middle or out on the side, you have to run with them. You have to be faster than the herd. You run forward with the mass and move slowly to the side and out of their ranks as soon as you can, but you never stop. If you stop, you'll be trampled. You have to run with 'em and move out to the side as soon as you can."

"Still think it'd be fun to run with the cow—steers." Sean tried to conceal his mild disappointment.

"Just keep drivin' these steers ahead of you. You're both doing a good job out here on your first day. Like cowboyin'?"

"I do Pa. Can't wait to rope a steer for real." Sean swung his loop over his head for emphasis.

"That day will come soon enough. For now, just keep drivin' them."

Luke the ever focused of the twins had never taken his eyes off the cattle in front of him. "We will keep 'em going Pa."

Will smiled. Good start to the day. He touched the gray's flanks lightly with his spurs. He turned to the boys as he started to leave.

"I'd better get up to the front and make sure there's no trouble brewing as we get ready to head into Carson City. You two keep up the good work."

*****

Henry Dangberg was riding point as Will pulled up just at the south side of Carson City.

"Henry, seen any sign of trouble yet?"

"No. I sent a note to two or three of my friends in the legislature. They are going to be sure and watch from the Capitol's window. Said they'd bring some others along. Might just pull my horse out right onto the walkway leading to the gardens in front of the Capital and turn and face the herd so my back is to that building full of politicians. I'll sit there as this herd of five to six thousand head moves by as if the legislature is irrelevant. I'm going to relish it."

"Should be a bit of a spectacle. You go ahead and pull off to the side, out in front of the Capital Building. While you rest on your laurels for a bit, I'll take over on point to make sure they keep heading out of town. We'll need to get some hands up ahead to make sure none of the herd starts taking any of the side streets."

"Just keep 'em moving nice and slow. Don't want anyone to get anxious and start the herd runnin'."

"That might detract from your show. Wouldn't want that." Will chuckled as he turned to assign some of the hands to ride ahead and protect the side streets.

After talking to several hands, Will pushed Powder to get to the front before the first leaders entered the south side of town. As he traveled by, they looked sluggish. Undoubtedly, they were thirsty. Didn't look like any of them were ready to run. As long as people kept off the street there should be no trouble.

Just as Will reached the southern border of town, Sheriff Zack Thompson came running up the east board walk flailing his arms. Will had little if any respect for the ineffective lawman. Beth had gone to

Thompson in Will's absence when the boys were kidnapped asking for help. But the man took days to move. Will had never forgiven him. Will and Beth had retrieved the boys without any of Thompson's help.

"Will, what ya doin'?"

"Drivin' a herd north to water."

Will did not stop. Thompson turned and jogged alongside of Will continuing to flail his arms as Will and Powder kept their steady pace at a walk.

"Ya'll got a permit?"

"Permit for what?"

"Bringin' those cows into the city limits."

"Nope. Don't think we do. Sheriff, you better stop waggin' your arms so, you're likely to start these steers runnin'."

"Then you gotta turn those things around."

"Can't do that sheriff. If we didn't drive them north today, this whole herd might of just stampeded right through town, headed north for water on their own. We're just protecting the citizens by moving them through under control."

Thompson looked dumfounded. Will smiled and kept on riding ahead.

*****

Main street ran north and south through the city. Smack in the middle on the eastern side of the street was a large plaza spaced with greenery and patterned walkways leading up to the Capital building. Henry Dangberg pulled his horse off to the side of the herd and just onto the main walkway. He then turned back to face the herd with the backside of his horse directed at the capital.

He stood right there like a monument in bronze. He'd tried to convince several of the legislators that something needed to be done about the water supply. For several years now Dangberg had pushed to create a reservoir and regular delivery system. The idea had come from Henry Millard of the Millard Luce Cattle Co. The Carson Valley Cattlemen's Association sold their beef to Millard. Both groups had offered to help build the necessary water system. But the politicians had procrastinated, saying that there was an endless natural supply of water and no need to build anything.

*Well,* thought Dangberg, *the last two years had proven them wrong. Maybe this little demonstration might just drive the point home.*

"Henry Dangberg, quite a show you're putting on here."

Dangberg looked to the rear in the direction of the walkway to the Capital. Erik Pasin, a representative from Yerrington, Nevada stood looking up at the rancher.

"Erik, you have a ranch, you have cattle. You are one of the few up there in that building who should know what we are facing here."

Pasin did not respond but the look on his face told Dangberg he agreed. Henry took the silence as an opportunity to continue with his sermon.

"I've been trying to get this legislature motivated to build a water delivery system but no one will listen. Well, my cattle are dying. I have to move them north. All of our herds are dying. Thank goodness Will Toal offered to keep them up on his northern ranch along the Truckee which is still flowing. Had Toal not offered to take in everyone's stock, there would be a mass of dead beef in the valley. And he's doing this even though he knows it'll ruin his ranch's grasses for years. There's more foresight in that one man than the entire collection of brains in that fancy building behind us."

"Quite a speech. Maybe you should run for office yourself."

"Waste of time. Erik, something must be done to protect the flow of water out of the Truckee. That's Nevada's water! Those greedy California businessmen are trying to take it and you all just sit up there in those meeting rooms watching them do it."

"Ah, Henry. We're not just watchin' them take it. We've already filed suit to stop that engineer A.W. von Schmidt's Tunnel of Doom as our local papers are calling it. They won't take Tahoe's water without a fight from us."

"That's all well and good Erik, but what's the use of protecting the Truckee if you don't create a method of delivery down here to the southern part of the Valley?"

"That's something we need to discuss. You willin' to step down off your horse and speak to some men I've collected back inside."

"I'll talk to them as long as it's quick. As you can see, we've got to move some beef."

"Come on inside Henry, it'll only take a minute. I've gathered several representatives who might be interested to push for legislation on a water system. Now's a perfect time to *drive* the point home." He smiled at his emphasis of the word drive and added, "If you get my drift."

# Chapter Seven

*August 1877*
*Forests North of Tahoe City, CA*

Silence. Peaceful, heavenly silence.

There was no human within miles of his position. No one cared about this section of God's creation now that it had been lumbered. The cutting crews were far to the south now. There were no birds, no animals. They had left. All that remained was man-made desolation. It was as if the land itself were injured. The damage was so serious it could not speak in its normal forest sounds as it tried to recuperate.

Silas Drummond sat on a rock amid a small stand of pine trees along Tahoe's rim looking north at the road from Tahoe City to the town of Truckee. The road was the main land access at the north end of the lake. It was one of very few that lifted up and over the mountainous bowl that cupped the waters of Lake Tahoe. Drummond sat deep within a small stand of tall pines set amid a host of large rocks. Most of the timber in this area had been cut to stumps. Only this one stand survived. The large rocks probably made it too difficult to harvest these trees. The rocks saved them.

From his vantage, Drummond was cloaked from sight, yet had a direct view of the road as it hugged the Truckee River. The road continued alongside the river on its path up to Tahoe behind him.

The access over the rim was only a dirt road. But Drummond had heard of plans circulated by Duane Bliss to build a new railroad spur which would connect Tahoe City with the Central Pacific Railroad's depot below in the town of Truckee. That rail line would snake its way up and over the crest of the Sierras right here on the same road.

Drummond knew of Bliss. They had been adversaries for years. Drummond had tried to convince the people of Carson City to stop Bliss denuding the forests around Glenbrook, Nevada. But Bliss had continued supplying lumber for the needy mines in Virginia City. In the process, Bliss had removed just about every pine tree on the twenty-two miles of Tahoe's eastern shore. Now Bliss intends to build a railroad from Tahoe City to Truckee. Drummond had heard Bliss wanted the railroad to bring San Francisco clientele to a new hotel he planned to build, the Tahoe Tavern in nearby Tahoe City. In Drummond's mind, all that would do is put Bliss in business with the bigger railroad interests who were already cutting trees here until there wouldn't be any forest left.

A six-horse drawn stage strained slowly up the dirt highway down below him. This was why he had been waiting here on the rock, the same rock and the same wait for the last three days. The driver pulled up the lathered team just down from Drummond's position. As dust glided to the front of the now idle rig, a lone middle-aged individual with a beard of long graying strands stepped down out of the cab. Despite the heat, the rail thin man wore knee length coat and trousers that appeared to be made of the same material. The outer clothing looked well-worn but sturdy. He wore thick boots that one might see on someone employed in the outdoors. The driver turned and tossed a small satchel down to the man. He also tossed what looked to be a long walking stick. Drummond watched as the slender silhouette swung the strap of his satchel over his shoulder, adjusted his hat and turned back to the driver. With a simple wave he bade the driver good-bye. The stage moved on.

Drummond stood up. His daily vigil was successful. He looked forward to meeting his spiritual mentor once again. It had been almost four years since they had last talked. Silas watched the man swing his long stick in methodical rhythm as he walked up to the stand of trees and rocks.

"Silas, your directions were quite exact. Sit on the west side of the stage and watch for the only stand of pine trees near the crest. Ask to be let off and I will meet you. And here you are."

"Mr. Muir, it is good to see you. You must be thirsty. I have a canteen."

"Call me John. Silas, we've spent too much time in the mountains to stand on formalities."

"Then John it will be. How was your trip?"

"I am not used to taking stagecoaches. I'd much rather walk. However, I wanted to spend as much time with you as possible before I head north to Alaska. So, as I said in my note, I'd take the stage on the trip here and back so I could spend as much time as possible with you walking over the mountains. I only have a few weeks and I then head back down to Truckee to pick up the train and travel to San Francisco to meet my ship."

"I appreciate you taking the time to journey here. There is much about to take place. I had run out of people who would talk to me. The land needs a voice, a sponsor. You have taken on that role before. There is no one else now."

"Come, let us walk. I assume you have a camp higher up. After sitting in that infernal stage, I look forward to a good walk."

"I do, it will take us only a couple of hours to get there."

*****

A campfire burned gently. Low flames threw specks of ash skyward from the pinnacles of their soft yellow reach. The blaze turned orange at its base hovering over the coals below. Heat wafted invisibly from its center. The two men sat inside the umbrella of that heat listening in silence to the consistent crackle of sizzling wood and occasional pop of burning sap. The dark serenity of the night mirrored the dejected emotion of the two sitting in silence.

Then, "Silas, you were right. They have ruined Tahoe's forests. When I was here last, you and I walked the eastern shore to see what Bliss and his logging company had done."

"John, back in 1873 when you were last here, it was only the forest around Glenbrook Harbor and here along the Truckee that had been cut. But they did not stop there."

"No, they didn't stop. Today's hike up to the crest here on Tahoe's north shore opens a window through which to view the devastation. As you said in your letter which prompted my return, that view provides ample evidence of the cutting here around the whole north end of the lake. There are precious few trees left. There has been a bloodless scalping of the forest."

Silas nodded, "Though we could not see the full extent, Bliss and his company have done the same along the entire eastern shore. Hobart and his logging company cut everything around the north east section. And the Central Pacific and their ilk have literally leveled this side of the north and down the western shore. The only old stand forest left is at the south end."

"And you tell me that this man Lucky Baldwin now wants to obtain rights to that stand."

"Yes, he wants to preserve some of the mature trees around his resort I think he calls the Tallac House after the peak behind him. But he's another of those rich barons from San Francisco. His plans are not well known, but the only reason he could have for purchasing over one hundred thousand acres is to make money. The only way to make money from that kind of acreage is to log."

"Tell me about the dam."

Silas sighed, "The dam of the Truckee is now complete. It has raised the level of the lake. I don't know how much, but I think it is at least three to four feet."

"That doesn't sound like a great deal for the effort."

"Oh, but John, four feet covering a lake twenty miles long and over ten miles wide is a lot of water."

"And you say that this man Von Schmidt wants to take that water down to San Francisco? I thought he tried that and lost."

Silas poked the fire with a stick angling the lower logs closer to the coals. "Yes, he tried but the Central Pacific's barons beat him with their Water Act. But word is he is again pushing the city of San Francisco to start the plan again."

Muir stretched his legs closer to the enhanced heat from the fire just created by Silas' adjustment. "If they start taking water from Tahoe, their greed will not stop. They'll continue until they drain her."

"I don't know that even the city of San Francisco could drain her, but they could easily ruin her shores. In fact, that might be another reason for Baldwin's interest. The dam raised the lake level almost flooding his resort. He wants the dam gone."

"And Silas, what do you think about that dam?"

"I think it should be gone too. I would do anything to remove that dam. On that topic I agree with Baldwin, probably the only topic he and I would agree upon. I think the whole lake must be returned to its natural state. God created something magical; it should remain so."

"You know I agree with you. The whole forest must be protected. From here to Yosemite is a footprint of God's work. I keep trying to make sure generations to come will be able to see how it looked when the Good Lord left if for us."

"It is a strange time. There are so many players involved. And all are driven by nothing other than self-interest."

Muir smiled, "Maybe we can use that self-interest to our advantage."

Taken aback by such a comment coming from one who Drummond knew to be as straightlaced a Presbyterian as any he knew, "I'm not sure how to take that."

With a wave of his hand Muir admonished, "Easily, we pit some against the others and let them fight. These people have power and financial might. We do not. However, all we must do is simply guide the fight in the right direction. That direction has an aim. That aim is to protect Tahoe and the trees around her."

"Who would you pit against the other?"

"You tell me that Bliss wants to build a resort. That must mean he needs people to come. He wants tourists. If he wants tourists, then he should want the natural beauty to return. He will also need to bring them up to the Lake. That has to be why he wants to build his railroad spur from Tahoe City to Truckee."

"Bliss has said he wants to have the forest return. But I have little trust in the man. He's devastated the entire east side of the lake. I think his turnabout is driven more by the fact that Virginia City's mines will not produce forever. Also, Bliss has logged everything he owns down to dirt. I think that is what is pushing him to look elsewhere for money."

"You might be right. But you tell me that Bliss is a wealthy man. Maybe he is struck by the damage he's done. Guilt is a powerful emotion. Could be a tool for use by us."

"How so? John, I still don't see how we can *work* with these people." The word work was expressed with no small amount of exasperation.

"I know a man with the Central Pacific Railroad. His name is E.H. Harriman. From all accounts, he is increasingly powerful in the operations of the railroad as the four old barons who started the CPRR move on, reveling in their wealth. I have spoken with Harriman on occasion."

With no small amount of exasperation Silas said, "You're not thinking of trying to work with the railroad are you John? Tell me that is not what you are thinking. They're worse that Bliss by several orders of magnitude."

"Harriman wants to protect his railroad, of that I have no doubts. But in our limited conversations, I detect a pragmatism in him I did not expect. They need lumber for their locomotives. The forests around Tahoe are petering out. They will have to look elsewhere."

"How could you possibly imagine a way to work with the railroad? It sounds to me like you could not have described a worse partner just now."

"The CPRR has connections in Washington to rival anyone. Even my connections respect the power they wield. The only way to ensure Tahoe has long term protection is to have the lake included in a federal park. If we are going to get the government to create a federal park out of these lands, we will need powerful connections to get it done."

Still highly suspicious, Silas asked, "And what do you have to offer the railroad in return for their cooperation, for use of their connections?"

"I have nothing. But the government has land; lots of it further to the north. I think we bait the hook with a plan to swap the CPRR's land around Tahoe with forests further north and let the railroad go fishing. I've walked the entire length of the Sierras. While pristine and beautiful in their own way, the forests to the north do not hold anything like Tahoe."

"Swap land?"

"Exactly. Direct the land grabbers to the north. Have them help to block any purchase by Baldwin and preserve what is left. Work to block Von Schmidt and any attempt to take Tahoe's water. We need to remove that dam. If the CPRR has trees to fell to the north, they don't need the flow of the Truckee."

"But what about the forests to the north?"

"Silas, they will suffer. But if this plan works, we protect the jewel of Tahoe. We need to protect the magic that was given to us that runs from Yosemite all the way north to Tahoe."

"And how does Bliss fit in."

"Bliss is the key. If he truly bears some measure of guilt, then he is the key to work with Harriman and the railroad. He needs his little railroad spur to run from Truckee to Tahoe City. That will be the glue that binds our band together. I'll go speak to Bliss first."

There was a long silence. "John, I think you intend to dance with the devil. But I must admit, I see no other alternatives."

# Chapter Eight

*August 1877*
*Road to Reno just north of Carson City, NV*

Will pulled up at the top of the gentle rise that formed a low subtle pass from Carson City to what the locals called Washoe. He looked north toward their intended destination. To his left was the ever-present wall of the Sierras. To the right and the east was a set of low foothills that would ultimately rise into Mount Davidson, which carried Virginia City like a sling on the side of its eastern slope. In between was a slender flat plain that stretched for about twenty miles toward Reno. The long slim sweep was further narrowed on the east side by a small body of water called Washoe Lake.

Normally blue and inviting, Washoe's fluid expanse was a mile or two long and half as far wide. At its center, the lake was only ten feet deep at its best. Fed by small streams coming off the mountains, it had no outflow. Essentially, it was a sump. Because of the lack of depth, each year the seasons drove the lake to expand and retreat far more than most bodies of water. With the exaggerated swell and shrink, one never knew exactly where the border of the lake was at any given time. While possibly good for some types of farming, the process of ever moving borders posed a special problem for the unsuspecting. The swampy fringes became a soft bed of tall tempting grasses. The combination of succulent green grasses, and lake beyond made for a colossal trap for steer or horse who could go belly deep in the muck and never get anywhere near the actual water.

Today, Washoe looked dry. Vulnerable with its lack of volume, the normal blue waters were gone with the years of light snowfall. All that remained was dark dirt in the middle of an expansive bowl. But that bowl could still be wet. The dark color of the dirt told Will to beware, it could be soft. The mud in the middle was an invitation to a herd of thirsty steers. Getting passed Washoe was going to be a challenge.

Will turned Powder around and motioned for several of the hands to ride up to his position at front of the herd. The hands were a collection from all the Carson Valley ranches. He knew them only passingly. Jed King, one of the other ranch owners, also rode up.

"Jed, we need to string a set of hands inside of Washoe's soft swampy borders."

Jed King looked out at the same scene Will had been assessing. "I agree. We need to keep them from running to the muck in the middle. What are you thinkin'?"

Will looked back at Washoe, "I'm thinkin' first we set up a string of hands inside of the lake. They need to be a solid barrier. They'll hold their position until the entire herd passes. They also need to be in position up ahead long before the leaders get there. We'll keep some extra hands on the right side of the herd up front to drive them towards the mountains on the left as much as possible."

"That's probably as good a plan as any. We need to control the leaders by pushing them left."

Jed turned to the other cowhands gathered in their small group. "Pete, grab the hands from our ranch and position them up ahead inside Washoe as Will suggests. Make sure each one knows to drive the herd away from the lake."

"Yes sir, Mr. King." Pete then spun his horse to head back to the herd.

Will then added, "I'll have Juan collect a couple of other hands and move to the right-side front. Between the hands from your ranch and some added help on the right side we should be able to keep them headed north."

King nodded, "Let's hope so. It's going to be a muddy mess if they get out there in the soft dirt."

*****

Will watched as the leaders of the herd came up. He sat on Powder with five of Jed Kings' hands strung out up ahead along the western side of Washoe. There was about a half mile between the string of hands and the dried underside of what had been the outermost part of the lake. The mounted cow hands faced the Sierras with Washoe to their backs. Will thought they looked like a calvary waiting for review. He saw Juan under his immediately recognizable wide sombrero working the herd's leaders on the right side. The steers were pushing against the hands trying to head to Washoe's inviting expanse. The dark dirt in the middle was the main attractant, but Will thought the leaders could probably smell more water somewhere out under the lakebed.

Will helped Juan and the hands at the head of the herd. The leaders moved alongside the barrier of cowhands strung along the lake. They kept moving north. Good sign. Will's plan seemed to be working.

The leaders of the herd moved further north of the dried lakebed. The main body of the herd continued on the road, but it also pushed to the right against the cowhand barrier. The rear of the herd was now approaching the southernmost hands along the line of cowboys. Will turned to see that all was moving north as he'd hoped. He left control of the leaders to others and beckoned Juan to follow him back to help the hands acting as a barrier. He could see Luke and Sean still swinging their ropes to the rear followed by Beth and Juliette in the wagon.

As he continued back south in between the herd and lake Will yelled out to the hands, "Let's get them north of the lake. Keep 'em moving'. But you men holding the wall outside of the lake, stay put until the entire herd is north. Let the other hands drive them along."

The main body of the herd had just cleared north of the lake and barrier of extra hands. Will was about to tell those hands to rejoin the herd when he saw a group of steers break toward the mountains. A couple of hands that had been riding at the left side of the leaders turned to move the breakout back into the fold. But there were only a few scattered men along the mountain side of the herd. The main worry had been keeping the mass from turning right toward what had been the lake. The two hands that headed to move the group back to the herd left a large space between them and the next cowboy to the north.

"Juan, they're turning left. What in the world?"

"Si jefe. They are heading back to Carson."

"Why would these stupid steers head back to Carson? We need more help on the left side."

Then it happened. It happened in a flash. The whole herd turned to its left one hundred and eighty degrees. It was if they moved as one unit and completely reversed their direction. There was no jostling, no bumping of bodies. The herd moved instantaneously as if it was a single mass, a single coordinated unit. The speed and the sheer volume of bodies that turned without any resulting chaos left Will speechless. The lack of cowhands on the mountain side must have left a gap of freedom sensed or intuited by the collection of thirsty beef. The opening gave way to follow instinct, instinct for water. What had been a movement north changed in an instant to now head south. And they began to run. Everything was out of control.

Will had seen it happen once before in New Mexico. A lightning strike hit near a smaller herd he and Juan had been moving. The entire group flashed in a different direction as if a leader snapped his fingers and on some prearranged command the group reacted in unison. It had been stunning to see the entire collection of bunched steers turn with such quickness in close quarters and not so much as bump each other. Here before him Will watched a similar astonishing change. The entire herd turned on an instant and began heading back south on the road. But now, steers in the north were now pushing what had been the laggards back south.

The new leaders started to veer back towards the lakebed. "They're headed to the lake." The rear now became the lead and the lead was running. Directly in front of them were Luke and Sean along with two other hands who had been working drag. Not enough to stop them. And there was Beth and the wagon. The entire herd was right on them.

Will spurred Powder to give him everything the mustang had. Juan followed. But they would not get to Beth and the boys in time. As he raced southward, he implored the hands between the herd and the lake.

"Get out your guns. When you hear me shoot, start shooting. It'll be the only thing to keep them away from the lake."

Will could see each hand reach for his sidearm. He could also see the tension in each of the faces as they stared at a wall of running steers."

*****

The rumble of a thousand steers running out of control was deafening. The horse pulling Beth's wagon panicked early almost at the same instant the herd turned. It reared. It's front hooves came back to earth and it made an immediate turn to race away from the oncoming amalgamation of beef. But the animal's turn was too tight for a smooth change of direction for the wagon. With the quick pull to the right, the wagon tipped violently downward on its left side in its shortened pivot. The right side rose lifting the inside front wheel off the ground. It was all Beth could do to stab her left foot out for a brace on the low side of the wagon and hold her seat. Juliette who had been riding to her left began sliding off the bench downhill and away from Beth as the rig lurched to its right. Beth dropped the reins and grabbed Juliette with both hands just before the child flew off the wagon altogether. Beth had all she could do to just hold her close as the wagon made its turn. The right-side wheels returned to earth, but the wagon then bounced wickedly side to side in its doomed connection to the horse now running free. Beth had clutched the baby to her with no thought other than simple maternal instinct. She looked over her shoulder. There couldn't be more than a dozen yards to the first steers.

Sean saw his mother grab Juliette. Having lost her hold of the reins, the wagon was now out of control.

"Luke, we need to get to Ma."

Sean possessed the only voice naturally gifted that could raise itself above the din of the oncoming hooves. His voice could carry for miles.

The twins had already turned to race away from the onrushing herd. They had been close to the steers pushing them forward. Those same steers were still close only now right behind chasing the boys. The wagon was just ahead. The harnessed horse galloped in full stride forward.

Upon hearing his brother, Luke looked away from the oncoming herd and glanced at the wagon. In a quick decision, he yelled back to Sean, "We need to grab the horse and do what Pa said. We need to run ahead of the steers but get it out of their path."

Sean had already turned his horse and spurred it forward. "I'll get one side and you get the other."

"Right. Let's go." Sean veered his horse behind the wagon and pulled along the left side. Luke went right.

Sean fought for control of his own mount as he reached for the bridle on the horse pulling the wagon. He tried to time the rise and fall of the animal's head. They were not in sync. He reached and missed twice. On the second reach he almost fell off in between his horse and the wheels of the wagon. He would have been run over by the wagon's wheels and then at the mercy of the herd still close behind. Momentarily frightened, he recovered more determined than ever to get a hold. On his third attempt he grabbed the harness bridle. The horse immediately began to quiet some, but still ran.

"Luke, grab the other side of the bridle. The horse's head is moving smoother now."

Luke rode up and got a hold of the opposite side of the bridle in his first attempt.

Sean then yelled, "Keep moving but head to the mountains. We have to get away from the herd."

"Got it." Luke then pulled with his left hand trying to get the horse to respond. The horse was still too panicked to do as instructed.

Seeing the lack of movement, Sean took his right hand fisted as it held the bridle and literally punched the side of the horse's head. "Move!"

The horse finally began turning gradually to the right following Luke's lead.

It took them several hundred yards, but the boys had pulled the wagon away from the onslaught of cattle. Now out of the herd's path, they both pulled up straining to get the wagon's horse to relax and halt. They both kept their hands on the bridle as the horse was slow to calm.

There, stopped far off the original road both boys turned to their mother.

"Luke and Sean, I could not be prouder of you. I thought Juliette and I were going to die a terrible death trampled by a herd of steers."

*****

Galloping to the south, Will had watched the scene unfold before him. He saw the boys run after the wagon and pull it to safety. Parental pride swelled, but he didn't have time to absorb it for long. With Beth and Juliette now safe, there would be plenty of opportunity for that later. He waved to Juan to keep with him. The herd was now trying to bend around the last of the cowboys along the barrier and head to the lake. Will and Juan had to get there first.

Only a horse with the quickness of Powder could have made it. The horse could get from a complete standstill to full gallop faster than any horse Will had ever ridden. Will and Powder pulled just ahead of the steers now leading the herd with Juan close behind him. Will saw that the other two hands that had been working drag with the twins now turned to help. Will then pulled his gun and Juan did likewise, motioning for the cowboys up ahead to do the same. Just as Will rounded the inside of the steers trying now to turn to the lake, he raised his gun in the air and fired. The lead steers stopped and tried to cut behind Will and still get to water. The two drag hands fired and blocked any further movement to the south. Juan followed to fill that hole behind Will and fired a round right into the ground in front of the closest steer. He kept firing in front of the herd facing him.

The herd's reaction to the gunfire was almost as instantaneous as the turning movement. Those steers closest to the string of gun firing cowhands stopped in their tracks. Normally, a herd would have bolted away from any gunfire. But here, the fear to bolt was balanced by the instinct to keep moving forward to water. The net reaction was to ease up. Those behind butted up into animals decelerating. To Will's relief, the collective result was a jarring halt.

Will had the leaders turning away from the lake and towards the mountains. Juan held his position. The barrier cowboys that had been further north trotted back toward Juan closing the gap in front of Washoe Lake even tighter. Almost as quickly as they'd started, the herd stopped. A brown snorting collection of muscle and hide massed in a standoff with the cowboys on the barrier.

Both cowhands and cattle stood eyeing each other not sure what to do next.

After what seemed to be minutes, Will yelled out to Luke and Sean, "Boys, start driving the back end of this bunch north up the road. We need to get them north of the lake."

Luke and Sean turned to their mother. Luke rode back alongside the wagons horse keeping the downed left side rein in his hand to ultimately give it to his mother. Sean watched and did the same with the right-side rein. Beth now had both reins she'd lost earlier.

Beth looked at her sons as only a proud mother could and said, "Go, your father and the herd need you. I'm fine now."

The boys turned off and headed to the back end of the herd and started yelling and exhorting the dregs to start their move north again.

*****

Will breathed easier when the herd cleared the Washoe plain and moved north closer to Reno. They would bed down the herd in a couple more miles. The whole group both human and bovine needed a rest. Everyone was exhausted.

Henry Dangberg rode up. "Heard I missed some excitement."

## Chapter Nine

*August 1877*
*Reno, NV*

Intermittent bursts of sun rays reflected off the wind ruffled surface of a water trough outside. The ripples were caused by an oven temperature breeze making its way down Main Street. The bolts of redirected radiance knifed through the outer window as if lightning on a dry day, striking the dangling crystals of the chandelier suspended from the ceiling. A wash of stippled glimmers showered onto the massive mirror behind the bar. He wondered if other people had ever experienced the same thing. He had felt it before. When the sun hits a chandelier just right and sprays dots of light all around the room, he could not escape the feeling those broken bits of light were raindrops. He stood across from the mirror watching a storm of light particles dance across the reflective glass. He marveled as the display drenched the interior with speckled illumination.

Only the most upscale of drinking establishments dared hang a crystal chandelier, and this was an upscale drinking establishment. He was here doing what he could to escape the early afternoon heat generated by those same rays now creating the light show of reflected beams.

Dale Paris stood at the bar of the Depot Saloon. Positioned directly across the street from the transcontinental railroad depot in Reno, Nevada, the bar was never at a loss for customers. This was the last stop before the train headed east into the Great Basin. The heat here was stifling and Paris could not imagine what the temperature would be like out in the desert. Many exited the stuffy packed passenger cars after a long day train ride from Sacramento and stopped in for a drink, maybe their last until they crossed the Rockies. As usual, here at six in the evening, the heat outside rose to its daily insufferable peak. The temperature late in the day often drove men inside seeking some cold libation, alcohol or not.

He lifted his beer and plunged his nose further into the mug than usual not only to savor the smell of the ale, but also to escape the odors leaking from his own body. Paris normally wore a thick woolen suit with vest and belly watch. But with temperatures in excess of one hundred degrees, today he wore only lightweight dungarees and an open collared shirt.

He was never without his bowler hat and sidearm. Despite the lighter garments, sweat soaked through the underarms of his shirt and lower back. Paris could not remember an August that was so hot. He hoped the man he was about to meet would not think him unprofessional to appear without a full suit. Paris had endeavored to join the Pinkerton Agency without success. But he wore his bowler hat and three piece suit whenever possible to create the illusion that he was an agent with that illustrious agency.

Paris had positioned himself in front of the bar's large mirror so he could see the reflected image of the entrance to the saloon over his shoulder. Angled as such, he could watch for the man he was to meet without having to stare at the batwing doors. According to the wire he had received from Charles Crocker, that man was to be on today's late train from Sacramento. The ale tasted good. It might be the only cool item for hundreds of yards. The saloon must keep their barrels down below ground surrounded by ice. Nothing left out in the open above ground these days would stay cool for long.

A whistle's shriek sounded the arrival of the evening train. Paris was about to order his second ale but decided to wait until he met this new potential customer. Shortly, a middle aged man with a gray beard extending down his chest walked into the saloon. He wore a dark suit with white pinstripes despite the heat. Obviously, he was a gentleman. Yet gentleman or no, he too succumbed to the ravages of the temperatures as he held his jacket over his shoulder with his index finger. In his other hand, the man held a brown small-brimmed hat with a crease that ran from front to back. It was a businessman's hat, not western at all.

Paris immediately felt more comfortable being under dressed without his own jacket. The bearded man stood just inside the doorway and scanned the room as the batwing doors flipped back and forth fanning his entry. Paris turned away from the bar and faced the entrance. He'd been told to watch for a man in a suit sporting a long gray beard. In return, Paris had responded to the wire that he would lift his bowler hat as an indication of his own identity. He raised his bowler hat above his head to garner the new entrant's attention. Spying the uplifted hat, the gentleman approached.

"I'm Dale Paris, I assume you are Mr. Hopkins." Paris offered his hand.

Accepting the greeting with a firm grip, "Nice to meet you Mr. Paris. Yes, I am Mark Hopkins."

"How was the trip?"

"Absolutely beastly. I'm not sure which town is hotter, Sacramento or Reno. Neither one is habitable."

"Hope you are not headed further east. Out on the basin might be so hot as to be dangerous."

"Unfortunately, that is exactly where I'm headed. But not until tomorrow."

Paris shook his head, "Too bad, I am not envious. It is plenty hot enough here for me."

"Is this weather ever going to break?"

Placing his bowler hat back on his head, Paris said, "Not for some time. This is the third year of hot summers."

"And hot winters. Which brings us to the point of Charles Crocker asking you to meet me. Is there someplace where we can get a meal while not frying in the process?"

"Where are you staying?"

"At the Little Big Town Hotel and Casino."

Paris smiled, "Nice accommodations. They have a restaurant. Why don't we just talk over dinner there. You can check in, freshen up and we can sit and discuss how I might be of service."

Hopkins lifted his left hand at the elbow, "Excellent idea. I'd love to be able to freshen up after which we can relax, eat and I can explain what we have in mind."

*****

Hopkins dabbed his mouth with the linen napkin. He then folded the cloth and set it to the side of his empty plate. A waiter immediately appeared to remove any evidence of the now consumed meal. Hopkins pushed his chair back from the table, reached down with each hand to spread his jacket and inserting his index fingers into the frontal pockets of his vest. With his jacket spread, a rather unique watch chain was exposed. It had thick alternating gold and silver links. Hopkins then pushed further away from the table and crossed his legs.

Paris admired the shiny fob. "Unique watch chain."

Hopkins smiled, "A present from my wife. I've become rather fond of it. Take it everywhere."

As the waiter was about to depart, Hopkins raised his hand and asked, "Would you please bring me a cigar?"

"Right away sir."

"Mr. Paris, would you like one?"

"No thank you, I am going to enjoy the effects of a wonderful dinner a bit longer."

"Fair enough. Then only one cigar waiter if you please."

Paris watched the man for clues. He had never met Hopkins. He had done considerable work for the Central Pacific Railroad several years ago, but all his dealings had been through Charles Crocker. Paris knew very little about the slender man across the table. Dinner conversation was pleasant but they had avoided all discussion of business. Paris got the feeling this man was quite careful with information and controlled his conversations. What knowledge he had of Hopkins came from offhanded remarks by Crocker. It seems Hopkins watched the money as the transcontinental railroad was being built. He approved each expenditure thereby effectively controlling the progress of the entire project. In those brief comments, Crocker had displayed the utmost respect. In fact, Crocker had told him his partner Huntington felt Hopkins was the most honest man he'd ever known. Both felt quite comfortable having Hopkins watch the money. No small task for such a monumental project.

But sitting across from him, Paris had trouble getting any read on what might have led to the fairly complicated arrangements to set up this meeting. Paris had been told the exact date and time to be present in the Depot Saloon. Hopkins must be on a tight schedule yet made the stop to talk.

Hopkins held the match to his cigar puffing repeatedly to light the tobacco. With each draw the flame sucked into the end of the glowing cylinder after which a small blaze reached higher on the exhales. Determining the cigar to be lit, Hopkins extinguished the match.

"There is nothing like a good smoke after one is refreshed and fed. A markedly more pleasant state of affairs compared to my situation walking off that train. I appreciate your patience in allowing me to change clothes and buy you dinner."

"Not at all," said Paris. "I'm the one who should offer thanks. That was a remarkable meal. Much appreciated."

"It was the least I could do as I have held you here all this time and have yet to explain why I wanted us to meet."

Paris waited.

"The Donner Boom and Lumber Company would like to retain your services."

Paris was puzzled. "I thought you worked with the Central Pacific Railroad."

"I do, but Leland Stanford and I are investors in several other companies, the Donner Boom and Lumber concern happens to be one of them. Mr. Stanford and I are responsible for its management and operations. That company operates the dam across the Truckee River at its origin up at Lake Tahoe. The dam controls the flow of the Truckee out of Tahoe. With that flow, we send timbers down the river to our milling operations in Donner near the Truckee train depot. Those timbers are milled and used to heat the boilers on our locomotives. Without that wood, the locomotives don't run. The flow of the Truckee is vital to the entire transcontinental railroad."

This was new information to Paris. But he knew these men controlled vast sums of money so it should come as little surprise they had investments beyond the railroad.

"We had an employee shot and killed recently in the area of the dam. We would like you to investigate and if possible, identify the perpetrator."

Paris had conducted dozens of investigations. Knowing now what the prospective scope of employment entailed, he felt right at home.

"May I ask a couple of questions?"

"Absolutely."

"What was the name of the person killed?"

"Walter Pritchard. He was our supervisor, a critical part of the operation."

"Do you have any further particulars?"

"Absolutely none. We got the information via third hand from another employee. We want you to pursue this irrespective of any investigative efforts by local authorities."

"I was going to ask if you had heard from any sheriff?"

"Despite requesting information from the Tahoe City authorities, we have heard nothing."

"When was this done?"

"Approximately 4 days ago. Sadly, we are not even sure of that date."

It was Paris who now pushed his chair back from the table. Muscles relaxed. Minor apprehension evaporated. He had not known what this meeting was about. The job outlined was exactly the kind of thing he did. He was good at it.

"I will be happy to be of service."

Hopkins took a drag from the cigar. "We were hoping you would. I assume your fees would be the same as during your efforts for the railroad back in Carson City."

"My fees would be the same."

"I am glad we can come to this arrangement. We need to find out who did this. There are significant stakes both political and economic. Also, we would like to be able to inform Mr. Prichard's family we found the perpetrator."

"Not all murders are solved. But I have a respectable record of results."

"I sent some wires earlier to check some contacts here in town and they have confirmed you have a remarkable record. More importantly, Mr. Crocker thinks highly of you. However, I must also hire some security personnel. To be blunt, Crocker told me not to have you hire any security forces. Something about past events in Carson City along those lines that did not work out well."

Paris stared at the ground in an obvious display of conscience then returned to look Hopkins directly in the eye. "Yes, some of those events did not work out as intended. In the push to find a solution to a critical problem for the railroad's right of way, I hired a man who disguised a grudge he bore with a rancher named Will Toal."

"And was this grudge a factor in what I'm led to believe was substantial gunplay?"

"He and his grudge turned out to be the one and only trigger. People died that day that did not have to. I'm not proud of how it worked out. It created a major bone of contention between me and Will Toal, but we later worked on another matter in Glenbrook which led to a mending of bridges to some degree."

"I was told by Crocker that while there was some unfortunate gunplay, the transcontinental railroad project was facing an untenable delay. Your actions ultimately led to a resolution of a seemingly insoluble problem."

"Maybe it did, Mr. Crocker told me the same thing. But I would rather the solution was arrived at without the guns. As a result, I am happy Mr. Crocker has recommended you pursue retention of any security personnel through other channels. I prefer the investigation work. I can certainly put you into contact with some folks who might be able to identify qualified men."

"That won't be necessary, I have a meeting tomorrow morning before I leave. I trust the person I am to meet will be able to find men capable of protecting our employees."

"I am looking forward to this job. Motive would seem to be elusive. Usually, if you can discover the motive for a killing, locating the perpetrator follows. So far, I have not heard anything that could lead to identification of a motive. Establishing that will probably be my first order of business."

"There are some things you should probably know. A man named Allexey Von Schmidt actually built the dam. Our railroad was instrumental in having a bill passed in the California legislature called the 1870 Water Act. We took control of his dam as a result of that bill. Obviously, he was not happy with that consequence. It seems Mr. Von Schmidt has recently made it known that he now wants it back. To complicate matters, the reduced flow of the Truckee has created havoc with downstream Nevada milling operations. The river's flow is used as a source of power to drive pulleys and machinery at these operations. Right now, that flow is not driving their machines. And, if that is not enough, the company is told we should expect a suit to be filed by the State of Nevada on behalf of its agricultural and ranching interests who are receiving little, if any, flow for crops and livestock."

"You have just taken me from a situation of no apparent motive to a multitude of possibilities. Sounds like I'll have a lot to check into. I look forward to the challenge."

Hopkins stood and offered his hand. "Perfect. I would like you to report to Mr. E.H. Harriman. He is an up and coming executive with the Central Pacific. I will be traveling out of the area and will not be able to manage these efforts. You can wire him at the railroad's main offices in Sacramento."

"I will start work on this tomorrow first thing."

# Chapter Ten

*August 1877*
*Campsite, Road to Reno*

A low eight foot circular blaze sent wisps of ash upwards against an indigo sky. The sun was down but a hint of light persisted to softly purple a darkening horizon. The small flying cinders burned bright orange and yellow when given birth at the base of the blaze only to meet their demise several feet above the flame. The once bright embers turned black as their energy dissipated. The fire kept regenerating a new population of embers minute by minute only to see another short life span end in the cooling air further above.

Beth sat mesmerized by the continuing drama of flaming birth and death. Some embers made it higher than others. Some were large and some were the barest of substance. She wondered if she was watching a microcosm of human existence reduced to a momentary vision of a coal's ash. Born in the heat of creation, the balls of life's energy rise to one's personal height only to meet our end in the blackness of termination. Her thoughts were darker than usual. Maybe the scare of the stampede had colored her outlook.

She held a sleeping Juliette in her arms. The two-year-old, oblivious to the day's frightening ordeal within an hour after things returned to norm, had pranced around the early campfire inspecting each cowboy's plate of food, their bedding, and clothes. The little one's bouncing personality with naturally flirtatious smiles captivated every one of the men she pestered. She was without doubt the princess of the campfire. But alas, her flame had burned too and she now rested comfortably asleep in her mother's arms.

"Heard our daughter has been the belle of the campfire ball."

Beth looked up at Will who had just moved close. He was attempting to collapse softly from a standing position to seated squat while holding his plate of biscuits and beans without spilling or waking the baby. He hit the ground after which a sigh escaped.

Beth said thoughtfully, "Big day?"

Will took a second to respond. Beth watched as he glanced at her before any answer. She surmised he was trying to get a read on her mood.

"I suppose. It ended well but could have been a lot different."

"Different is an understatement. There were several moments where I thought your daughter and I would be taking an early exit. I have been watching this fire and wondering if we are not just like the embers, born with burning ambition only to flame out into nothingness at some indeterminate level. From what I can see, what's left is darkness."

Will set his dinner plate down, food untouched. In that singular action Beth knew she had touched a chord in her husband. That he was so perceptive reminded her of the qualities that drew her to him time and time again.

Will twisted his upper body to face Beth. "You've been scared. Your foundation got shook. It's understandable. But you survived. Our sons played an amazing role in that. We should be proud of the way they took control."

Beth turned to face Will. "Oh, I'll get over this. When it happened, I just panicked at the thought that Juliette would not get to experience her life. She'd be like one of these coals, gone in a matter of moments. In those flash seconds, I wasn't worried about me, I thought I was facing the loss of our daughter."

Will did not answer. He reached out to touch Beth's forearm as it cradled their little girl. Nothing further needed to be said at that moment.

Beth now scoffed, "Ah, go eat your dinner. Everyone else around the campfire has already eaten."

"I had to make sure the herd was settled and calm for the night. The boys ate and are out there singing to the steers like some rusty old cowhands. I had to tell Sean to do it quietly. He's so naturally loud he would keep those heifers awake all night if he didn't tone it down."

Beth smiled, "He is loud. He just has a big voice. He can't help it."

"And it gets worse when he's excited. They're having the time of their lives. Both have told me they always wanted to be cowboys."

"Well, that part of your plan worked out."

"Now don't go getting swampy on me again. Gotta pull yourself out of this down spot. By the way, better not let Fr. Cecconi hear you talk about nothing but darkness once you die. I've always imagined you'd head to a place of sweetness and light. I'm the one who is playin' fast and loose with a trip to the darker side."

Now Beth perked up a bit. "And what makes you say that?"

After chewing a few beans, he answered. "Because I've sent a fair number of men to an early departure."

"None that didn't deserve it, and some who would certainly have sent you or I had you not acted."

She saw Will smile, a knowing smile. "You've got my dander up and you did it on purpose didn't you? Now you've got me up and fired in wifely protection mode."

Will grinned widely. "Could you tell?"

"Will Toal, you couldn't just let me wallow in my beer, could you?"

"Didn't know you had a beer nearby."

"You know what I mean."

"As I sat down, it was pretty obvious you needed a spark. You've done it for me on days. This was one time you needed it. I could've picked you up and given you a hard rap on the backside, but you had the baby in your arms."

"You men are all alike, you think a rap is somehow beneficial. The method you used is much more appropriate."

Setting his empty plate down, he said, "Anything that works." His grin was now unabashed. Will moved to sit right behind Beth. He wrapped his arms around her in silent support, non-verbal reassurance that he was there for her. Then he said, "Time will smooth over the scare you had today."

"You think you're so smart."

"Never made that claim."

Just then another presence came near. Henry Dangberg stood off to the side of the pair.

"Will, I hate to interrupt, but can I talk to you?"

Will turned and looked up at Henry. "About the herd?"

Dangberg shook his head, "No, it's about my conversation with the legislators."

Will turned back to Beth who saw the seriousness in his face and smile now gone. He asked, "Are you okay?"

Beth answered, "Yes, I'm fine. Go talk. I have to put the baby down anyway. She and I are going to sleep in the back of the buckboard. I do not look forward to sleeping on any ground. I will leave that to those of the male gender. They seem to think there is something spiritual in it." There was a playful sarcasm in the comment.

"I'll go talk to Henry and then come back and make sure you two are tucked in for the night."

*****

After Will stood, Henry Dangberg gently grabbed his elbow in what he took as a fatherly gesture to move away from the fire. "Let's go over here," motioning to an open area of now darkness engulfed grassland. As they walked Dangberg asked, "Will, is there something wrong with Beth?"

"No, she's just a bit shaken because of the stampede."

"Well, I can understand that. If I'd have been in her shoes, I'd have been more than just a little scared. I'd have been in an outright panic."

Will nodded his agreement.

Dangberg continued, "Several of the men told me what they saw. It sounds as if it was a close call. The men also said the twins were the ones who stepped in and saved their mother. You should be proud of your boys. They did a fine job."

Pride welled up deep inside Will. It was not the first time in the day he felt that because of what Sean and Luke had done. As soon as the herd had been settled and he and the boys had dismounted, he hugged them both and told them how proud he was. He didn't care if the rest of the crew saw the clutch. Will had witnessed how close he had come to losing his wife and daughter. The boys had prevented that. They deserved the hug.

Dangberg watched as Will seemed to leave the conversation without moving, his thoughts elsewhere, only to return to the present. He then continued, "Will, I need to talk to you about something, something quite disturbing."

The last comment pulled Will out of his thoughts about the boys. "What could make you say that? It must be troubling if you need to get away from the fire and the men to talk about it."

"Will, as you know, I stopped off at the Capital Building as the herd passed through Carson City. While sitting on my horse right out front of the building and relishing the sight of our herd passing through, Erik

Pasin came up and asked me to step inside to speak with some of the sitting representatives."

"Did you go inside?"

"I did."

Dangberg appeared to scrutinize the silhouetted horizon beyond which the sun had long since descended. A middle aged man of unremarkable features, Will thought Dangberg appeared to have aged over this last summer. He had known the man for some seven years now. Despite a lack of imposing physical size, Dangberg always seemed poised, composed, and full of substance. Henry didn't have to talk. He had a presence. Other men could sense it. Without any real effort, Dangberg immediately commanded respect. But right now, Henry looked less alive, weaker in some way; older. Maybe it was just the onset of darkness or a long day's ride.

Will waited.

"Erik and his fellow legislators walked me into a room just off the entryway and closed the door. I was waiting for some political pitch asking for money. But that wasn't it. They wanted to warn me."

"Warn you?"

"Yes, warn me. They said each had heard about a movement of ranchers and farmers up in the northern part of Carson Valley near Reno who planned to march on the Truckee Dam at Tahoe. Their plan was to destroy the dam and let the water flow to support their crops and grasslands."

"That would cause a flood," Will blurted.

"Probably right. Each of the men told me they had tried to convince their constituents to hold off. They got nothing but resistance. People are losing their livelihood, their ranches, their farms, their ability to feed their families. This drought is causing havoc up and down the valley."

Will now was the one to look away. He glanced to the north in the direction of the farms and ranches Dangberg was talking about, "I can understand their worry, we're in the same predicament. That's why we're moving the herd: to protect our livelihoods."

"True. But seems it's more desperate up north where we're going. We have the Carson River in the south end of the valley. That gives us a second source of water from the Sierras. Folks up here depend on the Truckee."

Will thought, "Are they telling us that people are going to be upset we're moving the herd north?"

"Part of it. They also wanted me to be aware that moving the herd was going to force their hand."

"Force their hand to do what?" Will was puzzled.

"File suit."

"File suit where, against who? And what would that have to do with us?"

"File suit in the new Carson City Federal court on behalf of the State of Nevada against a whole list of defendants. The idea is to protect the flow of water out of Tahoe down the Truckee."

"I'm still not makin' the connection as to how this affects us."

Dangberg sighed, then raised a finger for emphasis, "Because we might be defendants, along with the State of California, the Central Pacific Railroad, the City of San Francisco, the milling operations along the Truckee; everyone taking water from the river."

Will was stunned. "But I have property along the Truckee. I have rights to take water."

"Yes, so do all the others mentioned, with the possible exception of San Francisco. That's the point. The only way the legislators figure they can avoid what they are calling a 'water war' is to file suit."

"Sounds like a stunt, like a bluff in a poker match."

"Could be exactly that. But these men told me they had tried everything else to keep their constituents from marching on the dam. They're hoping this will keep them at bay. But they worried that by driving the herd north for all to see we were going to bring all this to a head."

"Do they think people will attack us or the herd?"

"I asked that. Most think people understand that we have grazing and water rights. Their problem is not with ranchers to the north or the south. Their problem is with the big money barons who are trying to control the Truckee's flow to pad their bank accounts while folks who need the water to survive will be left out. But some of the men present said we'd best be careful as they couldn't rule it out."

"Attacked by other ranchers? I can't believe that." Will took off his hat and wiped a bead of sweat from his forehead. The heat still lingered even in darkness.

Dangberg continued, "Most thought they'd leave us alone, but that seeing another large demand on the water arrive would push them to march on the dam."

"Henry, we can't turn around. There is no water back south."

"I agree. I think we need to continue to move to your ranch. But we need to keep a good watch."

Nodding his agreement, Will said, "We can do that."

"And I think we need to do something else."

Will looked back at Dangberg. What else could now be coming?

Dangberg held Will's eyes then said, "And I think we need someone to head up to that dam real quick and warn those in control to hold fast and be ready."

Relieved the suggestion did not sound ominous, Will answered, "We can send someone."

Dangberg shook his head, "The dam is controlled by the railroad barons through some company called the Donner Lumber and Boom Company. Erik Pasin has information that Duane Bliss is negotiating with the railroad to build a spur from Tahoe City to the city of Truckee in Donner Pass to start hauling tourists to Tahoe. Pasin speculates that Donner Boom would then use Bliss's railroad to transport logs down the hill, not the Truckee River. That would leave an opening for San Francisco to then say there was plenty of water to siphon off to California. Can't have that. Bliss is the key to stop any siphon."

Will could now sense what was coming.

Dangberg drove his point home, "If Bliss is the key to solving this, then someone needs to meet him in his brand new offices in Tahoe City which is also the location of the dam. Someone who has a history with Bliss."

Will clearly knew what was coming now.

Dangberg pointed his index finger straight at Will. "That person is you."

# Chapter Eleven

*August 1877*
*Purcell Ranch- Truckee, NV*

Sweat dripped down the middle of his spine, meeting his shirt just above the tension created by his gun belt. Will sat atop Powder looking down at the Truckee River. He had stopped above what had been a river of eight to ten feet deep in places. What he saw down below the soft sanded riverbank now would barely cover a set of ankles. But it was water. He took off his hat and wiped his brow with the back of his forearm. The sun overhead beat down in mid-day force. They had guided the combined herds to the west of Reno. While still moving generally north, they angled further west and headed uphill towards what he and Beth called their Purcell Ranch. Will had hoped the climb would lead to milder temperatures. But the land here was almost as warm as Reno itself despite the rise in elevation. A scent of pine trees spiced the aroma around him, but the heat was unrelenting. Maybe the trees would provide a welcome shade. The cattle would undoubtedly take advantage after a good drink. So would the hands.

Juan rode up next to him and pulled to a stop. A quick look spoke volumes.

"Is very low, eh jefe?"

"Not much there, but it is flowing."

Using only the visual picture before him and pulling from his instinct and experience, Will tried to calculate whether the stream would support the number of steers not far behind him. It was impossible to tell. No matter, the water levels on the ranches they left would have decimated the combined herds. Maybe not all would survive here, but more would live than had they stayed.

Will turned to Juan, "We'll have to watch the front of the herd closely. Once they catch the smell of the water, they'll try to run."

"If we put more of the vaqueros up front, maybe we can slow the cattle."

"Nah, I don't want too many in front. We can try to keep them moving slow and easy as long as we can, but when they catch the smell, they'll take off. I don't want anyone getting caught being run down because they were in front. Let 'em run. Just try to keep them slow until they just bust loose."

"*Si*. Once they gets here, they go no further until they drink."

"That's for sure. So, Juan head back and tell all the hands to keep them coming slow and easy. Hold them as long as they can but stay out of the way when they start runnin', okay?"

"No hay problema. I go right away."

*****

"Whoa." Beth pulled up the wagon's team. Directly in front of the horses was a stone spire, a rock column rising in the middle of an open space. The surrounding ground was covered with a bed of old dried out pine needles. She sat, speechless. Like a penitent before an ancient religious altar, Beth collected her thoughts. This place had a history, a history that she had a major hand in creating.

The stone obelisk had been a chimney. It was once connected to a home—her home. There was nothing attached to the rock tower now. The wooden structure she had lived in with her first husband and his Mormon wife had burned. The barn which had been to her left had also burned. The obelisk itself bore signs of dark charring on all sides. A black stain on a black day.

Will, riding Powder, had followed along with the twins on their horses. All three stopped to the rear of the wagon. Beth knew they were behind. She surmised that the boys knew to hold their questions. Or maybe Will had motioned them to keep quiet.

Beth still had not moved. Juliette sat next to her looking up at her mother as if to ask what was going on.

Finally, Will walked Powder up next to the wagon. "You okay?"

Beth did not turn. She remained focused on the chimney. "I'll be okay. I needed to see it. But the memories of that day still hit hard. They haunt."

"I suppose those memories will always haunt. You sure you want to camp here? We can always find plenty of space in the forest or other open ground on the ranch. We could stay at the bunk house we built not long ago too."

Beth turned. "No, I knew this would be a good spot to set up the tent. The river is close and we will need access to the water. That's why the house was put here in the first place."

Will glanced around, "It is open and cleared. Interesting how the forest provides the shade even though the ground is open."

Beth turned to face Will, "We never felt any sustained heat here. The sun might bear down in the middle of the day, but that would be it. As soon as it dipped into the afternoon, the forest outside the clearing would shade us all. It was a good setting."

Then, Beth returned her gaze to the chimney. Another extended silence followed.

"Will, have you come here before?"

"I did. When you first gave the deed to me, I came up to look over the ranch along with Henry Millard. I couldn't believe someone would gift over a full ranch, especially when you had just run off. I had to see it for myself. I needed to see how it would work for raising cattle. I came by this spot too. Curiosity maybe."

"I never thought I would ever be able to sit here again. Never wanted to be in this spot. How things change."

"No sin in picking another spot."

"I've addressed my sins. Probably good I face them. I told you last night back at camp that we should set up our temporary home here and I'll stick to that."

Will turned to the boys who had remarkably displayed a measure of respect. "Not sure I've ever seen the boys quiet for so long."

A wry smile etched its way to the edges of Beth's lips, "They probably are wondering what in the world happened here. I suppose part of my homecoming will be that I'll have to explain what took place all those years ago and try my best to justify why."

"Sure about that? I don't think their lives would be adversely affected if they remained ignorant of what happened."

"No, I'll tell them. I'll wait for the right moment and I'll tell them."

"With Sean, he might push the timing up a bit. He's an inquisitive thing."

"The timing will be mine. But I'll tell them. Meanwhile, I knew that we could use that chimney. To have a wind protected place to cook will be useful."

Beth looked up at Will again. She knew he had watched her face for any sign that they should pick another place. She nodded her approval to stay.

Will turned in his saddle, "Boys, unhitch the team. We will need to set up a picket line between some trees until we can build a temporary corral for the stock. Don't forget, the picket line should be high, as tall as you two. Remember, wrap the line around the tree once with a half hitch and then wrap it again with a half hitch on the other side of the tree. That will make sure the line won't give way. Like I taught you."

"Ah Pa, we remember."

"Let me see you do it right. Can't lose the horses up here tonight. They'll be gone. They don't know this area and if they get loose, they'll take off and we'll never find them. We can let them graze tomorrow."

Sean answered first, as usual. "Got it." Luke just started working.

Will added, "I'll start unloading the wagon. When you're done, you can come help set up the tent."

The boys set about unhitching the wagon team.

Beth returned her gaze to the chimney, "Maybe we can build a simple wood covering over the front of the tent. It'll be our porch, like a bit of home."

Will smiled, "Might be able to do that."

# Chapter Twelve

*August 1877*
*Tahoe City, CA*

Duane L. Bliss sat in his new office. The building was nondescript, a small structure in a small town. There were no stone or brick buildings in this small mountainous hamlet, not yet. Tahoe City almost looked temporary. The wooden buildings making up the town center were not old, but already looked weathered. Unpainted plank walls took a beating from the hard winters this high in the mountains. The constant cycle of snow buildup followed by the inevitable melting, stripped milled lumber of its primal essence. Carved from living trees, alpine weather sucked the once pinkish sheen of organic life from the pine slats in one winter. The boarded walls of this town looked gray, as if they were about to die.

It was his second office, the main one being in Carson City. He was a man of wealth and liked people to know it. Bliss stood well over six feet tall. Broad in the chest, he always wore a three piece woolen suit with vest to cover his expanding midsection. However, that midlevel widening created a perfect background for the ever present gold belly watch and dangling fob. His office in Carson City contained leather easy chairs, a large, impressive desk with leather blotter and paintings of striking mountain landscapes hanging on the papered walls. Here, the new office contained nothing but a simple wood table and chairs. The walls were bare. He'd have to change that.

Bliss had made his money lumbering property purchased or subject to timber license on the eastern shores of Tahoe. The lumber from his properties was milled into square set timbers which he then sold to the mines of Virginia City. The mines had a voracious need for those timbers. But the forests on his land would soon be completely gone. The forests had been clear cut. More importantly, the ore in those Virginia City mines would not last forever. The combined future of mines and trees meant his cash flow would not last either. He didn't want to lose the regular influx of money. He needed alternatives. That need led to the office here in Tahoe City. That need also led to the letter he sent to the man he was about to meet. A man who could give him some advice on building an alternative.

"Mr. Bliss, Mr. Baldwin is here to see you."

Bliss was about to tell his assistant to show him in when a boisterous voice bellowed, "Elias Jackson Baldwin, to be exact. But most folks call me Lucky. You're welcome to use the term."

Striding into the small office was a slender raw boned man whose medium brimmed Stetson perched on an abundant crop of prematurely white hair. His prominent nose stretched downward from a strong forehead and hung above a broad, thick, equally white moustache. A black string tie roped around a raised starched collar. Bliss had the immediate thought that the man could be in his forties or sixties. He couldn't tell. His stride across the room was agile and confident. The smile on his face was infectious and challenging.

"Some think the name Lucky comes from the fact that when I brought my family west, I turned three wagons of dry goods and eight mules into enough money to buy a hotel in San Francisco. I resold the hotel within months doubling my money and went on to buy and sell more real estate in that growing metropolis than anyone else. I also hit it big in Virginia City silver mine stocks when my agent was supposed to sell but was late to the stock market. The mine whose stock he was supposed to sell hit it big the day before my agent arrived in town. He heard the news and wisely kept the stock. I made a million on that gift of fate alone."

"I have heard tales of your fortuitous fortunes in business," said Bliss reaching to shake the man's hand.

"But I think the name truly stuck when two of my extra marital feminine liaisons attempted to shoot me from close range when I cut off the relationships. One barely missed when she tried to shoot me in my own hotel. The second one had a rather comely accomplice take a shot at me in court during a hearing on a charge of seduction against me. The accomplice narrowly missed shooting me in the back of my head firing just as I ducked down to reach for a fallen piece of paper. Now that was lucky."

The man tilted his head to the side as he delivered the last sentence. His grin broadened even further. Bliss felt he knew the man's life history and he'd only just shaken hands.

"So, Mr. Bliss, why was it you wanted to see me?"

"Maybe the best way to put it is that I'm looking for alternatives."

"May I sit?"

"Absolutely. Here, let me take your hat."

"Thank you, but I'll leave it where it sits."

Bliss waived him to one of the simple hard wooden seats across from his own position. Baldwin adjusted his lengthy black covert coat and placed his hands on the table now separating the two men.

"Alternatives you say. Alternatives to what? If you're looking for advice on women, I'm not the person to talk to. I make one mistake after another with the fairer sex."

Bliss smiled, "Based on your history as presented here in person, I would say you are correct. But no, I'm not looking for alternatives in women. Elizabeth and I are quite happy."

"Then, how might I be of service? Traveled all the way from San Francisco to be here. Have to say I was intrigued by your letter. As it happens, I might even have some questions for you on the business of lumbering."

This took Bliss back a bit. But he decided to push forward with his own questions first.

"How many people come to your Tallac House?"

Baldwin tilted his head in a movement of silent question. "Can't say as I was expecting such a line of questioning. Why do you ask? It's not for sale if that's what you're after."

"I'm not looking to buy, looking to imitate."

"That sounds like competition. Why would I give you any details if you're looking to *imitate* as you call it?" The word imitate was uttered with extra emphasis.

Bliss did not hesitate, "Because I think I can increase your business twofold. At the same time, I'd like to build something similar on the east side of Tahoe, in Glenbrook."

"If you *could* double my business, I wouldn't care if you built ten new houses. But tell me how you plan to do this?"

"Your season is limited to the summer and only part of fall, correct?"

"Yes."

"And I assume this is because all of your customers must arrive at Tallac House via the stage line over Echo pass at the south end of the lake."

"Yes." Baldwin's tone was more question than statement.

Bliss watched as skepticism spread across Baldwin's face. Bliss could sense Baldwin rise to the game of business poker, a game he probably was quite familiar with. As such, Baldwin kept his answers concise until the hand was revealed.

"What if I could deliver patrons to your dock from March to November?"

"Ha, my clientele is not going to ride on one of your lumbering tugboats Bliss."

"Not what I had in mind. But what if they were to ride on a one hundred seventy foot luxury steamer? We'd have an enclosed cabin, uniformed captain and crew, along with various services on board."

Bliss watched as the expression on Baldwin's face changed ever so slightly from skepticism to one of building interest.

"And who is going to build it? More importantly, who is going to *pay* to build it?"

"I would."

Bliss let the words sink in with a period of silence. He then continued.

"I've checked into companies who can send the manufactured parts up via railroad. I'd assemble it in Glenbrook."

"Okay, you have my interest, but right now this sounds like some kind of fantasy."

Bliss demurred, "Not really. I would build another hotel in Glenbrook, must nicer than the station house I now have. Planning on calling it the Glenbrook Inn. I'd cater to the same higher class clientele from around the country just like you do. But with a steamship, we could substantially increase the flow of customers. Right now, your clients must ride a dusty stage all the way from Sacramento. And they cannot get over Echo Summit in the winter. Your supplies must come via the same route. What if all customers and supplies came via ship?"

"I could do a lot more business. I agree. So, who would pay to ship these folks?"

"Patrons would pay a passage fee. But I am thinking you and I might come to an agreed upon monthly fee for their delivery as well as for supplies and mail."

"I wouldn't want to pay the same rate your walk on traffic pays. I'd want some discount."

"That might be done. I'd agree to a reduced fee, but I'd want to spread the amount over 12 months to cover costs throughout the year, even in the month or two when traffic would be slow or even non-existent in the winter."

Baldwin remained unmoved in his seat giving away no physical indication of reaction, "I'm getting more interested. But I have another question. How are you going to get the customers to Glenbrook? Won't they have to take the same stage up to Tahoe from Carson City?"

Bliss smiled, "No, my idea is to dismantle the small gauge railroad I have now running from the sawmills to Spooner Summit and float it across the lake here to Tahoe City."

Baldwin raised both hands placing fingertip to fingertip in a digital pyramid as he then displayed the sharp business acumen he was known for.

"At which time you would run that small gauge from Tahoe City down to the CPRR station in Truckee. It's probably about the same distance as your train runs now. With such a spur, you would connect with clientele in San Francisco as well as the rest of the country. Not bad Bliss."

"We could attract far more people who might come up on the train rather than those limited few who can spend the now required two weeks for a vacation with a stage trip on either end of it. They would have much more time to spend in our hotels if it only took them a day or two to get here."

"Yes, you might indeed. But where would you build the spur?"

"Down the Truckee River."

Baldwin stared right at Bliss. "But isn't that a right of way owned by the Central Pacific Railroad?"

"The rights are held by a subsidiary called the Donner Lumber and Boom Company. According to public documents I've checked, Donner is controlled by Leland Stanford and Mark Hopkins. So, for all intents and purposes, you are correct as Stanford and Hopkins are part of the CPRR. I'd have to make a deal for an easement to construct the spur next to the riverbed which is the most level route over the Sierras and down to Truckee."

Baldwin stood, his brain now working furiously.

"This could fit into the topics that led me to agree to the meeting, topics I wanted to raise with you. Your rail system would obviously carry passengers for the hotel business. But you currently have rail cars to transport lumber too do you not?"

"I do. That's the basic function of the railroad I built, haul lumber."

"Would you bring those same rail cars along with the rest of the system?"

"I could."

"Then you would stand ready to accept freight also, freight in the form of lumber down to the CPRR's sawmills in Truckee?"

Bliss now had an inkling of where Baldwin was going.

"Yes, I could haul the CPRR's lumber downhill rather than have them floating the logs down the Truckee River if that's what you're thinking."

Baldwin waived off the thought. "I suppose you could do that, but I was thinking of something else. You could also haul timber from my own logging operations down to those same sawmills, correct?"

Bliss now had a look of puzzlement. "What logging business?"

Baldwin's moustache rose at its ends as his cheeks lifted the blanched white fibers in an unabashed smile. "The logging business I'm going to start at the south end of the lake. The only stand of old growth forest you logging barons have not yet cleared. I have two thousand acres around Tallac House. I would leave the immediate forest intact, but I'm interested in obtaining multiple licenses from the Federal Government to log the upper reaches just as the CPRR did here around Truckee."

Bliss picked up the thought."

"If I can haul the CPRR's lumber, I can haul yours. For a price of course."

"If you can help me get a lumber license, I'll pay your fee for customers at Tallac House as well as for lumber freight."

Bliss felt this meeting was now heading in a very positive direction.

Baldwin, still standing, turned on his heel. "One thing though, that engineer Von Schmidt built his wretched dam raising the lake by five to six feet. I've lost twenty feet of a lovely beach my customers used to sunbathe on. If the CPRR doesn't need the water on the Truckee to float their logs downhill, I want that dam removed and the Lake back at its original level. If we are talking about building spurs along the river, let's push the discussion with the railroad to remove that stupid dam."

"I have no problem removing the dam."

Baldwin returned to his seat. "I'm ready to listen as to how you intend to proceed."

It was now Bliss's turn to smile. "Let's talk some numbers."

## Chapter Thirteen

*August 1877*
*San Francisco, CA*

Darkness worked to partially hide the detritus as it ebbed onto the edges of the dirt streets. The rejected material came in all forms, from all sources. It sprang from disposed food, rejected furniture, and discarded people. All lay about the edges of these streets only a short distance from the city's wharves. Jonas Greerson had passed at least two sailors prostrate and lifeless in the dirt amid the muck and other discards. They lay in all manner of posture with the appearance of being unceremoniously dumped off the brick sidewalks either drunk, injured, or dead. The debris also came with a smell, the smell of decomposition, a decay of hope. He had entered what was commonly called the Barbary Coast, the heart of San Francisco's red light district. It was the goal and often ruin of every sailor who entered the Bay.

Jonas walked passed the Old Ship Saloon, Whaler's Inn, and Bailey's Pub. He came to a stop across the street from the Bella Union. He turned to take a good look at the building, a two-story structure of indeterminate material. The ominously dark door was shielded by a deep overhang covering the brick sidewalk out front. Above the covering were three windows for second level rooms. The windows spewed forth light, one of which framed a backlit feminine silhouette. The projected vision above generated an enticing interest. However, there was no illuminating light on the foreboding entrance below.

Greerson looked left and right. Men lined his side of the street. There was no common thread to the manner of person present here at night. There were hard men, groups of young wide-eyed sailors, solitary men in suits as well as joyous or despondent men. But each had a common expression which he couldn't quite place. Maybe a fatalistic anticipation of the unexplored. He'd been told that if one continued further toward the wharves, they would find the opium dens. Those dens were the first enticement for the sailors coming from the ships, yet the ultimate rock bottom for those heading away from the city. While there were plenty of men on his side of the street, directly across the dirt roadway there was no one standing in front of his intended destination.

He'd been instructed to meet at the Bella Union. The man he needed to see came highly recommended. Jonas only hoped he could finish the meeting and leave unscathed.

Greerson had been charged by Von Schmidt to hire men, men who would not shy away from confrontation. Von Schmidt had even suggested it might be better if they were men who might *create* a confrontation—the type who could handle weapons. The Barbary Coast was the place to find such men. The contact he was supposed to meet was called Pin. Pin was reputed to have the ability to recruit others of like disposition. Jonas had no real idea how many would be required to remove the Donner Lumber men from the dam Von Schmidt had built back in 1870. However, his boss had instructed to find at least five men who could handle weapons.

The door to the Bella Union was extra wide. Inside was a small anteroom and another door. Standing to one side of the anteroom was a massive black man who had to be six foot five inches tall and almost as wide as the front door. The man had not one strand of hair and possessed a countenance as dark as the entrance he controlled.

"What business do you have here?"

Greerson was taken aback by the demand. There was no welcome in the man's demeanor, only challenge.

"I am here to see a man named Pin."

The doorman did not change bearing or expression, "Why?"

Greerson had the immediate thought he was going to be unsuccessful in his given task as his prospects to gain access to the facility appeared unlikely at the moment.

"I was referred to Mr. Pin who set this place for the meeting."

"He's occupied," came the response. "You should come back later."

"I was told to meet him at this hour. It's important that I see him. If he is meeting someone else, I can wait at the bar."

"He's up with one of the girls."

Greerson did not understand. "Girls?"

The doorman now displayed a derisive smile. "I thought so. You are not a regular customer. That's why I asked your business. Yes, girls. That's why men come to this establishment, to spend time with our girls."

Greerson now understood why the women lingered in front of the windows on the second story. The Bella Union was a bordello.

The doorman held his arm out to block any entry while he opened and looked beyond the inner door. After a brief look, he returned to Greerson.

"Pin is not in the lounge. Most of our customer's visits are quick. Pin likes to take his time. No telling when he'll be back down in the lounge."

Becoming desperate, Greerson asked, "Is there a place in the lounge where I can wait for him? I won't disturb a thing."

The Doorman took his time to answer. Greerson sensed his success or failure hung in the balance of this keeper of the gate's decision. Finally, there was a sigh and the man nodded toward the interior.

"Wait there to the side of the lounge. But don't talk to any of the girls."

Relieved, Greerson passed through the doorway but then stopped and turned. He hesitated to upset the doorman's recent decision, but Jonas needed some additional information. He decided he had to take the risk and ask his question.

"How will I recognize Mr. Pin?"

"It's Pin, not Mr. Pin. You won't miss him. He wears a black tricorn hat and has a scar that runs down the entire left side of his face."

Greerson raised his hand in silent thanks and turned to find a spot to sit. The nearest place turned out to be a couch. But this was no ordinary couch. It was wide enough to be a bed, curved into something of a kidney shape and was covered in the softest bright red fabric he'd ever touched. He took a seat facing the entrance. There was not another soul in the lounge.

The room was scented, probably to block the stench from the streets. The walls brandished gaudy colored paper coverings. The lamps were enclosed within cut glass. He could hear men and women talking in a room behind him, more to the rear. But as he had only barely gained access, Jonas wisely decided not to push his luck by moving any further into the interior. There were no tables. Nothing to hold a newspaper or pamphlet as with most waiting areas he'd been in. The room was full of seating arrangements, most for only a party of two. Clearly the room was meant for conversation.

Just as he was about to change seats, a man in dark trousers began walking down the stairway to Jonas's right from the upper story. He appeared to be in his mid-thirties and of medium height. He wore a white shirt with long blossomed sleeves and open down from the collar revealing a well-muscled chest. He hung a dark coat over his shoulder displaying a six gun at his side. On top of his head was a tricorn hat with the front lifted upward in relaxed fashion. The combined look was of a pirate on the top half and a gun hawk on the bottom half.

As he came close to the bottom of the stairs, the man wearing the tricorn hat turned and looked at the doorman. The keeper of the gate simply nodded in Jonas's direction with a wordless introduction. Upon hitting the landing, he turned and hung his jacket on the end of the rail as if any interruption would be brief.

"Are you here from Von Schmidt?"

Jonas stood. "I am. Are you Mr. Pin?"

"The name is Pin, not Mr. Pin. The name comes from a wooden dowel used on sailing ships. I killed a man using such a pin in a fight aboard ship when I was younger. The crew started calling me Pin and the name stuck."

Greerson had no idea how to respond. But from this brief history, he felt the recommendation to use Pin might be well placed. The man sounded like someone who was not going to back away from a fight.

"I would like to speak to you about hiring some men, men with particular talents. Is there a place where we could talk in private?"

"This is fine here. No one is about except Q there by the door. Q is short for Queequeg. That is not his real name but the sailors have come to call him that as he looks like a harpoon man they've heard stories about in a book of some fame. Q won't breathe a word of our conversation because he knows what I'll do to him."

Jonas hesitated, but before him was the man who could provide the necessary solution to the problem at hand. Greerson sensed he had to be quick, but he also had to choose his words carefully.

"We need men, maybe a total of five. Mr. Von Schmidt built a dam on the Truckee River up at Lake Tahoe several years ago. Another company has taken over control of the dam. Von Schmidt wants to take it back. I am to take a crew of men up on the train in two days. The idea is to appear like we are starting a survey for a new dam, close to the old one. I am an engineer with surveying tools and that should not be a problem. We are to look like we intend to build another dam to compete. Mr. Von Schmidt through his company owns property along the river near the dam previously built. He has the right to access water. However, the plan is to contrive a confrontation and take back control of the old dam."

Pin waited to make sure he'd heard the entire pitch.

"How long will we have to be up in Tahoe?"

Greerson did not hide his uncertainty, "Could be two weeks, could be two months. It will depend on how things develop."

"How many men now protect this dam?"

"Only one or two and they are clerks, not gunmen."

Pin then walked back to his jacket, lifting it from the rail and sliding each arm into a sleeve.

"I can have five men here in two days. We can meet out in front of the Bella Union first thing in the morning and then take the ferry across the bay to the railroad depot in Oakland."

Jonas was amazed Pin could agree that quickly.

"But it will cost one thousand dollars per man, half paid up front and half paid at the end of the job. The job will last no more than two months. If it does, you will owe each man another thousand."

Greerson who had been given authority to pay more said, "I'll agree to those fees." He then reached his hand out to shake.

Pin did not move to accept the offered hand. "There is another condition."

Dismayed, Jonas held his breath for the additional term.

"I am to be paid five thousand dollars. I will lead the men, and I will keep them in control. If there is shooting, I will decide where and when. As with the other men, if the job lasts more than two months, you will owe me another fee of the same amount."

This was now potentially more than Greerson was authorized to pay. If the job ended within the first two months, he could stay within the budget given by Von Schmidt. But if it lasted beyond that first period, it would exceed the amount authorized. However, he had no other options.

"I'll agree."

Jonas offered his hand again. This time Pin took it in a firm grip, then said, "In two days, be here at dawn in front of the Bella Union."

# Chapter Fourteen

*August 1877*
*Purcell Ranch, NV*

The hooves of his horse kicked up dried pine needles while a light breeze ruffled the branches of the Ponderosa pines overhead. That same breeze created a steady rain of dried out needles plucked from their tree limbs pelting anything below. His bowler hat did not provide much protection from the snowfall of needles. He had to constantly be on guard not to have a set of flying stems hit him in the face. However, the shade those pine trees presented was more than welcome.

Dale Paris had left Reno early. It was a two day ride from there to Tahoe City. He knew he'd have to camp out one night. His plan was to stop at the Purcell Ranch. Word was Will Toal had moved his herd here to the mountains. Years ago, Paris had investigated what had been officially called an Indian massacre on the Purcell Ranch. Josiah Purcell and one of his wives had been killed and brutally burned in a raid. When Paris checked the scene, he could readily see that the damage was not caused by any Indians. His pursuit of what he'd been led to believe was a surviving younger wife of the Mormon rancher led him to Will Toal, more particularly to Beth, the woman Will would eventually marry.

The clutch of trees opened to an alpine meadow. The break in the forest held a scattering of beef cattle feeding on what was left of the high mountain grasses. A rider sat watching. His chaps and lariat tied to the front of his saddle suggested he was a hand charged with checking on this group of steers.

As with the approach of any unknown rider, Paris watched the cowboy fix an apprehensive gaze on his approach. The cowhand didn't reach to cover his gun, but he freed up his right hand. As Paris got closer, the man was ready for a variety of possibilities. Paris would have done the same.

The ranch hand tilted his neck forward lowering the front tip of his hat ever so slightly and asked, "Can I help you?"

Paris did not fail to notice subtle the body movement which he hoped was just concern and not an indication of hostility. It could have been either.

"My name is Dale Paris. I'm looking for Will Toal. He and I worked together to solve a murder a year or so ago. Heard he was here on the old Purcell Ranch. Thought I might stop in on my way to Tahoe City and say hello. Would also like to pay my respects to his wife, Beth."

Paris hoped the reference to both Will and Beth would allay the man's fears. It took a moment, but the approach must have worked.

"Sounds like you know them."

"I do. I'd be happy to ride with you to wherever they're located."

Another pause. "Don't 'spect that'd be necessary. Not many would know the old name of this ranch as well as those of Will and Beth. You must know them. They're camped out where the old ranch house once stood. Know where that is?"

"I do. I am a private detective. I took part in the investigation of the killing of Josiah Purcell. I know exactly where the old homestead is. Much obliged."

Paris touched the front bill of his hat and reined a path around the cowhand towards the old homesite.

*****

Thick forest blocked the late afternoon light shading all beneath its reach. The sun would set soon. Here this high, the temperature was already beginning to back off. So different from the blistering late afternoons down in Reno. A scent of pine became more pronounced as the forest got thicker. Paris had to acknowledge that the smell had a way to revive one's outlook. He didn't know how, but the air seemed fresher. It filled his lungs with vibrance.

He was about to breach the opening where the ranch house had once stood. He stopped before entering the clearing. He could see a tent pitched next to the rock chimney along with a temporary corral fence. The pen was made of long branches set in an x pattern and tied where the limbs crossed. Rails so tied were then braced with posts at each end. He had to admit it was a good use of the material one could easily find lying around. Several horses milled about the enclosure. One was a tall gray Paris recognized as Will's horse Powder. Toal could not be far.

Paris knew Will had taught Beth and his sons to shoot; his entire family were quite capable with weapons. Best to announce an approach loud and clear before anyone reached for something with a trigger.

"Halloo the Toal camp. Possible for an old associate to approach without getting shot? It's Dale Paris."

Will came around the backside of the tent. He'd obviously been working with an ax cutting wood.

"Dale, come on in. I'll tell the boys to aim their rifles low to only wound you." A big smile spread across his face.

Paris returned the grin. "I knew I'd better announce my entrance. I figured you probably told those sons of yours to shoot first and shake hands after the victim hits the ground."

"Nah, we'd only shake hands with friends after we shoot 'em. Not sure you qualify." Will's smile became a bit sarcastic.

Paris urged his horse forward. "Glad to know where I stand."

Beth then lifted the flap on the tent entrance to stand before the temporary structure. "Dale Paris, can you stay for dinner? It's camp food, but it'll be hot."

"Mrs. Toal, I'd be much obliged to take a meal. Left to my own prospects I'd be lookin' at hard tack and bad coffee."

Will then said, "Step off and pull your saddle. You can sit here and talk to Beth while I take your mount down to the river and water him."

"That sounds most pleasant. Don't mind if I do."

Paris turned to sit on a log Beth now offered as if it were a place of honor. "It's not a padded seat, but it is one of the few around here that doesn't involve dirt."

"After a long day's ride, anything that doesn't move is welcome."

Beth then sat across from Paris rubbing her hands on a towel tucked into the apron tied around her waist. "It's been some time since we last saw you. You look well. Is there a Mrs. Paris yet?"

Paris laughed, "No, not sure the woman exists who would have me."

"Then you must be busy with work."

"I have been busy. In fact, I'm working on a job right now. Heading up to Tahoe City to investigate a murder. The supervisor of the Truckee Dam was shot walking across the structure. The railroad has hired me to find out who did it."

Will strode up having turned Paris's horse loose in the corral just as he finished his explanation. "Ah, still working for the Central Pacific Railroad, are you? Come to ask me to attend a meeting?"

Knowing the comment was a lighthearted reference to a past issue between the two men Paris responded, "Last time we attended such a meeting I believe we were on opposite sides and the meeting did not go well."

"That's an understatement."

Paris shook his head, "Then no, I don't think I want to stand across from you in any similar situation. I prefer to sneak up behind and save your life when you let some fire crazed bomber get the drop on you."

Not to be outdone Will retorted, "Was that before or after I shot Bliss's secretary just before she was going to unload her six gun into your mid-section?"

"I'm not sure who Ida Murray would have shot first, you were standing right beside me."

Beth then stood up, "I'm not sure I can handle any more of this male bravado. I had asked a simple question to be nice and you two cave men have to start beating your chests. I'll leave you two to drag your knuckles around some more while I go see to dinner."

Both men were speechless at the hostess's departing remarks.

Paris broke the silence. "Did I do something to offend?"

Will smiled, "No more than I. Let's call our joint history a draw. Thankfully, we have both been there to timely protect the other. For me, I'm glad you were on that pier late the night the men who intended to bomb Bliss's sawmills got the drop on me. As for Ida, let's just say she was about to shoot one or both of us. I was able to return the favor and prevent her from the clear harm she intended. Now, what really brings you up here into the mountains?"

"As I said, I am to investigate a murder."

"But you stopped off here out in the woods. I know you better than that. There is something else. What is it?"

"Nothing escapes you, does it?"

"I try."

Paris let the humorous mood up to this point evaporate. He responded in a more serious tone, "The CPRR controls the Truckee Dam. The man who built it, A.W. Von Schmidt, is trying to take it back. His aim is to have the city of San Francisco restart a project to pull water from Tahoe for the city's needs."

Will snorted, "There isn't enough water for those here in Nevada downstream. These folks need the river to flow."

Paris nodded, "The drought has hurt many. I talked to some people around Reno about the dam and flow of the Truckee after I took this job. One of them was your lawyer, S. Samuel Grande. He's in Reno meeting with people who are upset about the efforts of Californians to take Tahoe water when there is so little. He's using another lawyer's office for meetings over the next couple of days."

"Sam is a good lawyer. I'm sure lots of folks would like him to work for them."

"According to Grande, it looks like the railroad barons are fighting over the dam while San Francisco wants the dam to hold the water so they can siphon it off. He thinks there's going to be a battle."

Paris watched as Will took in the information. Toal then added, "Henry Dangberg had a conversation with some legislators back in Carson City who told him they had constituent ranchers who were threatening to march on the dam to destroy it. He wants me to go talk to Bliss."

"Bliss, what's he got to do with this?"

"Dangberg was told Bliss is planning on building a railroad spur from Tahoe City to the Truckee Depot on the CPRR's transcontinental line. He's going into the hotel business. Sounds like he's finally going to follow the suggestions Ida Murray told us she made to him."

Paris shook his head. "How strange. Ida did not have to go on her rampage of killing. All she had to do was wait a little longer and Bliss would be doing exactly what she wanted him to do."

"Yep. Sounds like it. A real waste."

Paris then extended his arm in question, "Doesn't your ranch here border the Truckee?"

"It runs right smack dab through it. I just watered your horse in the Truckee River."

"Then wouldn't you have water rights to flow out of the river?"

"I do. That's why Dangberg suggested I go to Tahoe City and talk to Bliss. I have water rights, therefore an interest in the Truckee and I have a relationship with Bliss. Dangberg thinks I can convince him to work with the CPRR and avoid a war with the Nevada ranchers. The legislators told Dangberg that they intend to file some suit naming a bunch of defendants. Dangberg thinks since the Truckee runs through the ranch here, I could be a defendant."

"Grande told me he's aware of that suit. Say, don't you have a pretty good relationship with that lawyer Grande?"

Will nodded, "I do. At least I think I do."

Paris pursued, "Maybe you should talk to him. If you have water rights or could get sued, maybe you should see him before you head to Tahoe City and Bliss."

"That's not a bad idea. Maybe I'll ride down to Reno tomorrow and then head up to talk to Bliss."

"As I'm planning on being in Tahoe City for some time myself, maybe I'll see you there."

"Good possibility."

"Do me a favor, if shooting starts, don't hit me."

"Paris, I used to be a sniper. If I hit you, it means I meant to hit you."

Paris now smiled again. "See you in Tahoe City. Any chance dinner might be ready? I'm starved."

"Let's go see."

## Chapter Fifteen

*August 1877*
*San Francisco, CA*

Leland Stanford sat in his office waiting for his dinner guest, the mayor of San Francisco, to arrive here where they could meet following their meal. Andrew J. Bryant and his spouse had joined Leland Sr., his wife Jane along with their nine-year-old son, Leland Stanford Jr., following a personal invitation. Generally, the Stanford's entertained large groups. This was different, a special limited solicitation. The setting of the engagement carried a heightened interest by the very nature of the selective guest list.

Bryant had briefly been called to see something in the other room as the wives talked about assorted charities. He would soon rejoin Stanford. Leland Jr. had retired to bed.

Stanford's office bordered one side of his mansion on Knob Hill. In daylight hours, a twenty foot tall window framed a peaceful view of a small garden adjacent to the main structure just outside that window. The master of the house sat behind a massive desk positioned in the middle of an oversized wood paneled office filled with memorabilia of his political and business career. Priceless paintings hung on all four walls. Various antique side tables and statuary rimmed the room filling spaces in between the paintings.

However, the focus of the room was the huge desk and two tall-backed chairs across from it surrounded by an extraordinary amount of space. Here was where Stanford did business. Here was where he now entered arrangements to protect and further his financial interests. He had his desk spaced between his guests and his own chair. The positioning of the furniture was intentional. His personality did not lend itself to closeness. He was more comfortable with a wide expanse of breathing space. He liked the intimidation the room created.

Stanford had given the upcoming conversation a great deal of thought. With Hopkins out on the road in Colorado, Stanford had spoken to Huntington and Crocker about the meeting with the mayor. Both confirmed that the flow of the water down the Truckee River remained critical for the operation of the transcontinental railroad. It would be several years until the Central Pacific could bring the coal production online as replacement. Until then, timber from the Sierras was the only source of fuel for the locomotives.

Huntington had offered to attend the dinner. Stanford had no doubt Huntington made the offer out of concern that Stanford might not prevail in the meeting with the San Francisco mayor. Huntington's offer was another indication of how critical the Big Four viewed this meeting to be. Huntington had been the member who obtained Washington's approval for the Central Pacific to build the railroad back in 1862. He was undoubtedly the ablest negotiator of the group.

But Stanford had said it was unnecessary. Huntington may be adept in national political circles, but this was California. Stanford had been governor of the state. He knew how the local political game was played. Further, he was the one who had a relationship with the mayor. Having Huntington present might cause an adverse reaction. One never knew how people would react to Huntington's gruff aggressive manner. Huntington had reluctantly agreed. However, Stanford now must deliver. He had to make a deal to block Von Schmidt.

Andrew Bryant entered the office rubbing his hands together. "You have a precocious son in Leland Jr."

Somewhat startled from his deep thoughts, Stanford looked up and responded, "Young Leland is a true blessing for Jane and I."

Bryant pursued the compliment. "The young man has a very agile mind and appears quite comfortable in conversation with both ladies and gentlemen of our age bracket. Most nine year old children would shrink from advanced conversation. He seems to revel in it."

Stanford smiled, "Yes, he actually does far better in that arena than does his father. I find it difficult to participate in most social conversations. Young Leland not only seems at ease, but he also enhances the exchange. He has a unique ability to connect with people of all ages on a wide variety of topics."

"That was quite obvious. The conversation at dinner tonight went far and wide, but your son was engaged throughout."

Stanford added with unapologetic pride, "His tutors constantly inform me that the boy is far beyond his years with his studies. They believe he could enter any university he wishes in only a year or two. Jane and I would not hear of that at such a youthful age, but we intend to let him pursue his interests as far as he wishes until age 16. Then we will talk about university."

"The dinner was delightful not the least of which was your engaging son. Thanks again to both you and your wife for the invitation. However, Leland, I've known you many years. I have no doubt the invitation was not simply to be social. You have some other aim. What might that be?"

Stanford knew his reputation as a man of flat effect. He found it easy—almost natural—to avoid emotional displays. He really didn't know why; it was simply his nature. Many had commented that they found it hard to generate any perceptible reaction from him. This moment was no different. Stanford did not acknowledge his guest's accurate perception. He consciously knew that he should try to respond with a compliment of sorts. But he just couldn't find the words in that context. For him, the next step was simply to get down to the business at hand. He wondered if Bryant thought him callous. No matter.

"Yes, Andrew, I did want to talk to you. It's about Von Schmidt."

"I thought that might be the case."

"I understand he made another pitch to the city council asking for funds to re-open his project to bring water from Lake Tahoe."

"Yes, Leland, he did."

Stanford could see Bryant begin to measure his words. Von Schmidt's water project was the most sensitive of subjects. Stanford had bluntly waded right in. Bryant undoubtedly had to consider the fact that San Francisco needed water. But the City did not want to disrupt the ability of the railroad to export trade goods to the east. Far too many businessmen whose livelihoods depended on selling that merchandise to the east would come down hard on the good mayor's party next election if the railroad service were diminished. Stanford had to play on his friend's dilemma.

"And has there been a decision?"

"No, there has been no vote yet taken one way or the other."

"That project was proposed all the way back in 1870. Von Schmidt could not make a run of it then, why would anyone consider the result could be any different today?"

"Leland, the city needs a water source. The Spring Valley service barely supplies enough water for the current city inhabitants. Projections are that San Francisco will double in population over the next five years. We need another source of water."

"Don't give Von Schmidt any approval. The Central Pacific Railroad needs the water to flow down the Truckee River. If you approve this project, Von Schmidt will go back to the California Legislature to revise the 1870 Water Act. He could gain control over the Truckee. We can't have that." Again, the comments were overt, blunt. Stanford worried that he had been too assertive.

Bryant did not respond. Almost without thinking, Stanford succumbed to his regular personality drive and simply pushed his agenda.

"Von Schmidt gets that city license and he'll maneuver it into a monopoly. He'll make a play for the Spring Valley operation and quietly shut it down. There will be no limit to what he would eventually charge the city once he controls the only supply."

"Don't you have a monopoly with your railroad?"

Stanford took offense. "Our railroad is what is going to bring that additional populace to your city borders. That railroad is what will transport your nascent growing Asiatic commerce to the east coast. That railroad is your lifeblood." It was about as emotional an outburst as Stanford could recall ever making.

Bryant looked out the large window now acting as a transparent border to the darkness of night beyond. Stanford could see that the mayor was struggling with the issues in play. He worried that he had pushed the conversation too far too fast. How would Huntington handle things at this point? Stanford could sense the scales of decision being balanced.

Bryant turned to look directly at Stanford. "The city needs the water. Very few on the council are fond of Von Schmidt, but the idea of access to hundreds of thousands of acre feet of water is a godsend. What other source is there to have such a great need satisfied?"

Stanford snorted, "They are all over the place! The Sierras have dozens of lakes that can be tapped in the same way. Dam up another river, there are plenty of those too. Just stay away from the Truckee. Why does it have to be the Truckee?"

"The dam has already been built. The extra water for the city has been developed when Tahoe was raised five feet. It's there to be had. All we have to do is convey it across the state."

This was not going well. Sweat dampened the armpits of his shirt. Shaken, Stanford hesitated for a moment. He did not feel completely comfortable as to how he could bring the conversation back to a more positive position. In a reflexive thought, he decided to highlight the benefits of the railroad, his railroad. With effort, he managed some incredulity in his speech. "And you would do this even though it might disrupt the railroad's ability to maintain service? How will that affect your constituents?"

Bryant looked out the window again. Stanford thought Bryant might want to magically move through the glass to the other side and enter some alternative dimension devoid of his present dilemma. The city needed the water source. However, the city could not hamper the railroad or make an enemy of the powerful forces behind it. It was a very close call. Both were vital needs. Stanford knew the discussion had reached a pivotal point as Bryant pondered his possible options.

It took several moments, but Bryant finally came back to the conversation at hand.

"If we need the water, what is the CPRR willing to provide in its place?"

Stanford silently exhaled in relief. He'd chosen railroad over water. Bryant had now opened the door of political concession. Eminently experienced with the rules, Stanford knew how this card game was played. The first response must not include any offer. That should come only after further pushback.

"The CPRR needs the Truckee to float its logs down from the Sierras so we can fuel our locomotives. Those locomotives are the lifeblood of your city's future. You know it and I know it."

"Close to a majority believe the city must push for the water. Von Schmidt will try to buy the votes he doesn't have with contributions to key councilmen's reelection funds."

"We can contribute more."

There it was. The cards were clearly in view on the table now.

Bryant appeared mildly uncomfortable. "This cannot be seen as a bribe Leland. The newspapers are becoming very hostile to the CPRR's own monopoly and what they see as financial manipulation of their own."

"Yes, I am well aware of the newspaper's current views of the CPRR along with their disapproving assessment of Huntington, Crocker and myself. But this is not bribery. Identify the local projects each of those councilmen are looking to promote for their own constituents and we will contribute. Very legitimate. We are only looking to accommodate the needs of the city. This is exactly how the state government functioned during my governorship. Call it pork barrel, call it give and take, call it what you want. I view it as nothing more than negotiation to a desired end."

Bryant smiled, "Does that include my own projects?"

"Absolutely, Andrew."

There was a pause. "Leland, maybe we can work this out."

"I am glad to hear that. If we are talking about shutting Von Schmidt down, I am sure we can be of great benefit to each other."

Bryant nodded in silent acknowledgement confirming their agreement. He then added, "Now if there were only some way we might extricate ourselves from the Federal lawsuit Nevada just filed."

# Chapter Sixteen

*Late August 1877*
*Road from Purcell Ranch to Reno, NV*

Distant clouds obscured the rise of the morning sun. The new day's rays were dispersed in Confederate gray tones. There it was again. Gray weather days reminded him of the forsaken time spent during the war. He had joined near the end of the conflict. His experience had been one loss after another. He had been on the wrong side opposing Sherman's march and lost each battle fought. To this day a gray horizon infused a sense of dread. He had never been able to shake the anxiety the color created deep inside. He couldn't explain it rationally to anyone. The gray clouded gloom still stalked him, pursued his inner fears and conjured memories he attempted to suppress. Despite the ever increasing years since the war had ended, it never seemed to change. His psyche had been branded by the color gray.

Will Toal settled into his saddle above Powder, his mount of choice. The tall mustang pulled against the bit, obviously happy to be out of the corral. Will knew this equine version of anticipation for the day was quite different from his own. He supposed he might possess a better outlook if he'd been released from a confining corral too.

Looking east he watched the new day's birth with the coming illumination. Hopefully, the dour gray morning clouds which caused him so much concern would lift heavenward into shades of preferred billowing white. He'd started early with the hope of riding the fifteen miles to Reno to meet his lawyer, S. Samuel Grande, and still have time to return in the same day. The combination of early hour and cloudy blanket over the horizon provided a brisk morning chill at this elevation. The cool morning was welcomed as he knew by the time he descended to the flat plane that cradled the town of Reno, the heat would hit.

The Truckee River was to his right. The trail would eventually become a road. The road would follow the river right into the town of Reno. In the two weeks since they had arrived at what they still called the Purcell Ranch, the flow of the river had continued to diminish. It would be nice if those gray clouds in the distance would bring some rain. But that was unlikely.

He thought about his coming conversation with Grande. Maybe he should take Dangberg's advice and use his water rights along with others to push for the destruction of the dam up at Lake Tahoe. He had never laid eyes on the dam. As a result, he had no way of knowing what might or might not be possible. Maybe a small breach could allow a steady flow to see them through the end of the dry season.

*****

Will had ridden beyond the borders of his Purcell property. The road now straddled another ranch further to the east. The change when dropping in elevation was much different here in the north portion of the Carson Valley. To the south, the Sierras dropped into a flat plane normally covered with green grasses year round. Here to the north part of the Valley, the Sierras dropped from pine forest to scrub and dust. The Truckee alone was not enough to convert the spread of the desert encroaching from the east. Unless the river had been diverted, there were no crops here. Beef cattle subsisted on the hard dry brush mixed with the life-sustaining flows from the Truckee itself. Just riding the road told Will it would be far more difficult to raise beef here, far more precarious. The flow of the Truckee was vital to those in its path.

About the time he had the thought, he saw riders ahead. There looked to be four riding abreast across the road. Will slowed Powder from his distance eating trot to a walk. The riders ahead slowed to a walk too. Both parties approached at a measured pace.

Will could see that the group looked like working cowhands. Each rider sported chaps, a lariat tied high and handy, and no bedrolls. These men worked nearby. They were not out on any long trip without a bedroll or at least a duster tied behind their saddles. As they got close, Will pulled up. The four riders opposing him did the same. Each man issued their own personal version of a locked stare all focused on Will. The cowhands appeared to be in their late twenties or early thirties. Each wore a light jacket, large bandanas around their necks, and sported a collection of well-worn dusty hats.

One of the riders tipped the bill of his head covering upwards off his forehead.

"Howdy." The comment came without any sense of welcome. It came with a serious dose of question, almost challenge.

Will returned the greeting trying to be a bit more genial, "Mornin'."

"My name is Dirk Ferguson. This here is my dad's ranch. Who might you be?"

"My name is Will Toal. I own the old Purcell Ranch upriver."

Ferguson's demeanor darkened.

"You're the one who just drove five thousand head of cattle into the mountains to suck off more water away from those here downstream."

It was now clear Will was not a welcomed neighbor. None of the other hands moved. Each had a side gun, but no one had reached to pull their jackets behind the grips. The tension brewed by Ferguson's last statement spread to his companion's faces. Will did an immediate assessment of the men opposing him. You could never be sure, but here and there you could get a clue as to the capability of the men you might do battle with. These four wore their guns high. None had leg straps. Standard fare for cowhands as opposed to gun hawks. Will could probably handle two or three, but they still had numbers. In view of the odds, he was careful with his reply.

"The Carson River dried up. Cattle were dying in the south. The Truckee is still flowin' and it runs right through my ranch. It wasn't much of a choice. Had to move the beef."

"Word is you didn't just move your own beef, you brought the whole South Carson Valley herd, each and every ranch."

Will looked right at Ferguson while still making sure to be aware of any movement from the men to his sides. He didn't think Dirk Ferguson was the type to understand or even care about the business considerations that went into the decision to move all the herds. He kept his response terse.

"Cattle Association in the south is a tight group. We have a collected obligation to provide beef to our buyers."

"So, you move all that beef up here where water is just as scarce."

Will looked down at the Truckee, "Seems to me there's water in the river."

Ferguson was not going to let up. "You have any idea who needs that water down river?"

Will wasn't going to back away either. "No, but I know I have rights to water that runs across my land."

He uttered the words without breaking the combined vision of the four men in front of him. His left hand held the reins leaving his right hand free to pull his new Frontier Colt. Since the war he'd used his Navy Colt but that required a paper backing and round ball load. His new Colt loaded a 44.40 cartridge that matched the ammunition he used in the Winchester rifle he purchased last year. He'd owned the gun for less than six months and had used it very little. He hoped he wouldn't need to add to that experience today. He also remembered he had only five cartridges in the cylinder. He had left one chamber empty as was standard practice when traveling. If shooting started, he had only five shots for four opponents.

Ferguson shifted his seat atop his horse, but more to his right. Because of the shape of the cantle at the back of his saddle, the move would obscure any attempt to pull his weapon. Will considered it an interesting move, maybe an easing of the encounter's friction.

"We're gonna head up to Tahoe and destroy that dam. Let the water flow. Seein' as how you have more beef than anyone on the river right now, you willin' to join?"

Though Ferguson's tone remained confrontational, the whole group eased just a bit. Will considered his response.

"As a matter of fact, I'm headed to Reno to see my attorney to ask him what my rights are to the water."

"We don't need no attorney to tell us the water should flow like it always did."

"I usually try to find out where I stand before I act. But let's say this, after I meet with my lawyer, my plan is to ride to Tahoe City and represent our Cattlemen's Association to find a way to increase the flow down the river."

"We don't see any need to talk. The dam needs to be broke."

"You might take care as to how you approach that. You destroy the dam and you might cause an immediate flood. There's a lot of water backed up behind that dam. It could destroy a lot of property downstream after which the river might look just like it does now."

Ferguson had no response. Will thought he could not figure out if he'd been given some good advice or his intelligence had been insulted. As Will imagined, he was not talking to a lead strategist. Someone else would be making the decisions for whatever group was thinking of heading up to Tahoe.

"Can I ask who all is planning to march on the dam?"

Ferguson again answered, "There are six ranches here downstream on the Truckee. My pa has the agreement of each owner to ride up with whatever hands they can spare."

"And when is this to take place?"

"Soon. No more than two weeks."

"You going to give any notice?"

"And why would we tell them we're comin' so they can get prepared? No, we ain't gonna provide any warning."

Will was glad the exchange had remained limited to words. He now hoped to end the conversation peaceably. "I'll probably be up in Tahoe City when your group arrives. As I said, I'll be working on getting more water coming out of the lake. I guess we'll be working toward the same goal."

Ferguson apparently did not know exactly what to make of Will's latest comment as he had no response. So, Will moved to end the discussion.

"Tell your father about our conversation. I'd like to talk to him if he's going on your trip."

"Oh, he'll be with us. I'll tell him we met. But once we get going, I'd doubt he's gonna stop and talk."

"Maybe we'll see each other at Tahoe, then maybe not." Will took the opportunity to move on. He tipped his hat while his knees gently squeezed Powder's flanks. Responding to the cue, the horse slowly moved around the group and continued down the road. Will didn't look back.

# Chapter Seventeen

*Late August 1877*
*Tahoe City, CA*

Duane Bliss marveled at the fact Tahoe City did not even have a boardwalk for its pedestrians. Oh, there were some businesses that had built a porch of sorts out in front of their establishments. But moving from one building to another required a trudge through dirt and muck. It was exhausting to lift his ample frame onto one raised porch, only to descend back to earthen drudge a few steps later. He'd decided to simply stay out in the street. Thank goodness it was dry. This walk would be intolerable if it were wet or covered with snow. That led to another thought.

If he were to bring wealthy clientele from the large cities around the country, it would not do to force them to walk around in dirt, snow or mud. Maybe he could build a pier for his railroad spur to run straight out onto the lake and disembark its passengers right next to his waiting steamer. The vessel could be docked on the opposite side of the pier. He had constructed pilings and piers in Glenbrook which supported his locomotives as they traveled out to the sawmills to be loaded. Why not do the same with passengers? He could even build the depot itself out on the pier. Again, he'd done the same in building the sawmills out over the lake in Glenbrook. Passengers could disembark from the train and move about the covered depot in any weather to collect their baggage and buy tickets for the steamer. He'd have to investigate that.

The town might be backward, but it had a kind of charm. The forest penetrated the city limits. Tall pines grew in between buildings on either side of the street. The scent of timber was everywhere. Obviously, the logging had not reached the immediate area around the town. One still felt they were standing in a small wilderness oasis. There was freshness, a newness to the place. It had possibilities.

Bliss approached his modest office. Standing out in front under the small overhang was a skeletal creature dressed in a long coat. The lengthy jacket hung down over sagging trousers that only partially covered a worn set of boots. He stood holding a floppy hat with modest brim uncovering an unruly, almost wild gray mane. The most striking feature of the man was his long beard. The hairline to the sides of his face barely covered cheeks so sunken as to be almost non-existent. But as Bliss came closer, he could see the man's eyes. The orbs were bright, lively and full of intelligence. They appeared to size up Bliss with botanical exactness, as if he were a new species. Bliss had no doubt that this was the man he'd been told he was to meet this morning.

"Mr. Muir?"

"I am." The words from the slim figure resonated with a baritonal vigor that seemed misplaced in the slight physique.

"My assistant tells me a Silas Drummond asked if I would meet with you. I have something of a history with Mr. Drummond."

"Silas was kind enough to point me in your direction. He is a good soul, but he tells me it would be better if he did not attend."

Bliss chortled, "He's probably correct. When we last met, he was leading a mob outside my door in Carson City calling for my head."

A bare smile appeared on Muir's bearded lips. "He mentioned that. He said he was doing what he could to protect the forest."

Bliss's shoulders sagged ever so slightly. "He was ranting for me to stop my lumbering business. He called for an end to the business I'd worked for years to build. End a business that was critical to the mining industry." Bliss paused and looked away then to return. "Funny thing is, I'm now looking to stop the lumbering. Silas pushed just a little ahead of his time."

"It is never too late to take steps to protect God's creation. It's the reason I wanted to talk to you. There is more forest that needs to be protected."

There was a hint of accent in the man's speech. Maybe Scottish. Bliss found it hard to place.

"I have heard of your efforts. I have not read any, but I am led to believe you have written books and articles calling for the government to take steps for the protection of special places here in California."

"California and beyond. I have had the privilege to publish articles in The Century magazine with the help of my friend Robert Johnson."

"And I am led to believe that Mr. Johnson has considerable influence with the government in Washington, D.C."

Muir smiled, the first indication of any real reaction. "We have tried mightily, but there has been little success. However, that leads to why I wanted to talk with you. I believe you might have a special opportunity to change that state of affairs."

"I am but a simple businessman here on the far western parts of the country. I have no connections to Washington whatsoever. I think you mistake my influence."

The pair had not moved from the porch. The impetus of the conversation had consumed Bliss completely. Muir had given no indication of moving inside either.

"I'm told you intend to build a railroad from Truckee up here to Tahoe City."

"That is true. At this stage, I plan to begin bringing tourists here to Tahoe to see the beauty of the Lake. The forest is part of that. It needs to re-grow." Bliss was amazed at how forthcoming he had been in the short time with this man. He was beginning to feel as though he were in a confessional. The slender figure before him could just as well have been a priest.

"The beauty of the lake. Mr. Bliss, I was not sure I would hear words like that from you."

"I wouldn't make too much of it. In reality, the forest is thinning on the east side of the lake. The mines are beginning to show a reduction in ore. We have drawn the resources needed to help the nation's economy. But now those resources are played out."

"How serious are you about bringing people here to see this magnificent place?"

"Quite serious. If successful in getting approval to build the railroad spur, it will be the focus of my business."

"And who will need to approve your railroad?"

"A subsidiary of the Central Pacific Railroad called the Donner Boom and Lumber Company."

"Is that company owned by the Big Four that built the railroad?"

Intrigued by where Muir was leading the discussion, Bliss answered, "It is."

"Then there is your influence in Washington, D.C. The Big Four has influence in substantial measure."

Now Bliss was completely bewildered. He had no idea as to how the disparate points of the conversation led to any focused conclusion.

Muir must have sensed his puzzlement as he then offered, "Confused?"

"Entirely."

Muir let another of his priestly smiles slip between his mustache and beard.

"If you build your railroad, you will be able to haul timber down from Tahoe City. The CPRR will not need the Truckee River. In fact, I have spoken to E.H. Harriman who works with the CPRR and has considerable rising influence in the company. He might be willing to use your railroad to transport lumber down to the sawmills instead of using the Truckee. However, he also might be willing to completely end lumbering activity around Tahoe if their licenses could be swapped for timber licenses further to the north on the other side of Donner Pass in a forested area with no special geographical significance."

"And if they have an opportunity to obtain rights to additional timber, they might be willing to use their influence in Washington to promote your idea to protect Tahoe."

"Ah, see Mr. Bliss, you are no longer confused. As I said before, you might just be in a special position to generate a great deal of influence in Washington.

"If Tahoe is protected, the forests will regenerate and it will be a draw for tourists into the next century."

Muir reached out with one of his skeletal hands placing it on Bliss's shoulder. "And you would have an extended future in bringing tourists here to see it."

Bliss had another idea. "I spoke with Lucky Baldwin recently. He owns the Tallac House at the south end of the Lake. He is looking to promote the tourist business too. But he wants the dam across the Truckee removed."

Bliss thought it best not to mention that Baldwin also wanted to do his own lumbering. Bliss would have to walk a precarious tightrope if he joined up with Muir and intended to continue his prospective arrangements shuttling passengers to Baldwin's Tallac House.

It was Muir's turn to now pause.

"If the CPRR no longer needs the Truckee to float its logs down to their sawmills, I see no reason why we could not ask to have the Truckee River and Lake Tahoe restored to its original condition by removing the dam."

"Mr. Muir let's go inside so we can talk more about this idea. I believe it has tremendous merit."

"Mr. Bliss, I have a better idea. Why don't we just take a walk beyond town into the very forest we intend to protect and we can talk further amid the grandeur itself."

# Chapter Eighteen

*Late August 1877*
*Reno, NV*

Reno lay a mile ahead, fractured by waves of heat rising from the baked dirt on the road. No matter how Will adjusted his eyes, the structures of the town moved in a soft, ethereal dance across his view like trying to see it through a bad glass window. Nothing stayed still. It were as if a rushing river of clear water hung in the sky and he was trying to look to the bottom as it flowed across his sight. He wondered how the heat affected the air so violently that you could not see clearly, even though it was transparent. Still early, the temperature was already blistering.

Despite the muddled translucent visage, he could see activity where the road met the town. Dust rose from all movement, lifted by the heat as if trying to escape the flat fry pan of the earthen street. The movement of those out in the sun was slow. The heat weighed on all. The sun's rays sapped any exertion.

The smell of Powder's sweat rose from the horse's steady effort. Will had peeled off his morning jacket tying it to the rear of his saddle. Rivulets of his own sweat ran down the middle of his back. And he was only sitting atop his horse. The animal was doing the real work.

It was still long before noon and the heat was already tough to bear. He had gotten used to the milder temperatures the elevations brought. He could not start his return trip quickly enough. He hoped Grande was in. Paris had said the lawyer was using another attorney's office on a temporary basis. That office was next to the courthouse. Will hoped it wouldn't be hard to find. The less time he spent in the sun, the better.

Will needed to take care of Powder and then locate Grande's office. He had used a livery stable on the outskirts of town on earlier trips to Reno. He stopped at the same establishment asking the proprietor to keep Powder saddled, but to water and feed him a touch of hay after he'd cooled out. He needed the horse refreshed for the trip back up the hill.

Once Powder was taken care of, Will headed to the courthouse. He soon found a string of lawyer offices. He asked at the first one he entered if the occupants knew where he might find a Sam Grande. He was told he'd find him two doors down.

Will opened the door. Silence. It was a one room office. Will could see the broad back of a man facing the opposite direction away from the front door. The man's size and physique gave away his identity.

"What no bell? I like that bell in your Carson City office. How can I generate a proper entrance without the irritation of the bell?"

Grande responded without even looking up or turning.

"Hearing your voice is irritation enough. Did you bring your beautiful wife? She would be more pleasant to talk to. All you bring is trouble."

"Ah, you love the trouble I bring."

"Says who?"

"Look how you solved the foreclosure war with the CPRR. You beat the railroad. You became famous after that win and I brought you that case."

"I saved your hide. Speaking of hides, have you been shot lately? Usually when you come to see me you have either been recently shot or are about to get shot."

"No shooting lately. Been quiet."

Grande finally stood and turned to face the entrant. "How pedestrian of you."

The friendly banter paused as the two men smiled at each other. Will offered no handshake. None was necessary. These two knew each other all too well.

Though some years older than when Will first met him, Grande was still a physical presence. Almost six foot five and barrel chested he loomed in the room. The office didn't fit him. It was too small. In his Carson City office Grande had stacks and stacks of thick books lining the shelves on his walls, piled on his desk, and strewn all over his floor. Some stacks rose higher than others like defensive bastions in a castle made of his books. Grande looked at home with his books. He loved them. But there were no books here. Not enough room. Standing before him, Grande looked almost confined.

The lawyer then broke the brief silence.

"You and your bride left town. I've missed our Sunday dinners. I might remind you that those dinners are payment for the back fees you owe me."

"Fees? With all the new clients my cases have brought, *you* should pay *me*."

"Lest you forget, it took some serious lawyering to save your backside with the railroad. And then we have the time I helped you when the law enforcement of Virginia City considered your arrest after you conducted a shootout raging throughout their town. Those efforts and results proved most valuable, and I don't recall ever seeing any cash."

"I paid for your help on the initial homestead."

"Oh, I had forgotten about that one. That was the beginning of our one sided relationship. I give advice and you ignore it requiring me to bail you out time and time again."

"Well, I've come for more advice."

"Oh no, maybe I should have thrown you out of my office instead of helping you homestead your ranch. The result may have been you'd have left town. My life would be remarkably less complicated." Good-humored sarcasm dripped from the comment.

"I need to talk to you about water, water from the Truckee. We moved the herds north to the spread we still call the Purcell Ranch. You know the story as to how I came to own a piece of that ranch from Beth."

Grande nodded. "Oh yes, I know the story."

"The Truckee runs through the land, but the flow is diminishing. A lot of beef could die. The other ranchers who came with us think I should head up to Tahoe City. Apparently, there is a dam across the Truckee at Lake Tahoe. The ranchers think I might be able to convince whoever owns the dam to increase the flow."

The good humor evaporated from Grande's face. His expression was all business. Will knew the look. It came when Grande initiated any analysis. Will had always been impressed with the speed and accuracy of Grande's mind. But the process usually began with questions. Lots of questions.

"And how do you think you are going to do that?"

"I think I'm supposed to have rights to take water from the river."

"That might be true. But even if we assume that, how do you figure you have any position to request an alteration of flow over the dam?"

"I was going to ask you how I should approach them."

"Without knowing anything more, I would say *carefully*." He issued the word *carefully* with emphasis.

"Something else you should know."

"Oh, here it comes. I'll bet this is the good part."

Will shook his head defensively. Grande had a knack of knowing when the vulnerabilities were coming.

"Dale Paris rode up a couple of days ago. He said the CPRR controls the dam through some subsidiary company. Also said he'd been hired by the CPRR to investigate the murder of a dam employee who'd been shot. Appears the original builder of the dam wants to take back control and has threatened to hire gunmen to do so. He also said a lawsuit has been filed by the State of Nevada regarding the dam and that I might be called into it as a defendant."

Grande sat down and motioned for Will to do the same.

"Have a seat. You're going to need it."

Will was left anxiously perplexed by the comment. He eased into one of only two other chairs in the office.

"Why do I need a seat?"

"Because you are a defendant."

"You've seen the lawsuit?"

"Yes, I have several businesses along the Truckee who are also clients. Sawmills who use the flow of the water to power their movement of logs. They've asked me about representation as they are defendants too."

"If I'm a defendant, I'd ask you to represent me."

"Like I said earlier, all you bring is trouble. Those sawmills are good paying customers. I could stand to receive a handsome fee if I take their positions in the case. It's a huge piece of litigation. Nevada has sued California, the City of San Francisco, the Donner Boom and Lumber Co., some business owned by a man named A.W. Von Schmidt, along with a slew of people who own property along the river. That's where you come in. They needed to sue anyone identified as having potential rights to the river's runoff. Nevada hopes to resolve all rights to the water. In order to do that they need to bring anyone with a claim to the Truckee's flow into the suit."

Perplexed by this news, Will figured Grande should have benefit of everything he knew of the dam and developments surrounding Tahoe City. "Something else you ought to know."

Grande sighed, "This could only get better. Why is it I have the feeling the worst is yet to come?"

Will shifted in his chair, "Henry Dangberg was approached by several legislators in Carson City when we moved the herds through. They told him about filing this suit you just mentioned. But they said they were doing it as lots of their constituent ranchers were considering marching up to the dam to destroy it."

"That sounds lawful." Again, the sarcasm was thick. "They can't be serious."

"As a matter of fact, I was confronted by young Dirk Ferguson just this morning on the way here and he told me his father has a group of other ranchers who are joining him to do just that. They intend to ride up within a matter of weeks to destroy the dam if the flow doesn't increase."

"So, let me get this straight. There could be a gun battle between the present people who control the dam and the people who originally built it. The City of San Francisco is making a play to take the water back down to the coast. The Nevada Legislature has pushed the state Attorney General to file suit against everyone connected with the dam or the river. We have at least one group of crazed ranchers, maybe more, who think the best thing to do is destroy the dam. And you think it wise for you to ride right up into the middle of this powder keg?"

Will now felt almost embarrassed. Grande had a way of putting things that not only called his plan of action into question, but also made it seem near ridiculous. He still felt the trip to Tahoe City might bear fruit. Getting more water was critical, not only for his own herd, but for lots of people downstream.

"Dangberg and the southern ranchers feel that Duane Bliss is in a key position to talk to the people who control the dam. He's intending to build some railroad and might be in a position to haul timber rather than having it flow down the Truckee. The ranchers think because of my past dealings with Bliss that I can talk to him."

"Oh, this just keeps getting better and better. What happened the last time you got involved with Bliss. Didn't you break an ankle and almost get killed?"

Will looked sheepishly at the ground in front of his chair. There was no escaping the fact that Grande knew exactly what had happened when Will tried to help Bliss and his lumber operations in Glenbrook. He had no defense to his friend's accusation, an accusation born out of concern.

There was another silence. This one more extensive than the last. Will finally broke the quiet.

"What would you do if you represented me?"

Grande sighed, collected his thoughts and responded.

"Since I've been talking to other potential clients, I've reviewed the law."

"You have always made it a point that I should review the law when there is an issue."

"Well, I have yet to observe you taking that good advice."

"I have you to do that." Will waited. He knew the man's mind was working and the assessment would soon follow.

"Though you do not normally examine your legal rights before you start pulling your trigger, I always do. In this case, the key is California's Water Act of 1870. They authorized a license for the Donner Boom and Lumber Company to manage the flow of the Truckee River water. What is important, what is critical, is that this act does not give the Donner Boom company rights of ownership to the water. Those rights belong to whoever owns property along the watershed. Like you."

"So, I do have rights?"

"Yes, you do. Problem is you are a small player in this mess. But a small player with the same size right to take water. If I were to represent you, I would file an emergency motion in the Federal Action seeking a court order that the flow of the Truckee remain uninterrupted."

"Would that work?"

Exasperation could be heard in the tone of Grande's response. "Lord knows. Depends on the judge. Depends on what the opponents say. Depends if the sun is up, or on the weather in general. Depends if the judge had a fight with his wife on the morning of the hearing. The variables are endless."

"Then I'll ask again, will you represent me?"

Grande stood. Will had seen the movement used often by the lawyer. The action created time, time for thought. It was as if rising to a standing position led to a decision. He turned in his confined little office space as if he were looking for something. He didn't seem to find it. Grande turned back to Will.

"Against my better judgement, yes, I'll represent you in the suit. I won't get a dime, but maybe I can figure a way to keep your delightful wife from becoming a widow."

## Chapter Nineteen

*Late August 1877*
*Tahoe City, CA*

Forms covered in shimmering iridescent scales slithered to and fro in the lustrous clear water. A large round utterly transparent Tahoe pool spread below him. Dozens of what he assumed were trout undulated slowly, maintaining a static position in the flowing crystalline fluid. Were they eating? He could not tell. They hung in indecisive suspension amid the liquid's gentle flow—neither retreating nor moving forward. Like so much of the human populace, there was movement but little progress.

But as he stood on one end of the dam across the Truckee there was a peacefulness in the pool before him. Strange to think a corpse with a bullet deep inside had earlier invaded that peace. He wondered what the fish had thought about the crash of a body hitting the water. Some of the fish almost looked as blue as the lake. Some looked dark, malevolent. Just like the people who threw hooks at them or shot bullets.

Dale Paris stood waiting at the dam. He had checked in with the new superintendent. The man's name was Mark Shaver. Shaver had said he needed to finish something and would join him in a minute. It gave Paris time to look over the dam, the current focal point of collective angst from the California coast to Nevada. The structure seemed benign enough. Simple rocks and timbers jammed together with only a limited rise above the level of the river. It was not very impressive. It looked like no more than debris a storm had washed up to block the waterway.

However, it didn't take an expert to see what was causing the anger downstream. Even Paris could see that very little water ran over the rugged cutout in the dam's structure. To the east side of the dam there looked to be a large wooden door of some type. That must be where the logs were pushed when the buildup of water emptied through the opening. On the lake side of the dam, Tahoe's rim was low. Granite rocks bore signs of the normal water line. The lake's usual level lined the boulders like a thin blackened stain. That stain rose at least three to four feet above the current level of the water. The whole lake was low. If it got much lower, Paris could readily see that it might not crest over the dam's cutout through which the water was obviously meant to flow.

"It's called a spillway."

Paris turned to see Shaver standing back in the tree line. He waited for the man to approach, but he did not move.

"If this heat keeps up, there will soon be no flow over the spillway at all. The Truckee will dry up altogether."

Paris turned to look down at the thin level of water cresting over the section of the dam Shaver now referred to. He spoke again from the trees.

"Why don't you come over to the office. I don't like to walk the dam in broad daylight because that was when Pritchard was apparently shot. I don't want to be the next target."

Paris adjusted his bowler hat and moved off the dam following Shaver's path of travel. When he got to the door, Shaver offered his hand.

"Sorry for the way this looks, but I've got a wife and family. Pritchard was a good man from all accounts. I look to do what is required but survive."

There was a pervasive nervousness in the man's demeanor.

Shaver continued, "I can see from his logs that Walter would do his inspections early in the day. I do my inspections in the early morning when it's close to dark. I hope I make a tougher target at that hour."

Paris was now quite taken aback by the man's obvious fear. He was not sure how to initiate the conversation with the man in his current state of mind. Without any other alternatives, he decided to simply start asking his questions.

"Did Mr. Prichard have any enemies?"

"I didn't know the man, only knew of him. Seemed to be the solitary type. If he had been born a couple of decades earlier, he'd have probably been a mountain man trapping beaver."

"Did he list any strange occurrences in the logs you've read."

"No, those are mainly technical journals. The information includes nothing but water levels, flow rate and the like. I have seen no personal entries. Don't know if he kept a diary. If he did, I haven't found it."

"Did you speak to the local sheriff?"

"No, I've only been here one week. My understanding is that whatever the sheriff did happened before I arrived. My hope is to hold the fort so to speak until a replacement for Prichard can be found. I'm doing this as a favor to Mr. Hopkins, a favor for which he is paying me quite a bit. Don't plan on being here any longer than it takes."

Paris asked, "Why did you even take the job?" He wondered why the man was here in view of his obvious reluctance.

"Family needs the money. Mr. Hopkins is paying me three times my normal wage. They could not find anyone to take the job after hearing Walter got shot. Were it not for the money, I wouldn't be here."

"Is there anything you can tell me about the murder at all?"

Shaver shook his head, "Not really. I wasn't here and haven't spoken to anyone locally about it."

Paris nodded, trying to cover his disappointment with the lack of any leads.

"Have you received any threats, any sign of additional violence?"

"No, but Mr. Hopkins said he would be sending some men for security. Haven't seen anyone yet. But that tells me even my boss is concerned for the safety of whoever is working here. All that does is make me feel more uncomfortable."

Paris hesitated to add to the man's fears, but he needed to know what he might be confronted with.

"Has Mr. Hopkins told you that there might be an effort by people connected to A.W. Von Schmidt to try and take control of the dam?"

Shaver nodded. "He told me about that. If there is any indication of violence, I will leave. I am not a gunman."

Paris figured Shaver was so afraid he didn't need to tell him about the chance of ranchers coming to destroy the dam. Shaver would probably leave right now if he told him. Paris did not want word to get back to Mr. Hopkins that Shaver left because of something he said. He tried to think of something to allay Shaver's apprehension.

"I spoke to Mr. Hopkins personally. He's the one who hired me to find the murderer. He told me that the company would be hiring personnel to protect you up here. Those men should be coming soon. I would guess no more than a day or two."

"They'll be a welcome sight."

Paris added, "I'll be around. I'm going to check with the local authorities to see what they know. After that I might be back. Would you be willing to talk to me again after I've had a chance to speak with the sheriff?"

"Sure. Mr. Hopkins wired me to cooperate with you in any way I can. Frankly, it's nice to see a friendly face."

Paris smiled. "If I were you, I would be on the lookout for anyone who tries to do any surveying or construction down river. If you see anything that looks like that, tell your security people. I'll be staying in Tahoe City if you need me and I'd be happy to help. Oh, and I wouldn't confront any other work force alone if I were you."

Shaver had not looked comfortable during the entire conversation. His demeanor had not improved following Paris's advice.

"Thanks for that offer. I will definitely look you up if I see anything before the security people arrive."

Paris turned to head out the door. "Then I'll take my leave. Thanks for talking to me. I'll check back in a day or two."

Shaver looked like a man living on a thin string of hope. "Much appreciated" was all he could say.

# Chapter Twenty

*Late August 1877*
*Along the Truckee River*

Razor thin dust floated upwards. The glow of fine particles lifted in momentary triumph over gravity as Powder stopped. The disruption of the soil floated forward to engulf both rider and horse. Tiny earthen bits floated high above their station turning toasted orange before the setting sun only to slowly return to the roadbed.

Will knew Powder needed a rest, a blow. Fifteen miles downhill this morning and fifteen back uphill all in a day was a grueling test. They were almost back to the family's camp. Darkness would fall soon bringing an end to the day. Will couldn't help but feel there could be a different type of darkness befalling future events. He waited until the dust settled back to earth. The air was again crisp and stung his throat with its purity. Powder took advantage of the stop to dip his head and rub each side of his face on first one front leg and then the other. It was the horse's way of wiping his brow.

Will sat wondering if the dam at Tahoe city might soon resemble the fallen collection of dust and road residue. A bomb could reduce it to similar shards. Could he prevent that destruction? Will squeezed Powder gently, barely touching the animal's flanks with his spurs. The horse needed little encouragement to get home as he was as anxious as Will to end the day's journey.

The sun had long since dropped beneath the unyielding mountain peaks further to the west. The day's heat waned here in the forest heights. They approached the camp's clearing. The chimney obelisk ahead rose skyward, a marker in his life's history. That history had led him to meet Beth. The destruction that occurred here gave birth to the things he held most dear, his family, now covered by the adjacent tent.

As he broke free of the tree line, he decided best not to startle anyone.

"Luke and Sean, it's your father."

The boys came running out of the tent. Beth soon followed lifting the shelter's flap high over her head. Even at a distance he could see her smile. Welcome enough.

"Pa, you're home."

"Yes, Sean. Do me a favor tonight and unsaddle Powder. Between you and Luke rub him down and give him some water but not much. Then tie him to the picket line. We'll have to wait a while before we can feed him. He's worked hard today. Don't want him to colic. Only give him a little water right now. We'll feed him after he cools out and take him down to the river later for more. Then we can turn him out in the corral."

Luke popped up. "Sure Pa, we'll take care of him."

Will stepped down out of the saddle. His left ankle felt stiff and mildly non-responsive when his boot first hit the ground. His left ankle was the one he had broken during the gunfight on the Glenbrook piers. He didn't trust himself to take an immediate step. He waited until the feeling resumed before he turned to face Beth. She walked up and gently laced her arms around his neck.

"Long day?"

"It was."

"Don't look like you're ready to run any races. You're not getting old on me, are you?"

"Like to see you ride thirty miles up and down hills."

"You never know, might look better than you do right now." She grinned at Will's rise to the baited banter.

"Just like you, strike out at a man when he's vulnerable." The words were issued with a face of feigned pain.

"And I thought you were made of stouter stuff. I must have been misled into this marriage."

With that he swooped his right arm down and behind her knees lifting her up into his arms. Thus ladened, he began walking toward the tent.

Beth's grin broadened. She leaned into his shoulder and whispered into his ear.

"Might be enough left in this old horse to keep me interested."

"Oh, I bet I can think of something stout to keep you interested for a bit. Might just have to take a walk out into the forest after dinner."

"That's if you can still walk after I feed you. My guess is you'll be asleep before dessert."

"Despite the bite of the welcome, it is good to be home."

Beth kissed him softly on his cheek, "It's good to have you home. Even if you do show signs of early arthritis." She laughed at her own jibe.

Will dropped his wife's feet unceremoniously, "Woman of the house, I'm famished and in need of food. Make haste."

Beth stood bemused, meeting his gaze eye to eye.

"Returning to your ancient Scottish roots will not get you far. However, in view of your feeble condition, go wash up and come get your dinner. Bring the boys with you."

*****

"The stew was good. Where did you get the onions?"

Beth looked up while grabbing the dishes from the flattened log that served as the family's dining table.

"Those and the carrots were brought from home. I probably have enough for another week or so."

"Maybe one of the boys can find a deer and bring home some fresh meat. I was about their age when I started hunting for the family meals back in Georgia."

"Not sure I want those two walking around in the woods shooting at things. You never know when they decide to pick a fight. If armed, they might only shoot each other."

Will smiled. "Nothing wrong with a little temper."

Beth shook her head, "Not when armed at the age of nine. Come with me down to the river. You can help wash the dishes."

"But that's woman's work." The exclamation sounded tinged with false disfavor.

"You'll not fool me with that attitude, get up and grab some dishes."

Will obeyed with a smile.

"When I said we should take a walk after dinner I did not think it would be limited to doing the dishes."

"If you help proper, you never know. The sky's the limit." There was an enticing grin shot over her shoulder as Beth walked out of the tent.

Will ducked out behind her hands full of pots and pans. "Sam said to say hello."

"You have not said anything about your conversation with our consigliore."

"Our what?"

Beth chuckled. "It's his word. He says it means special advisor in Italian. He says his family is from Sicily, an island off the coast of Italy. They have gangs of bad men roaming around doing all kinds of things outside the bounds of the law. A consigliore advises the leaders and they go about disregarding the advice to do what they please. He says he's always advising you only to see you step outside the bounds of normal law abiding citizenry to do what you please."

"I'll bet you agreed with him too. Lots of support I get from my bride."

Not giving Will the benefit of an answer, Beth changed the topic.

"So, what did he say?"

A serious look came over Will. "According to Grande, there are a lot of upset people. A lot of people who might start doing some crazy things."

"Such as?"

"There is a man in San Francisco named A.W. Schmidt who apparently built the dam to raise the level of Tahoe so he could siphon off the excess for the city's water supply. But the railroad took over the dam and he wants it back. Might use force to do it. On top of that, there are ranchers here along the Truckee who are considering riding up to destroy the dam and let the river flow naturally."

"That's silly. If the dam has created extra water, why don't they just let that extra water flow. No one would be that crazy to destroy the dam."

They had reached the river with their batch of pots and dishes. Beth began washing. After she finished each dish, she held out her hand to Will in a silent request for the next. Will hesitated to tell her about his meeting with the cow hands, but he figured Beth ought to know.

"On the way down to Reno, I met up with some working cowboys on the road. Turns out it included a young man named Dirk Ferguson. His dad owns the ranch to the east of us. I think Dangberg told me on the way up that he knows the owner of that ranch. Dangberg said the father's name is Angus Ferguson." Will hesitated again.

Concerned at his reaction, Beth pushed Will to finish the thought, "And?"

"Well, it was sort of a confrontation. Least that is how I took it. There were four of them total. When I told them who I was, they reacted real angry at the fact I'd brought the herds up to the Truckee. This Dirk kid made it clear they weren't happy with the additional drag on their limited water supply."

"Did they threaten you? Should we be concerned here in camp?"

"The four of them were armed and there was a moment or two when I thought it might come to shooting, but it didn't. They wanted to know if I'd join his father and some other ranchers when they headed up to blow up the dam."

"So, they really are going to do this?"

"Sounded like they are gonna try."

Will watched as Beth seemed to scrub the dishes even harder. The plates were taking a beating as she became more and more concerned.

"What did you say?"

"Told 'em that I was headed down to Reno to ask my lawyer what water rights I have. Also told 'em I was then going to head to Tahoe City and talk to the people who control the dam. Plan in our group is for me to ask for them to increase the flow."

"And what did they say?"

"Dirk didn't strike me as the sharpest knife in the drawer. I don't think he knew if I was offering to help or telling him he was nuts. When he hesitated, I took the opportunity to ride on by."

Beth returned to scrubbing the last of the dishes.

"Did you find out anything more from Sam Grande?"

"Said we've been named as a defendants in a lawsuit."

"Defendants! Why would anyone sue us?" Beth's voice rose an octave.

"He said we were sued only 'cause we're a landowner with water rights. The state of Nevada filed the action. The aim is to settle all disputes to the water so they must include anyone who has potential rights to take from the river."

"And what is Sam Grande going to do?"

"He says he's going to represent us. Talked about filing some motion. Claims it'll be worth ten years of dinners."

Beth stopped washing altogether and looked directly at Will.

"Are you sure you have to go to Tahoe City? This sounds like a battle brewing if there ever was one."

"The water keeps getting lower and lower. I have to do something to try and save the cattle."

"Will, be careful."

"I'm plannin' on it."

*****

The aroma of smoke never left the room. Though there was nothing burning in the fireplace, years of use left everything in the simple house smelling of past blazes. The bare plank floor supported an assortment of axe hewn furniture and creaked as its owner stood and walked to the gun rack.

Angus Ferguson was not tall, but he was wide. Broad shoulders were touched by long gray strands of unkempt hair. His stout frame was set in a low center of gravity. He wore tailored wool trousers that draped over well heeled boots. The cut of the clothes were his only concession to vanity. Home, barn and ranch were models of necessity. His garments were a statement that he'd prevailed in decades of toil to build a successful ranch from hardscrabble soil.

"Did he say he would join us or not?" Angus had turned to address his son. The words carried a distinct Scottish brogue clinging to the man from his birth in the Hebrides.

"Pa, your limp is getting worse."

Angus looked down at his left side. "The leg that took the arrow in the Paiute wars gets worse with age. It'll nae hinder me though."

Not to be deterred, he pressed his son for an answer to his question. "Will he join?"

"I told you, he said he planned to head up to the dam to ask them for more water."

"And he thinks they'll listen? He's an idiot. Dangberg told me this Will Toal was young but not to be trifled with. Doesn't sound too sharp to me."

"The four of us looked real menacing but he showed no fear."

"Ah, he might have some substance, but if he thinks he's gonna talk his way to more water, he's daft. We're dealin' with the railroad here. They're not the type to shake hands and roll over."

Ferguson lifted one of the rifles out of the rack. He pulled the lever to make sure a cartridge was jacked into the magazine. He admired the weapon.

"Wish we'd had these here rifles back during the Indian wars. I wouldn't be limping if we had."

Ferguson was thinking as he spoke. It was his way of working through his thoughts toward a decision.

"I'll not lose everything I've worked for because robber barons want to take our water to California. I'll not stand and watch my beef die of thirst. Your departed mother and I worked too long and too hard to build what we've got. We can't wait any longer. There's barely enough water flowing in the Truckee. If we wait, it'll only mean more steers will die."

Angus looked up from the gun to his son. Dirk listened intently. His boy had become a man, but he lacked sharp judgment. Angus knew this. But Dirk had been the only child to survive. He and his wife had lost three babies at birth. With his wife now gone, Dirk was all he had. Dirk was the reason he was going to ride on the dam. He had to leave the ranch in the best shape he could. He was not sure how Dirk would see it into the future. All he could do was pass it to him intact. A ranch with cattle dying of thirst was not a stable circumstance to give to his son. He had to change that. He had to destroy that dam.

"Dirk, tomorrow you ride to the other owners. Tell Bob McCollum, the Brady's and Carter McKinnon that we ride in four days. Tell them to bring as many hands as they can. They each told me earlier they could spare two apiece. With you and I, that should be ten to twelve men. That should do."

"I'll ride tomorrow Pa."

# Chapter Twenty-One

*Late August 1877*
*San Francisco, CA*

Deep green ferns lazed in the corner of the room. Rows of manicured hedges and flowering roses bordered crushed rock walkways in the garden just outside the office window. The flora both inside and out sprawled in static peace. Leland Stanford reclined mutely in his chair, yet he was anything but peaceful. The man who had been invited, more ordered to appear, stood in the doorway behind a servant.

"Mr. Harriman to see you sir."

Stanford's consciousness appeared to lift but only momentarily. There was a dark look in the deep set eyes, a spiral of anger if he was not mistaken. But the guest had rarely seen any such pronounced emotion in his host, so it was difficult to tell for sure. Better to wait and tread carefully. Without looking at his butler, Stanford answered.

"Please send him in, Gerald."

E.H. Harriman entered the spacious office. Stanford did not rise. He did not look up in anything that resembled a normal welcome. Harriman stood just inside the door as if waiting for formal permission to enter.

"Good morning, Leland."

"Sit. Look at this." Stanford pushed a folder with fifty or so pages included inside across the surface of his desk inlaid with rare burl wood.

Harriman approached the large desk halting directly opposite his host. He lifted the folder quickly assessing the volume of paper inside. He stood before one of the two guest seats and unbuttoned his suit jacket then lowered a thin briefcase made of fine leather to the floor. He adjusted the egg round rims of his spectacles and removed the business day hat from his bald pate and set it on the adjacent chair. He then sat, never taking his eyes off his host, expectantly watching for a clue in the man's body language. Stanford had yet to say another word.

"What am I looking at Leland?"

"A lawsuit. Donner Boom and Lumber was just named as a defendant in some infernal suit filed by the state of Nevada. They dispute our right to the waters of the Truckee."

"I thought we were going to be talking about Von Schmidt's efforts to retake the dam."

"We were, but this was just dropped off this morning. It has ruined my day." Stanford could not suppress a weary sigh. The effort to keep the Truckee flowing continued to cause him grief. It had been a thorn in his side and a drain on financial resources for almost a decade. It just never ended.

Harriman interrupted the silence. "I received a wire from Mark Hopkins yesterday confirming that we have hired men as security for our employees up at the dam. Three men have been hired to work around the clock watching out for our folks. But Mark did not say anything about a lawsuit."

Stanford swiveled his chair, turning his gaze from the view outside his window to look at the man now seated across from him.

"I'm not sure Mark knew about this. We both had heard rumors of some suit, but we thought it was some political stunt, a hollow threat."

Harriman began thumbing through the papers. He spoke while still looking at the various pages he skimmed.

"On first blush, this does not look like some political stunt. This complaint has some solid legal footing."

"I read it carefully and would have to reluctantly agree. We'll need to send it off to our lawyers. And Edward, we need to tell the lawyers this is big. They must do everything they can to keep the flow of logs headed down the Truckee River."

"Who is behind this?" Harriman was still reading through the document quickly.

Stanford shrugged, "No idea. Says in the papers that Donner Boom and Lumber is blocking water which otherwise would flow east to the state of Nevada."

"They are saying that the dam at Tahoe City is holding water they would normally receive?"

Stanford sighed, "That's how I read it."

"So, they want the dam removed?"

"Not sure what they want to do with the dam. I think the main thing they want is more water. We all want more water. But right now, there just hasn't been enough snow."

Harriman set down the folder.

"Funny, this is the second request I've recently received concerning removal of that dam."

"Oh, who else wants to interrupt our business?"

"A man named John Muir. I met him a couple of years ago. He just sent me a wire from Tahoe City. He asks that I meet a man named Duane Bliss to discuss granting an easement along the Truckee River. The purpose of the easement is to build a railroad spur from Tahoe City to the CPRR line at the Truckee depot. He also wants our support in Washington to make Tahoe a protected national park. He thinks this might be a way to block all other uses and claims to the water and land around the lake. In return for our assistance in the political arena, he will back any request we make to obtain timber licenses north of

Donner Pass. Included in the overall concept is the removal of the dam across the Truckee."

Stanford sat up. Displaying a face now bright and interested, his expression alone acted as if he had just joined the conversation.

"If we grant the easement and this Bliss fellow builds his railroad, what does he intend to use it for?"

"Tourists."

"Tourists?"

Harriman nodded.

"As I understand it, the thought would be to bring people from San Francisco and other parts of the country up to the lake via a rail line the entire way."

"They'll never make any money doing that."

"Might be difficult in the short run, but if there was a federal protection of the lake and the area around it, there could eventually be a steady business for decades."

"Not interested. But there is something much more important here." Stanford paused as if to process a thought. Harriman watched the normally unanimated face display the rise of an idea. And even from his vantage, Harriman could see it could be a potentially big idea.

"What are you thinking Leland?"

"If this man Bliss wants to haul people up the hill, will he haul lumber down the hill?"

"Ah, that could be a bit of genius Mr. Stanford. I think I see where you might be going. To answer your questions, I don't see why he wouldn't."

"Do you know this man, Muir?"

"Passingly, yes. He is a crusader for the protection of land, areas he considers pristine forest or mountains. He's intelligent, well read and describes his earthly objects of preservation as victims teetering on geological mortality. At first glance you might think him irrelevant. However, he is anything but. More importantly, he has developed substantial influence in Washington."

Stanford now stood. "Can we trust this man to work with us in Washington?"

Harriman remained seated spreading his arms. "I believe so, but nothing in Washington is predictable these days. We are not a well-liked business. Politicians treat us at times as if we suffer from some communicable disease."

Stanford was again looking out through his window deep in thought.

Harriman continued, "What about the dam?"

Stanford scoffed. "I don't care about the dam. If we can get lumber hauled down from Tahoe City by a railroad line and have potential access to new timber forests to the north, then we don't need that silly dam. It's been a nuisance to our business operations for over seven years now. But the trick will be timing. We need the dam until we can get the spur built and access to other forests."

Stanford walked across the broad space to stand at his window. At eight or nine feet wide and over twenty feet high, it provided abundant light for the office. It was also a visual link to the outdoors that called to Stanford. With his hands clasped behind his back, he turned again to face Harriman.

"I think we need to pursue this. It just might be a pleasant opportunity. Edward, you need to get up to Tahoe City to talk to this man, Bliss. Make a deal for some special rate to haul lumber downhill in return for the easement. If we have a railroad, we don't need the Truckee."

*****

Six men proceeded Jonas onto the boat, the last one wearing his signature tricorn hat. They had met at dawn in front of the Bella Union. One half of the agreed upon fees were extended in cash as confirmation of the monetary arrangements. With the payments thus made, the group moved to the dock to pick up the first morning ferry across the Bay. The Oakland depot for the Central Pacific Railroad lay on the other side of the sound. They would pick up the train there and head east to the Sierras.

Jonas Greerson followed the group thinking this must be what it's like to hire a mercenary army. The men looked like hired soldiers. All wore small arms at the waist. Pin carried a wooden club in a special leather holster on his left, and a gun to his right. Greerson remembered the man's story as to how he got his name. The small club must be one of those shipboard items sail lines were tied around. All carried what looked like heavy bags in which he believed were more weapons. He had been introduced individually to the men. Each was called by some sort of nickname. One was Bull, another was Sniper, and another was simply called Muscle. Greerson could not escape the feeling he was headed into battle.

A foghorn whistle sounded from somewhere near the raised captain's perch and the ferry pulled from shore. Pin took a position next to Greerson looking him up and down as if to assess how he would do on the open water. Early morning's on San Francisco Bay were never warm no matter the season and today was no exception. A stiff breeze pushed its way into the large inlet and with it came waves. Heading northwest across the bay exposed the boat to the windswept mounds of water blowing east into the bay from the open ocean. The liquid fusillade broadsided the portside freeboard producing a constant series of splashes heaving spray over the side. Standing just inside the railing, Greerson turned his back to the onslaught lifting his collar in futile effort to shut out the moistened cold. Pin didn't seem to mind at all. In fact, he seemed most at home on the water.

Greerson wanted desperately to wipe the smile from Pin's face. He did not know why, maybe to establish some form of command authority. Not a word had been spoken about the upcoming task, but Greerson struggled to muster respect from a man who had undoubtedly seen action in armed conflict whereas he had not. Respect might be hard to achieve from such a man.

"Will these men fight?"

Pin answered in an overly casual manner, "If I ask them to, they will fight." Implicit in the comment was that the result might be different if Greerson was the one doing the asking.

"A camp is being set up for us near the Tahoe dam. We will stay in Truckee tonight and take a wagon to Tahoe City tomorrow. We can then take a day to make sure everything is in order. If so, then three days from now we can start taking mock survey readings. Hopefully, the occupants of the dam soon take offense and we can physically remove them."

"Why wait for them to take offense?"

Pin issued the words in an ominous tone. He spoke with a sense of confidence, but the attitude also carried a strong hint of malevolence.

"We need to try and provoke the dam personnel to action first."

"Why? If the object is to remove them from the dam, why not just get to it? The sooner we finish, the sooner we can return to San Francisco."

Greerson now knew controlling Pin was not going to be easy. He already felt a slippage of authority and they had only just begun.

"Mr. Von Schmidt wants to take control of the dam under the premise that he has the right to do so. We need the other side to take overt action so that we look like we are simply defending our rights."

"Sounds way too complicated."

Greerson took a chance, a chance to keep this effort in line before it escaped his control altogether.

"Pin, you seem like an intelligent man. Maybe uneducated, but intelligent. Why don't we use our combined intelligence and experience to set up the situation to obtain some advantage. It will be like a game, a game with a known ending."

Greerson could see that the idea had some appeal. A smile spread across Pin's face.

"It might be fun to play a bit, and we can see if we can provoke the other side. Might be something to keep the men occupied. But it cannot last too long. As you said, the game has a known end. The sooner that end arrives, the better my men will like it."

Greerson did not know if he had won or lost this small battle. At least he'd made some headway.

*****

A.W. Von Schmidt sat at the New World Coffee Saloon. Waiters moved quickly through the tight hallways between sectioned rooms swishing by each other in their short-waisted black jackets and ankle length white aprons. Gruff to the point of rudeness, the waiters expected their customers to sit, read the menu, and order quickly so they could be fed and move on for the next patron. Business was always brisk. Von Schmidt had been a customer for years and knew the drill. He did not know if his patron would approve.

The patron in question, James Leicester, made his money in gold. Leaving the hardscrabble slums of London earning his passage aboard ship as an assistant to the boatswain's mate, Leicester docked in San Francisco and immediately headed to the gold fields. He started to work his claim in 1849 by panning rivers. From that beginning he moved on to building sluices, then hiring others to work the lucrative stretch of riverbed that was his claim. He never admitted how much education he'd had. But he had told Von Schmidt many times men of his class could never own property in England. He intended to own as much land here in America as he could afford. Leicester now invested in real estate, office buildings and, hopefully, water companies.

Von Schmidt watched as the well-dressed Leicester entered the Coffee Saloon, looked about, and moved toward Von Schmidt through the throng of customers at the bar as if barging through a mess hall. He was stocky and possessed a florid face partially covered with a now graying well-trimmed beard. He removed his hat revealing a thick shock of salt and pepper hair. He stopped and stood behind the only other chair in the partially sectioned room that Von Schmidt had selected. He turned to look at the Saloon behind him before taking his seat.

"I remember this eating establishment when I hit the docks in 1849. They sold good coffee and cheap grilled fish. I had just been given my wages and though I was bound and determined to use it all for my stake, I treated myself to a cup of that dark chocolate-colored American replacement for tea called coffee and a good meal."

Von Schmidt took the opening comment as acceptance of the choice for the meeting. Leicester lifted the menu and was quickly ready to order when the waiter appeared.

"Coffee only for me. I will not be staying long."

Von Schmidt now felt his chest cave inwards as if his lungs had been depleted of oxygen. He had to consciously force himself to suck in his next breath to replenish that which had been lost upon hearing Leicester order. Von Schmidt needed money from this man.

Agreements to fund what he intended to ask for did not occur in quick chats over nothing more than a cup of coffee.

"Allexey, may I call you by your given name?"

"Of course," said Von Schmidt.

"Allexey, the only time you contact me is when you need money. I have heard about your efforts with the City Council. Do you really intend to try to start up the Lake Tahoe and San Francisco Water Works Company again? That did not go so well back in 1870."

"Mr. Leicester, the city needs water. Growth projections show an exponential need for water over the next ten years. The Pilarcitos dam and Spring Valley Water won't be able to supply enough. The business doesn't need a model, the potential for revenue is astronomical."

"But you have to get the water. That fundamental little problem is what doomed your first attempt."

"We created the water. Our dam raised Tahoe by five feet as planned. The amount of water stored in that five feet is more than San Francisco can use in twenty years. We just need to move it from Tahoe to San Francisco."

"You don't even have control of your dam."

"That's why I need money. I have hired men to take back control of the dam. We built it; it bridges the Truckee River from parcels of land we own on either side. It is not the property of the Donner Boom and Lumber Company. It is ours."

"And who is *ours*?" The last word was spoken with sarcastic emphasis.

Von Schmidt knew this was the key question that needed to be answered if he was to have any long term traction in getting the pipeline built.

"Me."

Leicester scoffed. "You? And how do you come to that conclusion?"

"Because I still own the land abutting the dam. That ownership brings with it rights to take water from the river."

"I thought Spring Valley bought your old now defunct business. If I remember you called it the Lake Tahoe Water company. Didn't that company own the land?"

"No. The land was kept in my name personally. Lake Tahoe Water leased it from me."

"That was pretty diabolical. However, I have to admit it was shrewd."

Leicester paused collecting his thoughts.

"And how much money do you need?"

"One hundred thousand."

"Allexey, I gave you five hundred thousand back before 1870. I have absolutely nothing to show for it. What would you use this money for that is going to make this different?"

"I need twenty thousand to pay the men who are going to take back control of the dam. The rest will be used to pay city councilmen. I need three more votes for approval of the new plan. Most of the money will go to those three with a sprinkling among other councilmen to make sure their votes stay solid."

A dubious grin spread across Leicester's face. "Even if you take control of your precious dam, that doesn't get you a pipeline to San Francisco."

"First, I intend to get control of the dam. I have men on their way there to do just that as we speak. If I get the votes from the council, then their approval will come with a ten million dollar bond issuance. That is what I've asked them for. I can build a pipeline for that."

The coffee was served. Leicester stirred in some sugar twirling the deep brown mixture as if business justification would rise along with the steam from the liquid. He put down his spoon and looked across the table.

"Allexey, I will give you the one hundred thousand. But if you don't get the city council approval, if you don't start some building of the pipeline, I will make sure you never work again here in San Francisco."

Leicester took a tentative sip of the still steaming liquid peering over the edge of the cup at Von Schmidt. The look was menacing. He then set his cup down, stood and walked out. Von Schmidt did not know if he should feel elated at obtaining the vital funds or doomed in the face of daunting odds.

## Chapter Twenty-Two

*Late August 1877*
*Tahoe City, CA*

A pallid full moon desperately clasped the night's horizon in a doomed effort to flaunt its diminishing brilliance as long as possible. The sun had not yet risen. Dale Paris was caught between darkness and light.

Paris sat atop his mount, back erect, almost stiff. While not tall, his frame was muscular and solid. On the ground his stance was naturally stable. But his frame was not particularly cast for riding. Others had told him his riding seat lacked any supple communication with his horse. It was if he was too hard, too rigid. He did not ride smooth. But on the ground, many a man had tried unsuccessfully to knock him from that stance. His father had been a blacksmith. Paris had begun working in the smithy with his father as a young boy. The broad fibers in his arms and legs were a result of those long hours at an early age. The work had built muscle, but those hours also convinced Paris he was never going to make it a career. He liked using his head to solve mysteries. Better than swinging a hammer.

Paris had ridden out from Tahoe City heading for the Truckee River dam hoping to catch Mark Shaver on his early morning inspection. He wanted to see what that process looked like without letting Shaver know he was watching.

Paris stopped. The river was not far ahead. He listened but could not hear anything; maybe the river had stopped flowing. Silence blanketed his path on the road. An uneasy stillness pervaded. Even the nocturnal animals had given up their efforts. He felt abnormally alone.

He usually liked the feeling. Yet here an uncertainty crept into his thoughts. It was not that he heard any ominous sounds. The problem was the *lack* of sound—a complete scarcity of life. Perhaps it was the lingering lack of light, but he sensed he should be cautious. Despite the quiet, something told him he was not alone.

Paris pulled his collar tight, glad he had brought a coat. Reno had been unbearably hot for months down in the valley making it unthinkable to wear any outer clothing. But the morning's here in the mountains were always brisk no matter the season. The air was dry, devoid of any moisture and cleansed by the scent of pine. The ground beneath was a collection of well-trampled dust, dirt that had not seen rain for weeks if not months.

Nothing moved. He waited. Still nothing.

Paris lightly squeezed the sides of his horse with his knees, moving the animal forward in a slow but steady walk.

The sun strained to make its regular daily appearance. In the distance behind him, a soft pale blue began a slow cosmetic resurfacing of the receding black ink of night. However, just yet the sky above him was still dark and low. He felt confined as if he had entered into a long tunnel. It would be some time before the cobalt color of day would lift the ceiling heavenwards.

Soon he heard the lapping sounds of the river. The road would continue right over the top of the dam and the connected short bridge over the small spillway on the far side of the structure. Paris pulled off the dirt path into the forest. He wanted to stay out of sight. He pulled his horse up at another stop.

Paris placed his elbow over the crest of his saddle horn and leaned forward to get a view through the branches. He did not have to wait long. A man exited the supervisor's shack across the river and walked to the dam. Paris figured it was Mark Shaver. While he could not see the man's face under his hat and tall collar, the figure moved furtively. Frequent stops and rapid glances up and down river interrupted his progress out to the dam. Based on his earlier conversation with Shaver during which he conveyed his fear of these morning inspections, it had to be the same man. Shaver held a board with paper on it. He reached for something inside his coat with which to write.

A shot rang out. Shaver dropped to the top of the dam.

Paris could tell that the shooter was down river, but upslope. The sound of the shot told Paris it had been a rifle. He spurred his horse racing to the downed man. He pulled his gun from its holster and fired in the general direction of where he thought the shooter might be. He knew there was almost no chance of hitting the shooter who was undoubtedly out of range and out of sight. But Paris wanted to create a diversion until he could reach Shaver.

He pulled up on top of the dam where the path was only four to five feet wide. Paris jumped off his horse on the opposite side from where the shot was fired using his horse as a shield of sorts.

"Are you alright?"

No answer.

Paris dropped his reins and ran in a crouch to the prostrate figure. It was Shaver. His eyes were closed in a pained wince. Shaver's body had collapsed parallel with the path over the dam. His head was closer to the opposite side of the river from where Paris entered. Paris ran all the way around to Shaver's head. He could see the man was trying to speak. Paris leaned closer in effort to hear anything he might be able to say.

"I . . . I, didn't see him"

They were the only words Shaver uttered. His head then dropped to the side, limp.

With his left hand, Paris pulled at Shaver's coat. The wound was at the upper right shoulder away from the heart. He slowly lifted Shaver to check his back. The bullet had passed all the way through the body, additional evidence that the shot had come from a rifle.

Paris looked again toward the spot where he thought the shot had come from. No movement. No smoke. He pulled his scarf from his neck and placed it over Shaver's chest at the bullet's entry point, applying pressure. The wound oozed red fluid, but Shaver was still breathing. Paris was about to holster his gun and grab the man to start pulling him to safety when he heard a voice behind him, coming from near the superintendent's shack.

"Don't move. You have three guns pointed at you."

Paris was about to turn.

"I said don't move. One more flinch and you're a dead man. Drop the gun."

Paris did as he was instructed. He raised his hands.

"Get him boys. I'll keep a gun on this guy while you both grab him and drag him off the dam."

It dawned on Paris what was happening. These men thought he was the shooter.

"I did not shoot Shaver. The shooter was upriver in the woods."

"You expect us to believe that? You probably shot him and ran out here to finish him off."

Two sets of hands grabbed Paris, one set just outside each shoulder on the arm. They started dragging Paris backwards in what would have been the direction to the superintendent's shack.

"Shaver is not dead. If I shot him, why did I put my scarf into the wound to stop the bleeding? He needs a doctor."

The men had pulled Paris completely off the dam. They turned him on to his stomach and one man pinned his knee into his back while holding both arms. Paris struggled to get some air free of dirt and dust as his face was now jammed into open ground. The same man who had done all the talking so far spoke again.

"Houston, check the man's handgun to see if it's warm, if it's been fired."

After a moment, "Yep, it's warm."

"So, you didn't shoot him, did you? We caught you with a gun right in your hand."

Paris found it hard to speak with his chin and jaw driven into the dirt.

"Check both sides of the man, if you know anything about weapons, you can easily tell that wound is clear through his shoulder. It was caused by a rifle. No handgun would do that. Go check the rifle on my horse. It has not been fired."

A pause. "Go check the rifle, Houston."

Paris could not see the activity behind him out on the dam. He heard movement but could not see what was taking place.

"The rifle is cold boss. Hasn't been shot."

"Miles, can you lift Shaver?"

"Sure. I gotta tell ya, the man's right, Shaver's still breathin'. We need to get him to town."

"Ok, let's pull him into the shack before there's any more shootin'. We'll load him onto the wagon and take him into Tahoe City. Miles, you keep a hold of Mr. Gunman here and we'll tie him to one of the chairs in the shack until we can sort this out."

*****

Duane Bliss sat in his office. He'd arrived before time to get work done. Usually an early riser, he was away from his family back in

Carson City. He wanted to get some things done before he rode across to Tahoe's east side on one of his tugs. He would disembark at Glenbrook, the base of his logging operation. It would take at least half the day to ride across the Lake and then the rest of the day to drive his buggy over Spooner Summit and down to Carson. If he got his work done promptly, he might be home in time for dinner.

A knock came at the door. Bliss stood to open it.

"Good morning Mr. Bliss. Thought I might find you here early. Decided to take a morning walk on the chance we could talk."

"Mr. Muir, I wasn't expecting you."

"I apologize for the interruption. But I got a wire yesterday from Mr. Harriman. I'd sent him a note after our earlier meeting. He has responded."

"Did you tell him about our idea?"

Muir smiled, "I did not go into detail, but I conveyed the basics."

"And what kind of response did you receive?"

"Quite favorable. Mr. Harriman is taking the early train today to Truckee. He would like to meet you here tomorrow."

Bliss returned the smile. "Then I should probably wire my wife and tell her I will not be home for dinner tonight."

# Chapter Twenty-Three

*Early September 1877*
*Purcell Ranch, NV*

The canopy of pine treetops bent in obedience to a strong, high wind. The sound of oncoming squalls could be heard pulsating through the woods, approaching with invisible stealth. Will heard the next barrage approaching through the dense stand of pines in front of him. After dropping two more logs into the wagon, he watched the forest tips bend to their limit like greenstick twigs when the force of the blow hit them. More impressive was the sound. The cycle would start with a low whispery murmur in the distance and then crescendo to a howl as it blew passed. In the process each individual gale tried to lift and take everything in its path with it. Then the blow would subside as if mother nature were sucking in volumes getting ready to exhale the next gust. In the lower earth bound levels of the forest, the breezes swirled around stout trunks with less power but still lifted-up pine needles and flung them in a fusillade of small irritating arrows stinging any exposed skin.

Will and Luke had been cutting and gathering wood for their temporary home. An open meadow was behind him, a large space of relative peace. On the opposite side of the forest's opening was the tent of their makeshift homesite. The meadow's grasses swayed back and forth violently but it was nothing like the wind's effect on the trees. Nights were cold here in the mountains. Overnight fires in the chimney had kept the tent warm.

A loud snap boomed above.

Will whipped his head upwards at the sound of a good sized branch about to break.

"Luke, get out from under that limb! It's about to fall. Can't you hear it crack?"

The youngster looked questioningly at Will. Above the rush of another loud blow Will yelled again.

"Up above you, listen. That thing is about to break. Bring your ax over here and help me stack the wood in the wagon."

Luke had no sooner reached his father's side when the branch broke free amid another gust and crashed to the ground. It was not a big branch, but thicker than a man's leg and large enough to cause injury. It had landed exactly where Luke had been hacking at a chopped log.

Will lowered his forehead in the direction of his son in a well-used paternal gesture. "Good thing you listened to your pa."

Luke appeared nonplussed, maybe shaken. Will could see the boy could not find appropriate words for the moment. His eyes had widened at the sight of the branch on the ground near where he had stood. After a pause and still wide eyed, he turned back to Will.

"That would have hurt."

A fatherly smile spread as he answered. "Yep."

Will reached out and laid his hand on Luke's shoulder. He could feel his touch steady the young man.

After a moment, "Here, help me put these last logs into the wagon and then we'll see if we can get your mother to fix us something for lunch."

Luke blinked and with that small movement seemed to return from a far off distance.

"Ma is out riding with Sean and Juliette."

Will nodded, "That's right, I forgot. Well, maybe she'll be back soon. Not a good day to ride. Horses will be spooked by the wind and whatever is blowing at 'em."

Luke looked back at the downed branch, "Hope they don't get hit by a branch like that one.

Will grinned. Luke had already shown a maturity beyond his years. Here again he displayed a concern Will would have expected from someone much older.

"Let's finish and drive the wagon back to camp."

They lifted the last logs onto the wagon and headed across the meadow. About halfway into the open space Will saw a rider approaching their temporary home. Though the rider's hat was pulled low and jacket collar lifted high around his neck, he could tell from the horse and silhouette it was Henry Dangberg.

Will leaned just a bit toward Luke to his right, seated up on the wagon's bench.

"Wonder what Mr. Dangberg wants. For him to ride across the ranch in this weather it must be important."

Will pulled the wagon around the front of the tent and stopped at the nearest set of pine trees.

"Luke, you start unloading the logs. Stack them good, like the rest. I'll see to Mr. Dangberg."

The lone rider strode into the clearing. The wind continued unabated. Will had to turn away from his oncoming guest during a particularly strong burst which lifted both dust and needles.

"Henry, you picked a poor day for a ride. Let me take your horse."

"That would be appreciated Will. I am forty-six years of age but right now I feel eighty. Wind cuts right through you. It's been so hot, now this."

Will reached out toward their small collection of stumps and one rough-hewn chair. "Have a seat. Beth is not here but should be back shortly. Will you stay for dinner?"

"Thank you, but I don't think so. I would like to get back before dark. In this wind, no telling what might come flying at you. Be best if I did the ride in daylight. At least I might see what's about to hit me."

Dangberg's accent still carried tones from his native Germany. Will remembered his own efforts to drive the twang from his own Georgia roots as he came west. The thought struck that you cannot ever completely change signs of your origin.

"What brings you here Henry?"

"What has brought us to the mountains? Water. Or maybe the lack of water."

Will nodded, "The meadows are getting dry. But we still have grass."

Dangberg slumped into the rough wooden chair. "Yes, we still have grass. I suppose that is something of a minor miracle as we've had no rain."

Will waited. He knew there was more to come. Best let the man move at his own pace.

Dangberg extended his arm and held his hand up to block the flying pine needles targeting his direction as the next gust hit. When the blow subsided, he looked back at his host.

"Will, Peter King and the other ranchers are getting concerned, very concerned. The flow in the Truckee has slowed to almost nothing. The cattle are starting to look like they did back home. Most are listless, some are getting weak. There is just not enough water."

"Henry, we've been here in the mountains for almost a month. The herds are doing a whole lot better than if we'd stayed home."

Dangberg nodded, "No one says otherwise. They are just worried as to how long the stock will last."

Beth then rode up with Juliette sitting on the front of her saddle and Sean following on his own horse. Will rose to take hold of Beth's bridle. Her horse was normally steady, but Will could see its eyes were wider than normal, likely anxious in the wind.

Will could see that upon lifting the brim of her hat from a pine-needle-protection-level, Beth realized they had company. "Mr. Dangberg, so nice of you to drop by on this lovely day. Did the wind carry you over the ranch and deposit you here? I felt we were going to lift off the ground on several occasions."

Dangberg stood and tipped his hat. "Mrs. Toal, it is a pleasure to see you out and about."

Will grabbed Juliette with one hand and offered the other to Beth as she dismounted.

"I know it seems like a silly day to go riding, but I've been planted here for over three weeks and just felt the need to saunter through the woods a bit. What brings you here Henry if I might call you that?"

"Please, use Henry. I was just about to tell your husband why I had come."

Beth extended her hand, "May I join the conversation?"

Dangberg took off his hat, took Beth's hand and looked warmly at her as she walked toward the collection of temporary seating outside their tent.

"By all means. Maybe you can come up with some ideas as to how we can survive this current predicament."

Will handed the reins from Beth's horse to Sean, "Son, put the horses in the corral and take their saddles off. You know what to do. Give them a good brushing and walk them down to the river for a short drink."

"Yes Pa."

Will then turned to follow his wife but not before he touched his two year old daughter's perfect little nose and tickled her stomach leading to the anticipated giggle.

Beth handed Juliette to Will, then sat on one of the short stumps that served as a place to sit, offering the makeshift chair to Dangberg once again. "And what about the current predicament needs to be discussed?"

Dangberg waited for Will to join, then he too sat. "The river is getting too low. The other ranchers and I hoped to convince Will to head up to Tahoe City to talk to this Mr. Bliss or anyone he can to increase the flow over the Truckee dam."

Will sat still, holding Juliette. Looking at Beth he answered, "We had talked about this before."

Beth paused, then "How long will you be gone?"

Will now looked at Dangberg, "I don't think I'll be more than two to three days. It's only a day's ride up and another back. That gives me a day to find and speak to Bliss or anyone he might suggest."

Dangberg must have perceived concern in Beth as he said, "I can have one of my men camp close here to help keep an eye on you all."

Will shook his head, "No need. Juan went down to the ranch to pick up his wife Maria and they'll be back later today. Those two should be all the help Beth might need."

It was now Beth's turn to interject. She looked at Will, "Maybe I should go with you."

Will was a bit taken aback. "Honey, I've never been to Tahoe City. Don't know my way around. Don't know what I'm going to find. It might be best if you stayed here."

"You've rarely call me 'honey'. Makes me wonder if you expect trouble. Is that because of what Dale Paris said?"

Will shrugged, "Not sure what I expect. Bliss might have no idea on how to help. Shoot, he might not even be there. I might have to wire him in Carson City and hope he can refer me to someone at the dam. I just have no idea what might happen."

Dangberg turned to set his hat on another stump. "What did Paris have to offer?"

Will began to answer but Beth cut him off. "Mr. Paris rode through a few days ago and said he'd heard that some group of San Francisco investors were going to start a fight with the railroad barons to take control of the dam. Both sides were hiring gun hands. He thought there'd be a battle."

Dangberg then looked at Will, "Didn't you go down to Reno recently to talk to your lawyer, Sam Grande? What did he say?"

Will had been looking at Beth trying to figure out if by butting in she was sending him some unspoken message. Still unsure, he turned to Dangberg. "Sam said pretty much the same thing as Paris did. He thinks there could be trouble."

Dangberg looked down to the dirt between his boots. "Then you could be heading into a hornet's nest. We've got the local ranchers telling us they intend to head up to the dam and blow it up. Maybe we should send you with several hands."

Will gave the suggestion some thought but shook his head. "I think that would send the wrong message. I'm going to talk, not start a war. It might spark the tinder box if we ride in with multiple hands. I think it best to go alone. 'Sides, Dale is up there already. We work well together."

"Those ranchers told Peter King they intend to head up to Tahoe City in a day or two."

Will rose, "Then I'd better leave tomorrow." He looked at Beth. He could see disappointment in her eyes, maybe fear.

# Chapter Twenty-Four

*Early September 1877*
*Truckee River Dam, CA*

A bead of sweat dripped from his hairline into the corner of his eye. The salt stung. He could not wipe it away. His hands were tied behind him.

Dale Paris sat in the middle of a room. He had been dragged unceremoniously upside down into the dam supervisor's shed and tossed into a wooden chair. His hands had been tied while outside on the ground. The rope binding his wrists had now been fixed in the rear. Additional lengths strapped his ankles to the legs of the chair. He could not move.

It was now hot. Sun beat down through a window focused on his unprotected position. The morning chill hovered beyond the shed's plank walls. Dry heat crept through the transparent glass warming everything within. They had not taken off his jacket. Paris had seen dark interrogation rooms where a single oil lamp would blare overhead blinding the subject of the inquiry. He felt the sun do the same here.

He blinked. The salt from the sweat now burned at the edges of his eye sockets. It was as if a river of sweat had now been formed such that the perspiration flowed freely down this new tributary to a point of maximum irritation. He shook his head. The flow of sweat remained unchanged.

"Can someone wipe my face?"

There were only two men left inside. Both stood at the ready watching out of their respective windows, designated sentry posts.

"Shut up."

Paris had seen that both men displayed a cool ease handling weapons. One man, called Houston, wore a tan dust covered beaver had with at least a four inch brim. The other, called Miles, wore a black flat brimmed hat with a circular crown. The dark color of his hat contrasted with the trimmed gray beard. Both men appeared fit. Obviously, these men were part of the security force hired by Mark Hopkins. They appeared professional.

Houston now turned to Paris.

"You even have the look of a guilty man. You're sweating bullets."

Paris scoffed. "I'm sweating because I'm sitting in the sun with a heavy jacket. If you won't wipe my face, at least take off my hat."

"Miles, take off the man's hat."

"You do it." Miles kept and intent watch out one of the windows constantly scanning his field of view. "Bryce said to keep a lookout and not to move this guy until he got back from taking Shaver to the doctor."

Paris shook his head. "You guys are letting the man who shot Shaver get away. If there are any tracks, you risk having them blown over with pine needles and lost."

"And what if you were the only shooter?" The man called Miles did little to hide his skepticism.

"You men seem to know your weapons. You saw the wound. That was caused by a rifle. You checked mine; it had not been fired."

"Then what were you doing out there? How were you out on the dam so quick?"

Paris felt he had an opening to talk his way out of being confined. He just needed to take one more step to set up his idea. "I was hired by Mark Hopkins to investigate the murder of Shaver's predecessor."

Houston now entered the exchange. While still looking out one of the other windows to the shack he asked, "How do you figure we are going to believe that?"

"Because I can describe Mark Hopkins, the same man who hired you."

Houston turned and glared at Paris; a questioning look spread across his face. Paris could tell by the man's expression that he had at least opened the door of opportunity a crack. He had to hope Hopkins wore the same outfit he'd seen him wear when they met outside the railway depot.

"Mark Hopkins is about fifty, long gray beard almost reaching his waist, wore a dark suit with vest and a brown hat with small brim and crease running down the middle."

Houston sneered, "All you did was describe about half the businessmen in Reno."

"But Hopkins always wore a watch chain with thick links of alternating gold and silver. He was never without it. Said it was a gift from his wife. I'll tell you something else; he probably also told you he had already hired a man to investigate the murder of Shaver's predecessor. And he gave you his name. The man he hired was Dale Paris."

Obviously surprised, Houston now said, "And what if he did?"

Paris smiled, he was winning the battle and he knew it. "Reach into the pocket inside the right side of my jacket. You'll find a handful of my business cards."

Houston now turned to his partner, "Miles keep a bead on this guy, if this is a trick, shoot him."

Miles turned away from the window and aimed his six gun at Paris. "Go ahead."

Houston walked over also keeping his aim on Paris, reached inside his jacket, and pulled out a group of business cards. He looked at them carefully. Surprise now turned to concern.

"Miles, the cards say this is Dale Paris. The man's right, Hopkins told us he'd hired an investigator of that name."

Paris moved to finish his plan, "And you have now tied and bound the person responsible for finding the murderer. Whoever fired that shot is probably the same man who's been shooting at Mr. Hopkins's employees, and you are preventing me from finding the shooter. Not something I would want to get back to the man who hired you."

Still unsure, Miles asked, "Then why were you out there so early in the morning?"

"Waiting for the murderer who shot the first supervisor at the exact same time of day. I had a chance to pursue, but now that trail is stone cold. Although I might still be able to track the man if you would let me."

"We have to wait until Bryce returns before we can let you go. He's in charge."

"That could take hours. I've already lost the better part of a day. I need to try and find the spot where the shooter set up for his shot."

Neither of the men responded. Undoubtedly neither knew what they should do.

Desperate to canvass the side of the hill where he thought the shot came from, Paris floated an idea.

"Ok, look. One of you stay here. The other can come with me. We will walk up the side of the hill. Keep my gun. Keep my horse. I'm not going anywhere without both of those. Just let's take a look at where I think the shot came from. If we find something, I'll make sure Hopkins hears good things about your efforts."

Houston looked at Miles, "Can't hurt. The man appears to be who he says he is. If there was another shooter, Hopkins will want to pursue whoever did it."

After thinking a moment, Miles waved the end of his gun as if it were linked to some thought process. "Ok, I'll take him out to the forest, but untie only his feet. Leave his hands tied. You stay here and keep a lookout."

Houston untied the bindings around Paris's legs. "Don't be long."

Paris did not waste any time. "I hate having my hands tied, but let's go. The sooner we get up that hill, the sooner I might be able to show you how wrong you are."

*****

Greerson ripped back the flap of his tent. He, along with Pin and his men, had arrived at the campsite near the dam the night before. Tired and sore from the combined travel by train and wagon, Greerson had slept soundly only to be awakened yesterday just at dawn by a gunshot. He stood outside his tent trying to get his bearings. To his amazement, a fully dressed Pin stood out in front of his tent looking upriver toward the dam.

Greerson move to his side. "Where did that shot come from?"

Pin had fixed his stare on the dam and did not alter his line of sight.

"I was about to start getting coffee ready. A shot was fired. Not sure from where. I did see a man who'd been walking on the dam fall. Right away a rider came up and fired in the direction of the slope there to the right. He then bent down to help the man who'd been shot when three others ran out of the shed there and looked like they arrested the one helping. They kept him in the shack."

"Arrested?"

"That's what it looked like. The three men all had their guns aimed at the man and made him drop his weapon after which they flipped him over, tied him up and dragged him into the shed."

Intrigued, Greerson asked, "See anything else?"

"The three men lifted the wounded worker into a wagon and one of them drove off, probably to a doctor in Tahoe City. So far, that's it."

Greerson followed Pin's gaze toward the shed. At that moment two men came out of the door.

"Look, there's someone coming out."

Greerson heard someone coming up from behind. He turned to see Pin's man—called Sniper—walk up. He cradled in his elbows an exceptionally long rifle.

"Didn't see anyone."

Greerson chose to remain silent. He just watched.

Pin spoke without taking his eyes off the pair exiting the shed, "Are the others out and ready?"

Sniper replied, "Everyone's in position."

Greerson did not understand. Things were moving far ahead of his perceptions or knowledge. He now fought to get caught up. "What position?"

Pin continued to watch the two men on foot. He barely acknowledged Greerson's existence, but he did respond.

"As soon as the shots rang out, I sent four of the men out to set a perimeter and had Sniper go out to explore. I told them to wait until they saw further movement."

The speed and execution of strategy impressed Greerson.

Sniper moved closer and stood by Pin also looking at the men on foot.

"What do you think they are doing?"

Pin adjusted his tricorn hat to block the early rising sun.

"Hard to tell. Almost looks like they are walking that man in front out to execute him. His hands are still bound."

"Did you see him shoot the workman?"

Pin shook his head. "No, and he didn't look like he was the one who fired the original shot. As I told you earlier, I only saw the man ride up fast and pull his handgun out to shoot in the direction up the hill where I sent you. He never looked like he had taken the first shot. If he'd wanted to kill the attendant, he would have finished him off when he got close. He didn't."

The two men walked into the forest. The man in the rear continued to hold his gun aimed at the man in front.

*****

Paris turned and looked down toward the dam gauging whether there was an open line of sight.

"He had to be up here close. See, he would have set up in a spot where he had a complete view of the dam. He wouldn't want to have any trees in his line of sight."

Paris saw that Miles had not taken his eyes off him. There was no attempt to get engaged in any search. Paris turned away from the dam and moved uphill at one hundred eighty degrees keeping the line of sight to the dam open. He walked about twenty more yards, then he stopped.

"Here, look at the pine needles. They've been churned by boots."

Paris spun around taking in the immediate scene.

"There's a log here and he set up behind that using it to brace his shot."

Miles now looked down at the area near the downed log. "Someone has been here."

Paris circled around the footprints. He stopped, knelt, and reached out with his still bound hands.

"Well, well. Take a look."

Paris was careful not to touch the shiny object. He wanted Miles to see it as he did.

Miles lowered his gun and knelt next to Paris who pointed at the object of interest.

"That's a Sharps .45-70 cartridge."

Paris turned to Miles, "You in the war?"

"I was."

"You know your weapons?"

"I know that's a cartridge from a Sharps. They don't take Winchester ammo. Sharps originally made muzzle loaders but later shipped out breech loading single shot rifles of different lengths. The longer barrel versions were used by snipers during the war on both sides."

Paris nodded. "You *do* know your weapons. The original infantry issue Sharps used percussion caps. Later versions used cartridges. I heard that you could even modify the original percussion cap versions to take cartridges."

Miles picked up the cartridge. "Looks new. Anything out here more than one night would have changed to a slightly darker color or even started to rust. This hasn't been out here long at all."

Paris inspected the dirt for a trail away from the lair. He could see a set of footprints that led uphill. No sign of a horse.

"Whoever did this picked the spot carefully. I don't see where he tied a horse. Must've walked here in silence and waited. Probably did the same thing to shoot Pritchard."

Miles holstered his gun. "Guess you've been telling us the truth. Here, give me your hands. I'll untie you."

Paris turned so his bound hands could be freed. In doing so, he looked back down to the river. He noticed a group of tents down river from the dam.

"Who are those men down there, the ones by the tents?"

"Don't know. Shaver told us that the camp was set up a few days ago. Shaver was worried that these were the men he'd heard Hopkins say were hired by Von Schmidt."

Paris rubbed his hands as the rope came free trying to work some feeling back into his fingers.

"There's a man down there with a very long barrel rifle. Maybe we should walk down and have a chat."

Without waiting for any reply, Paris started walking straight down the hill toward the camp. Miles began to follow but stopped.

"You sure this is a good idea? We don't know what those men are up to. And you are not armed."

Paris did not stop. "Only want to ask some questions. Need to check that gun. If I'm not mistaken, that looks like a sniper weapon."

"Might take care not to start any trouble. Word we've gotten is that there will be trouble soon enough."

Still trudging downslope Paris again responded just as he came clear of the forest.

"Just want to ask some questions. I must investigate all angles. Right now, that rifle is the only angle in sight."

Paris arrived at the outskirts of the camp. Several men stood watching his approach. "Who's in charge?"

A man in a strange tricorn hat answered, "I am."

"My name is Dale Paris, I'm an investigator hired to find the man who murdered the prior dam superintendent and probably just shot the current one. I need to talk to your man there with the long barreled rifle."

Pin took a single step towards Paris. "You'll not be talking to any of my men."

Paris could not mistake the confrontational tone. He also took immediate note that all the men he could see were well armed. But he pursued. "What's your business here?"

Another man next to the tricorn responded.

"My name is Greerson. Gesturing to the man in the tricorn hat, he added, "And this is Pin who works for me. We all work for Colonel Von Schmidt. He owns this property and intends to build another dam at this location. We are here to survey the area."

Confused, Paris asked, "Why is there any need for a dam when there is already a dam less than a quarter mile upriver?"

Greerson replied, "Because the man who I work for believes that dam will be removed." Greerson now pointed to the dam upriver.

Miles retorted, "The men I work for have been hired to protect that dam."

Pin now glowered, "If it is decided that the dam is to come down, you protect it at your own peril."

Paris cocked his head, "That sounds like a threat."

The man in the tricorn replied with a sinister if not confident smile. "Consider it any way you want to."

Paris tried to pursue his original intent, "The superintendent just shot was hit by a sniper rifle. The man next to you is holding such a gun. We just found a Sharps cartridge up on the hill that has been recently ejected. I want to ask that man their next to you whether he has fired that sniper rifle and I want to look at it."

The man standing next to the tricorn hat answered for himself in a low confident tone, "No one touches my rifle. If you found a typical Sharps cartridge you are barking up the wrong tree. This here is a Remington, sometimes called a Rolling Block. It's used for buffalo hunting. It's cartridges are called Bottlenecks and run at only forty-seventy. Your Sharps there is probably a forty-five or even a fifty caliber. My rifle does not take any of the same cartridges that are used in a Sharps and it's easy to see the difference. The bottleneck cartridges are used only in a Rolling Block such as this one." The man held his rifle out ever so slightly in emphasis.

Miles touched Paris on the shoulder. "The man's right. Can't use the Sharps ammo we found in that Remington. Let's go."

Paris initially resisted. He looked back at Miles, "You sure he's carrying a Remington?"

Miles nodded. Look at the hammer. Sharps has a unique curve at the top. That gun don't have the same curve so it's definitely not a Sharps.

Paris then relented and along with Miles began walking back upriver to the shed. But he looked over his shoulder at the man in the tricorn hat as he left. He did not have a good feeling about the man or his operation.

After the two men moved a distance upriver, Pin leaned over to Greerson. "You wanted a game. Well, it just started."

# Chapter Twenty-Five

*Early September 1877*
*Tahoe City, CA*

Rather proud of himself, he had done his best to look 'western'. A leather coat shrouded a muted paisley vest and extended far below the top of his pleated wool slacks. A broad brimmed hat covered his receding hairline. All were purchased just for the trip. Not bad for a railroad executive who was trying to blend in.

E.H. Harriman brushed off specks of light dust that had found their way to his knees. The road over which the stagecoach ran was a dusty avenue. He had ridden from the east side of the San Francisco Bay in a special car reserved for the owners of the railroad. Soft couches and leather chairs provided the utmost in comfort on the rails. But the stage was the only mode of transportation from the Truckee depot to Tahoe City. Dust was inevitable in such a carriage. He had stayed last night in the city of Truckee down near Donner Pass. The only stage from Truckee to Tahoe City ran from mid-morning to mid-afternoon, right in the heat of the day when it could stir up the maximum clouds of dust.

He sat at the rear of the stage on the right side. He had taken his seat intentionally. The Truckee River bordered the road out to the right of the stage line the entire way uphill. He wanted to see what the flow was like on the river. It was not impressive. The flow, such as it was, ran meekly through about one quarter of the riverbed. Numerous logs were jammed on exposed rocks down what was now more a stream than a river. Several timbers were high and dry in stretches of the river's regular path, but now carried no flow of water at all. He was amazed any logs could make it down this vital corridor from the logging operations to the sawmills below in the town of Truckee. He had been told that they would collect a load of logs and close the gates to the dam so as to build up water levels. Then teams of horses would pull the gates back and a rush of water would flow down in volume, carrying the logs as they were sucked along with the flow. But this riverbed did not look like any rush nor any volume could carry logs downstream at all. To think, the fuel for every locomotive plying all sorts of trade across the western expanse of the nation depended on logs flowing down this river.

"What a ridiculous state of affairs."

"What did you say?"

A man sitting next to Harriman had heard his comment uttered to himself yet out loud.

"Oh, nothing. Just looking at the lack of water in the river. Is this normal?"

The man leaned forward to look out passed Harriman to the Truckee.

"No, usually the water runs all across that riverbed, even in September. Come winter and spring the current reaches up to the top of those walls bordering the bed, even overflows at times."

Harriman nodded, "Thanks, I'd heard it was low."

"Lower than I've ever seen it and I've been here in Tahoe City for ten years."

Harriman returned his gaze out the window. In addition to viewing the river itself, he also wanted to assess the width of the stage road. He had been self-taught as a banker, not as a surveyor. But even his untrained eye could see there would not be enough room in the river's canyon for both the rail bed and the stage road. The stage line would have to find other access up the hill if Bliss were to be granted use of the easement over ground the railroad controlled. He made a mental note to check for any contracts that had been issued to the stage for use of the easement. Donner Boom and Lumber might have to reach a settlement with the owner of that company. The stage would probably fail altogether if there was now a rail line hauling passengers. But that was the way of the world in business these days. The country was becoming more and more modern. Business and profit would dictate who would survive and who would not. The railroads would survive, at least as far into the future that he could see.

Harriman's mind began to spin with possibilities. He had often considered his brain to be twisted. He felt he could see opportunities for growth and additional profit where most others did not. He could not understand it. He thought the ideas were most often obvious, simple, and straightforward. Whether rooted in management, organization, or expansion, he regularly saw something that could be improved and profit enhanced. Here before him was another example. How had Stanford and Hopkins opted for such a vulnerable method for shipping lumber that was vital to the railroad? He began to think how a new railroad spur could increase the movement of timber and fuel more rail passage east. That could easily lead to more revenue.

His father had been a pastor. His father in law was a banker as well as owner of a small railroad in the east. Harriman had left school at the age of fourteen to work as a messenger boy on Wall Street in a financial house. He had been focused, dedicated, even driven. Never a large man, some had described him as a "small, sort of bantam rooster type." Probably accurate he thought.

He had fought for every positive event in his business life. He learned finance by watching it happen. He scraped enough earnings together to buy a seat on the New York Stock Exchange by the age of twenty-one. Next, he left the brokerage life to help his father-in-law's struggling railroad. In a short time Harriman turned the railroad around and sold it at a handsome profit. At age thirty-three he purchased another railroad which led to another turnaround. He now worked at the Central Pacific Railroad. He saw big things for the rail industry. One of his visions was to buy the Union Pacific and join the two largest rail systems under the same corporate roof. He knew he could do it once he got control of both. Not bad for a boy who left school at fourteen.

Trips like this enthralled Harriman. His possibility-generating brain was already germinating ideas. The Truckee River did not strike him as a viable or even reliable force upon which to base the foundation of the railroad's fuel source. If the flow were not increased, the entire stock of timber necessary to fuel the locomotives would have to be pulled down the mountain by wagon. That would take days or even weeks instead of hours.

One trip, one view of the river, convinced him that he had to make a deal with Bliss to build the rail spur from Truckee to Tahoe City. The company's logs could then be transported over a set of rails, far more reliable than the river before him. And what a switch: he would not have to pay for building that spur. He would get Bliss to do that.

"Coming into town."

The man next to Harriman nodded up to the left at the first set of buildings they had seen since cresting over the Sierras.

The mountains and the scenery were impressive. The expanse and majesty of the multiple crests almost captured his interest. But even those unique creations could not hold his attention for long. What did capture his notice was the landscape further down the slopes left by the loggers: nothing but stumps where a forest had once stood. Here near town, the forest remained untouched by the railroad's saws. The tall trees were impressive. He could even understand what Bliss now saw in the potential for tourist traffic. The forest would return. One day it would all look like this again.

Harriman stepped out of the stage onto Tahoe City's main if not sole thoroughfare. Dirt, more dust. Not anything like downtown San Francisco. He had been told where to find Bliss's office. Not one to waste either his own or other's time, he headed off to follow the given directions without hesitating.

*****

Will Toal rode into Tahoe City on his gray mustang Powder. It had taken the better part of the day to arrive. Beth had expressed concern at his leaving, more than ever before. He had ridden out on several potentially dangerous trips before and while Beth always told him to be careful, she had not appeared worried. This time she was obviously troubled. Maybe it had something to do with the fact they were not in their normal home surrounded closely by the ranch's hands. Maybe it was because the boys were getting older and needed a father around more so than before. Then again, it could be simply because the situation he was headed into had a lot of wealthy people butting heads with a lot of money at stake. And those people had hired guns. From the sound of it, they had hired several guns on each side.

Will stopped at the livery stable. A blacksmith hammered a horseshoe on an anvil. The sound echoed up the slope behind the establishment. The smithy had a hold of the shoe using a set of thick thongs while he swung at it with his hammer in the other hand. He lifted the shoe and apparently it met his approval as he dropped it into a box next to the anvil. He reached to a rack with the tongs to pick out another shoe.

Will caught the man mid-swing, "You know where I might find the office of Duane Bliss?"

The smithy looked up. Mild annoyance spread across his face but soon changed into something that looked more welcoming. "Bliss's office is across the street and halfway down the block. In fact, you see that man standing on the boardwalk with the long leather coat? That's Bliss's office."

"Much obliged."

Will lifted Powder's reins and moved to the hitching rail outside the door the man had pointed to. Duane Bliss was about to close the door when he noticed Will riding up.

"Will Toal, what brings you to Tahoe City?"

"Mr. Bliss, I'm here to see if you can help me go about getting more water to flow down the Truckee. I represent several ranchers who've brought our herds up to my property along the river, as the Carson Valley is parched. But the Truckee is now drying up too. Cattle will die."

Bliss made no response. Will felt he had to press his mission.

"I'm hoping you can tell me who controls the dam so I can ask them to consider our position."

Bliss stood sideways with his back to the opened door. He looked inside then back at Will as if in thought.

"Maybe you should come inside and join the meeting I'm about to have. I think the man you actually need to talk to just walked into my office. Come on in and I'll introduce you."

Will stepped off, looped one of his reins over the hitching rail and entered the room while Bliss continued to hold the door. Bliss closed the door behind him and followed Will into the office.

"Gentlemen, this is Will Toal. I've known him for years. He's a rancher down in Carson Valley with a large spread and a couple thousand head of cattle. He is here representing himself and other ranchers with the same goal. He wants to speak to the man who owns the dam across the Truckee. Mr. Harriman, I understand that might be you. As

I believe we are here to talk about the dam and the flow of the river, would you object to Will sitting in on our meeting?"

The man Bliss spoke to was peeling off his thick leather coat. The heat of mountain mid-day did not call for a coat of that weight. Will thought he must be quite hot. After placing the coat at the end of a long table flanked by chairs, the man turned, thought a moment, and responded.

"I have no objection. Sounds as if Mr. Toal wants the river to flow just as we do. He might bring some added support to our cause."

Bliss then turned, "Will, this is Mr. E.H. Harriman. He is a high executive with the Central Pacific Railroad. We are here to talk about building a rail spur along the Truckee. And this other gentleman is John Muir. He has an interest in protecting the forests and lands around Tahoe. He too would like to see the dam removed."

Will reached his hand out to each man. When he shook the hand of John Muir, he held it just an extra moment.

"I think I heard a man name Silas Drummond speak of you a year or so back."

Muir smiled. "I do know Silas. I hope he had good things to say about me."

"I took it more that he held you in something close to awe," said Will.

Muir now chuckled. "The only thing awesome in this vicinity is Tahoe."

The men sat. Muir and Bliss on one side of the table, Will and Harriman on the other.

Always the one to drive any agenda, Harriman started.

"Bliss, I am led to believe by my friend Mr. Muir here that you want to build a railroad spur from Tahoe City down the hill to Truckee. Is that correct?"

"I do."

"Well, there is no sense beating around the bush. You need access to our easement right of way that follows the river. Laying track on any other path over the mountains would cost far more *and* that assumes you could even find another route a train could travel over."

Bliss put both hands on the table in front of him palms down. "I would agree that the only real viable rail route would border the river."

Harriman plunged ahead, "The stage line now uses that easement. I just rode up on the stage and it is readily apparent that if a rail line were to be built, there is not enough room for any stage road."

Bliss nodded, "But if I build the railroad, there won't be any need for the stage."

"True, but there is undoubtedly going to be an expense to buy out the stage line's interest in using the easement. That will cost Donner Boom and Lumber. We have no intention on paying off the stage and also paying to build the railroad."

Bliss had been involved in his share of business negotiations. He knew he would be talking to a man who was comfortable throwing around the weight of Central Pacific's considerable clout. He had given this upcoming meeting a good deal of thought.

"But Mr. Harriman, I think you have an interest equal to mine in seeing a railroad built."

"And why do you say that?"

A wry smile wafted across Bliss's mouth, "Because if the river gets any lower your logs are not going to flow down to your mills. I would think you might be quite happy to ship those logs downhill using a much more reliable mode of transportation."

Harriman now mimicked Bliss's grin, "I agree a spur might be of joint benefit. Would you consider giving a volume discount for freight fees in return for specific quantities of timber?"

"I would for Donner Boom and Lumber. I won't commit for any others."

Harriman stared across the table. The room was quiet.

"Then I would propose the following: Donner Boom and Lumber will buy out the stage line. Better than waiting for them to sue over some contractual issues on the easement. You, Mr. Bliss, can access over the easement but you will have to pay out of your own pocket to build the rail line. Donner Boom is not going to buy the stage and build the spur."

Muir now interjected, "And what about the dam? Also, what about helping in Washington to have Tahoe made into a national protected area?"

Harriman turned to face Muir. "John, timing is everything here. We need the logs to keep flowing now and through the winter. In fact, the river must flow until Mr. Bliss can build his line. The grants to take lumber here on the west side of the lake south of Donner are crucial to the Central Pacific. But if you were to lend your assistance to a request by Donner Boom in Washington to swap the grants for additional lots north of Donner Pass, then we might support your efforts to protect Tahoe. We might be able to collect our separate goals into a single piece of proposed legislation."

Will had been listening, fascinated as to how business worked. "How does this affect the flow down the Truckee? Sounds to me you need the flow just as much as we do."

"Mr. Toal, you are correct. What would you suggest?"

"I have no idea, but I know there are other ranchers in Nevada who do not belong to our group that have threatened to blow the dam up."

Harriman frowned, "After our prior supervisor was shot, we heard about possible further unrest. We have hired men to protect our people."

Muir pushed his chair away from the table, "Destroying the dam would only lead to a flood. It would cause huge damage along its way and then the flow would be done. Whoever thinks that is a solution is silly."

Will hesitated for a moment but then responded, "They are desperate. Their livelihoods are at stake."

Bliss now offered, "Why don't we simply start a controlled increase in the flow, lowering part of the dam so that both logs can flow and there is more water downstream."

"That is the solution," said Muir. "We can start a slow release of the water Von Schmidt's dam has created. That should certainly last until next spring when, hopefully, the snowpack will provide adequate melt to replenish the river's flow."

Harriman shrugged, "I don't see why we couldn't agree. The only person who will oppose that plan is Von Schmidt himself."

Muir lifted his hand as a form of concluding agreement, "Then I will help with the land grants in Washington in return for your support for a Federal plan to protect Tahoe."

Harriman looked at Bliss, "Are we agreed? We will buy the stage and you will build the rail spur? And Donner Boom gets preferred treatment and available space to haul timber downhill."

"Agreed. But you handle Von Schmidt. I am a resident of Nevada. I have no ability to deal with your San Francisco political battles."

"Done."

The men all stood and were about to shake hands when there was a violent knock on the door. A man barged in without waiting to be invited. All four who had been sitting at the table looked up with anxious faces. Will covered his handgun.

"Mr. Bliss, there's been another shooting at the dam!"

Bliss jumped out of his seat. "What?"

"Yes sir, someone shot the current supervisor. They just brought him into town looking for a doctor. Best we have is Ely who tends to injured stock, but he's trying to help right now."

Bliss turned to Harriman. Did you not say you'd hired men to protect your people?"

"We most certainly did," replied Harriman. "We also hired an investigator named Paris to find whoever shot the original supervisor."

"Dale Paris?" asked Will.

"I believe that was his name."

The man who had brought the initial news tipped up the front of his hat displaying a confused look.

"The man who brought in the fella who'd been shot said they'd arrested someone named Paris for the shooting."

Bliss looked at Will, "We need to put a stop to this."

Will now rose, "There is no way Dale Paris shot any supervisor. He headed up here to find the shooter. I'd better ride out as soon as I can. Mr. Harriman, would you consider writing out a quick note indicating that Dale Paris is an investigator you hired?"

"I'd be happy to. Bliss, can I borrow something to write on?"

"Absolutely."

After waiting for it to be written, Will took the note and moved to the door. "Gentlemen, I'll leave the politics to you, but I would recommend thought be given as to how we can lower the dam without starting some war."

Bliss then offered, "From what we've heard today, the only person who might object is Von Schmidt."

"Exactly," said Will. "And he's hired guns too. Give it some thought."

# Chapter Twenty-Six

*Early September 1877*
*Tahoe City, CA*

The rhythm of Powder's gait at a canter pounded its own percussion tune on the road. Bliss had described the route Will should take. Pretty simple: follow the road east out of town until you hit the river. Will pushed Powder. He knew it was not a long distance from town to the river. The sooner he got to Paris the better. Powder had plenty of stamina for a short run at speed. It would be a good workout for the big gelding.

Will had to admit he worried over the news that Paris had been arrested. The man had saved his life back in Glenbrook at Bliss's sawmills when Will had tried to stop two armed arsonists. A broken ankle had hobbled Will. He had underestimated the jump to a position of strength. The injured ankle had failed and the resulting fall left him exposed. The two arsonists took advantage and forced Will to give up his gun. He was about to be shot when Paris killed one of the assailants. The second man had jumped into a rowboat and headed across Glenbrook Bay. Will picked up his rifle and blew out a hole in the side of the small vessel. Both he and Paris watched as the man sank into the moonlight depths of frigid Lake Tahoe in winter. Had it not been for Dale's timely arrival, Beth would have been a widow.

The azure blue waters of Tahoe came into Will's view to his left. There was no wind. The lake was calm. He had seen it otherwise. Tahoe could lift into nasty rows of unrepentant fast paced waves two to three feet in height. The constant barrage devastated all but the largest vessels on the lake who dared challenge those afternoon squalls. But when placid, the cold depths cast a magnificent blue that could not be described. Its color had to be seen in person.

Will stopped. To his left, the indigo hues of the lake were severed by the dam. The river's barrier stretched out in front of him. To the right, a meager flow of clear water moved slowly into what had to be the riverbed for the Truckee. The road he'd been on from Tahoe City led to a narrow path over the earthen works of the dam. Will took in the scene. Powder's sides heaved in and out as the animal tried to catch its breath. So, this was the cause of his herd's thirst. This haphazard looking collection of rocks and logs had stopped the flow of the Truckee River and lifted Tahoe's brim. The dam looked anything but imposing. He had the thought that it would not take much for Ferguson to blow up the blockage.

But he could not stop for long. Will spied a building across the dam. The structure looked to be nothing more than an oversized shed. But there was a chimney and some windows. More importantly, there were horses tied up near. One of the horses had been ridden by Dale Paris when he stopped by their camp. He headed over the path.

As he pulled up, he heard voices inside.

"What do ya mean, ya lost his trail?"

"There wasn't any trail to follow. It just ended."

"How can a set of hoofprints just end. Horses don't fly."

"There weren't no hoofprints. Boots yes, but no horses."

Will came closer to the partially opened door. His right hand covered his holstered gun. He did not recognize either of the two voices he could hear.

"And you untied this guy's hands. What made you think that was a good idea?"

"Because everything he said 'pears true. We found a brand new casing, a Sharp's casing. The man don't pack a Sharps. He couldn't have been the one to shoot Shaver. Mr. Paris, tell him."

Will pushed open the door. His gun was leveled at the now exposed room. He could see only three men.

"This man is Dale Paris, an investigator. He's been hired by E.H. Harriman and the Central Pacific Railroad to find the man who murdered Walter Prichard. I just came from a meeting with Mr. Harriman and I have a note to confirm what I just said."

The two men on either side of Paris reached for their guns.

"Don't," said Will. "Just leave the guns be."

The man wearing a dark flat crowned hat spoke, "And who are you?"

"Name's Will Toal. I'm a rancher. I know Dale Paris here. I can vouch that he's an investigator. I've worked with him before. Mr. Harriman is going to tell your man in town the same thing. He should be here soon and he can tell you for himself."

Will watched carefully as both men slowly edged their hands away from their guns. Tension eased.

The second man wore a wide brimmed tan hat. He now offered, "We turned the man loose. Don't think he shot Shaver. But we seen him near the body soon after the shot and thought he'd done it. We know now he didn't."

Will holstered his gun. "Here's the note from Harriman."

Paris watched Will reach out and hand over the note. "Nice timing, but I think I'd already convinced these two I wasn't the shooter."

The men looked over the note. Tan hat lifted his hand in the direction of Paris, "Miles, that about confirms it. Paris here ain't the shooter."

Miles pushed up the front brim of his black hat, "Probably, but Houston I'm not full sure. Mr. Paris, I'd like to wait until our boss gets back before you leave." Miles then looked at Will, "He's the man in town you spoke of."

Paris replied, "I'll wait. In fact, I'd like to walk Will here out on the dam to show him how I think the shooting took place."

"That's fine," said Miles. "But we'll just walk out with you."

"C'mon Will, let me show you what I think the shooter's angle would have been. It was probably the same guy who shot Prichard. I am betting he sat in the same position for both."

Will followed Paris out the door. Miles and Houston trailed behind.

The four men got to the center of the dam and Paris stopped. He looked down river with his back to the lake. He then pointed slightly uphill to the spot where he and Houston had found the cartridge.

"Will, look there through that gap. You can't really see it, but there's a small flat spot with a downed log that has a full view of the dam. The shooter could wait until his target made it to the dam and he'd have a perfect angle to take the shot any time he wanted. The log would have made a perfect brace to steady a long range rifle."

Will looked up into the woods. "Can't say that I can see the spot you are talking about, but the shooter would have to have clear view of the whole dam so what you say makes sense."

Paris then bent at his waist and knees. He extended his arm as his whole body lowered down. He pointed to a spot on the path.

"I found Shaver here . . . "

Just as Paris bent over a shot rang out. A bullet whizzed over the now kneeling Paris and slipped into the calm waters on the lake side of the dam with a quick sucking sound. From the angle the bullet took to reach the lake, Will could tell with his experienced eye that had Paris not knelt down the round would have caught him right in the chest. All four men dropped to their chests flat on the road. There was no cover. The instinct had struck each with the same reaction: hit the deck to minimize yourself as a target. Will immediately pulled his gun and noticed the two CPRR men did the same.

Paris did not yet have his gun which was still in the shed.

Will heard no small amount of frustration when Paris said, "Do you believe me now? I need my gun."

*****

Greerson jumped up in his tent and exited quickly. Pin was standing at the edge of camp very near where he had been earlier when shots rang out at daybreak.

Greerson reached Pin's side. "Again? Another shot? This is getting serious. Did you see the shooter?"

"Don't need to see him. I know who it is."

Greerson was shocked. "What do you mean you know who it is?"

A leer spread across the lower part of Pin's face. He turned to Greerson.

"I don't know who took the first shot, but I told Sniper to pick a good spot and fire another. I told him not to kill anyone, just send another calling card."

"Why on earth would you do that?"

"All part of your game Greerson. All part of your game. Just upping the ante."

# Chapter Twenty-Seven

*Early September 1877*
*Carson City, NV*

His suit was snug as befitted the new fashion. The heat made wearing any form of full clothing uncomfortable. The fact that he chose to wear this new suit on a hot day like this now seemed a poor decision. His mind had been on other things as he got dressed this morning such as the matter bringing him to this structure.

Attorney Samuel Grande walked up the short flight of stone steps to the Federal Courthouse in Carson City. The Romanesque design rose to three stories of red block limestone. A broad peak capped the impressive edifice. A soaring clock tower bordered the facia beginning at the base and rising higher than any other part of the building. Grande mused the tower could have doubled as a lookout turret in a military structure.

The building was brand new. It stood as the first Federal building in Nevada. Ulysses S. Grant had appointed the only Federal Judge in the entire state, Judge Edgar Winters Hillyer, in 1869. Judge Hillyer, never shy to display his authority, now felt further empowered as he presided in his impressive new courtroom finished just last year.

Grande made it a point to learn as much as he could about the jurists he would appear before. Judge Hillyer had been a colonel in the Union Army during the war. A transplant from Ohio, Hillyer had mined for gold, speculated on silver, and practiced law all the way from Placerville, California to Carson City. But his roots were now firmly planted here in Nevada and he was fiercely devoted to the State's interests. His new imposing courthouse only served to enhance the Judge's view of his high calling. Grande hoped that devotion would help the cause he carried under his arm today.

Grande did not expect to see the judge on this trip. All he needed to do was to file a motion. On most occasions he would simply walk into the courtroom and hand his documents to the judge's clerk, Sandra Goern. Grande was a single man. He had never found a woman who could put up with his devotion to his work. He knew Sandra was unmarried too. Tall, slender, and quiet unless called to speak her mind, Sandra daily dealt with all manner of the lawyer personalities. From the bombastic to the borderline helpless, she dealt with each in various measures of assistance to deflection. And she did this always maintaining absolute decorum as only appropriate in the surroundings of a Federal Court.

Men normally filled the role of clerk to a federal judge. Sandra was unique. It could have led to distain or derogatory remarks from some quarters, but all save the most pigheaded of those lawyers who appeared in this court displayed the utmost respect for Sandra. That might often be a result of their attempt maintain good relations so as to curry any and all favor when they appeared before the judge himself. But most lawyers offered their deference because it was immediately apparent that Sandra was extremely competent at what she did. Grande was deferential for additional reasons, he liked her. However, there was a significant hurdle, she was considerably younger.

Samuel Grande was approaching forty. During the early years of his practice, he worked from daybreak long into the night. His normal workday did not leave any time for socializing. He had been focused on building his practice such that meeting the right woman, any woman, just did not fit into the schedule. His only days off were Sundays and he spent those driving his buggy out to the Toal ranch for relaxed end-of-the-week dinners. However, dinners in houses on the wide expanse of a cattle range did not lead to many meetings with those of the fairer sex.

Grande had made several appearances in Judge Hillyer's court. Not near as many as the county courts, but quite a few. Each time, he went out of his way to talk to Sandra. He thought she enjoyed their conversations too, but then again, he might be deluding himself. She could just be simply extending professional courtesy. In any event, he had planned this visit to take place after the court's morning business had been completed and there would be little chance of anyone else being present.

Grande pushed through one of the two heavy doors to the courtroom. At a quick glance he was pleased with his timing. The courtroom was completely empty. Grande made his way to the low railing that separated the public seating from the area where clients and counsel sat. Two waist high swinging doors crossed the aisle that ran down the middle of the public seating through which counsel entered to approach either counsel table or the clerk's desk. The combination of the low railing and swinging doors made up what was technically called 'the bar'. Only lawyers admitted to practice or special invitees could cross this barrier. It is where the term "admitted to the bar" comes from. Grande passed through and walked to the clerk's desk. He turned again to face the entry doors to make sure he had not overlooked anyone.

"Mr. Grande, to what do we owe the pleasure?"

Samuel turned to see Sandra enter from a door that accessed the judge's chambers behind the courtroom. Usually seated when they spoke, Grande could not remember seeing her standing no less moving. She had an exceptionally extended yet flowing stride. Long legs he thought. Her effortless motion belied the speed with which she covered ground. It caused the fabric of her lightweight summer dress to press against her feminine form. It did not go unnoticed.

"Miss Goern, I had begun to wonder if the Federal system had shortened their work hours." He delivered this lighthearted jab with a broad smile hopefully to convey the humorous intent.

"Are you implying that those of us who work here in the Federal building are slackers?" The retort took Grande aback. But it too was accompanied with an ever so slight break of a grin. He knew at that moment he had not overstepped. He continued the exchange in like kind.

"I think the evidence is clear. I believe the calendar says the court is open, yet upon my entry the clerk's desk was unmanned, or should I say unwomaned?"

"I was speaking with the Judge regarding tomorrow's hearings. I can return to his chambers to inform him that there is a very impatient and impertinent counsel here who insisted that the court was shirking its duties." She issued the retort with a look of extreme offense which Grande dearly hoped was feigned. Being unsure, he decided to alter his tact.

"I would endeavor that you remain here so as to confirm my prior experience of your limitless capacity to assist, particularly those who are undeserved such as myself."

"I would not consider you undeserved at all. I might think speaking to the judge about your behavior is most deserved."

"Ah Miss Goern, you have me at a disadvantage."

"How so?"

"You hold the keys to the gate. Should you fail to accept my emergency motion, I fear there will be repercussions far worse than my falling out of favor with the judge."

Sandra now hesitated upon reaching the back of her chair. "Repercussions?"

Now quite serious, Grande pushed forward. "Potential violence."

Sandra reached out to take Grande's filing. She clutched the paperwork with one hand and momentarily placed the other lightly on Grande's forearm.

"I should hope you will not be a target of any violence." She looked directly at him as she spoke the words.

The simple unanticipated act braced Grande. On one of the rarest of occasions, he had no words.

Sandra sat now looking at the face sheet of the motion.

"Oh, Mr. Grande, you have become involved in this one?"

"This one?"

She looked up from the paperwork. "The case of Nevada vs. California has caused no small amount of consternation here. The issue of Tahoe's water has many people at each other's throats. You should have seen the last set of motions argued on this case. The lawyers almost came to blows."

"I can imagine. But yes, I am involved. I have undertaken to represent a group of ranchers whose herds are dying of thirst. The Carson Valley cattle business is on the brink of disaster."

"And violence?"

"As you will see in my papers, there is threat from multiple quarters that I must emphasize do not include my clients. Those bearing threat are both corporate, political and private entities."

Sandra looked back at the motion before her. "An emergency injunction? I am not sure we have ever heard such a thing. Most injunctions are time critical just by the nature of the relief they seek."

"This motion for injunctive relief is even more time critical."

"When are you looking for this to be heard?"

"At the earliest possible date."

There was an audible exhale. "The judge chastises me if I set any motion to be heard in less than thirty days. What is your hope here?"

Grande now sucked in an extra volume of air. "I am holding out hope I can convince you to set this to be heard in fifteen." He knew that in the world of plodding court systems, this was asking a lot.

"The judge will have an issue with getting your opponents served with these papers such that they will have time to prepare a response."

"I have already sent out copies of the motion to all parties. I have messengers who stand ready to serve them today if you accept the filing. They will have fourteen or fifteen days to prepare for their appearance to respond. Under normal conditions of a thirty day motion, it would take at least half that time to get the parties served. I have undertaken to make sure the timing for response to my filing here will be the same as for any normal motion."

"My, a bit presumptuous are we not?"

"How so Miss Goern?"

"It sounds as if you anticipate success at achieving this clerk's agreement to accept the filing." Sandra looked up from her seated position with an unmistakable coquettish smile.

Grande placed the palm of his right hand against his chest and then waved it outward in overt Shakespearian artifice.

"All my efforts are to make your job so much easier Miss Goern."

Sandra flashed a look of artificial offense. "You would not be trying to take advantage of our relationship would you Mr. Grande?"

Though he knew he now stood a good chance of getting his motion filed on an extraordinary fast track, he quickly decided to take a further substantial risk, "Miss Goern, may I call you Sandra?"

"You may as long as there is no one else in the courtroom."

"Then Sandra, would I be at peril of being conflicted out of this case should I ask you to dine with me this coming weekend? I hesitate not with the invitation, but with the danger that I might have to withdraw from the case so as to avoid any appearance of special favor. If I were to be forced to leave the case, it would have an adverse effect on my clients."

Sandra smiled. "I have often wondered if you might have the courage to extend such an invitation. There are no rules as to who I might accept an invitation to dine from. I just cannot extend any improper advantage to any such person. Considering your very proper concerns, let me approach my answer in this way. Based on your representation that the parties will be immediately served, I will accept the filing of your emergency injunction and set a date for hearing in fifteen days from today's date. Also, I will gladly accept your invitation to dinner but that will have to occur on the first Saturday evening following the hearing."

Grande beamed. "Splendid. I could not have devised a better all-around solution."

"But Mr. Grande . . ."

"Call me Sam."

"Samuel, you had better get those parties served or I will be looking for another job."

"Sandra, I will see that they are served before the end of the day."

Grande walked out of the courthouse thinking of how he was going to get word to Will Toal. He had people in place in Sacramento, Reno, and San Francisco waiting for his wires. Serving the parties in those locations would be easy. Getting word to Will at his ranch along the Truckee would be more difficult. He had a rider waiting, but it would be a long hard ride to get word there by nightfall.

# Chapter Twenty-Eight

*Early September 1877*
*Forest Above the Truckee Dam, CA*

The crunch of fallen pine needles crackled underfoot with each step. The dry mountain air had lost its morning brisk. A direct beam of the sun needed only a short time to fry any exposed skin. As he climbed upward, the stunning expanse of Tahoe's blue spread further and further into the distance as the increase in elevation created an ever broader vantage. The deep royal blue seemed lighter today as if the lake's normal sapphire hue paled under the burning rays. Despite the shade provided by the thick stand of pine trees, heat penetrated the stagnant air of the forest. Climbing uphill generated its own source of heat. Will could feel sweat collecting at his belt-line.

He had followed Paris as they traversed the western slope upwards from the Truckee River. He estimated that they had to be at least four hundred yards from the Superintendent's shack by now. If Paris was bent on showing Will the spot where someone took the shot that hit the man who was now back in Tahoe City, the shooter must have had some skill. It would have been a fair shot even at this distance.

"Not many could take a shot this far away."

Paris did not break his pace. Though his legs were not nearly as long as Will's, Paris and his shorter stride seemed better suited for this side-step traverse uphill. His frame seemed to be in constant balance lower to the ground. As Will found himself correcting his equilibrium upon the frequent slippage of a boot, Paris climbed like some machine that could grab the ground.

Both men carried their rifles in front of them. His earlier guards had agreed to give Paris his firearms back.

"This is the second time today I've climbed up to this spot."

Paris stopped and scanned the slope for movement or sound. Will did the same. Not observing anything of note, Paris started to move again. After only a step or two, he stopped and turned to face Will. He motioned with his index finger that they should remain silent. Will felt that it had been at least fifteen to twenty minutes since the shot had been fired at them. He thought the possibility of encountering anyone up here now was slim. But he nodded assent.

Paris came to a small level section deep within the shade of the forest. Again, he motioned to remain quiet. Paris took off in one direction and pointed in the opposite noiselessly suggesting Will look around there. Nothing appeared out of place. Both returned to the center of the flat section.

"This is where I think the shooter took his first shot today. It's where we found the spent cartridge."

Will looked back towards the Superintendent's shed. Paris watched Will assess the view for a moment and then said, "You're right. Anyone taking a shot from this spot had to be a fair marksman."

Will did not answer right away. He knelt and held his Winchester aimed toward the dam as if to calculate the chances of hitting a target.

"The trees would seem to make the shot more difficult, but if the shooter sat here and used this log, he'd have a full view of the dam just as you said and the log would act as a natural brace to steady the shot. The distance is not all that far if you had the right firearm. This Winchester here would not be able to carry the distance with any accuracy, but I'd have no trouble at all with my Enfield."

"The cartridge we found was a Sharps, Miles said it was probably a forty-five - seventy."

Will turned from his seated position to respond to Paris. "Then, I would say the man who was shot is lucky to be alive as that means he was hit by a weapon normally used for hunting buffalo at distance."

"Miles described it as such too."

Will glanced around the immediate area, "But do you think the shot we just had fly over our heads came from this same spot?"

Looking around at the area behind the fallen log Paris ultimately shook his head.

"Can't tell, but I don't think so. There are no more cartridges here. So, either the last shot was taken from a different spot somewhere near, or our shooter is getting smart and picking up his cartridges. I wasn't looking uphill during the last shot. I don't have a good idea as to the direction it came from, do you?"

Will now stood. "No, I was watching you so I didn't get a good look either. Sound can be deceiving in a canyon like this too."

"When Miles and I were up here last time, we followed a foot trail up the hill for about fifty yards, but then it disappeared."

"No hoofprints?"

"None."

Will turned slightly to look further downriver. "Is that the group of men you talked to earlier?"

"It is. I saw a man holding a gun with what looked like an extended barrel. Thought it might be the type to shoot someone at distance."

Will cradled his rifle into the crook of his left elbow.

"Well, we can look around up here some more, or we can go back down and talk to those folks again. Do you see the man with the long rifle?"

"As a matter of fact, I don't."

"If the shooter covered his tracks before, he probably did the same for the second shot. More than likely we'd be wasting our time walking around this hill."

Paris shrugged, "Then, let's go down and have another chat with those men. Maybe the fact the man with the long rifle is missing could be significant. He might be the shooter."

The path to the camp fell directly downhill from their position at the shooter's lair. This time Will led the march with Paris behind. It did not take long to drop downhill. Will kept a look on the collection of tents. Men standing out in front of them were watching their descent.

"Who is the guy with the funny three-pronged hat?"

Paris chuckled, "He's the man who seemed to be in charge. Said his name was Pin. Strange name."

"He looks more like a pirate than a gunman."

Will's longer stride now made it difficult for the shorter Paris to keep up. Skipping down the slope with a hop in between Paris came back abreast of Will.

"He may look out of place from this distance, but the man had a malicious manner. There is something about him that makes one take notice and take care."

Will noted the advice while keeping his eye on the encampment.

Just then, "That's far enough." The man in the tricorn hat issued the statement in a clear form of a command.

Will stopped. Some twenty yards separated the two. He decided to try an approach he had used on several occasions during his days with the Texas Rangers: ask questions and investigate. People usually understood if you want to find a criminal, you must investigate.

"Someone just took a shot at us. Any chance you saw the shooter?"

"No, but if you keep coming around, I might send one of my men to take some shots at you myself."

"We need to find out who is doing this. Might help you. You could be the next target."

"We can take care of ourselves."

"I'm told you have a man with a long range rifle. Is he here?"

"I wouldn't tell you if he was."

"I don't see him; know where he is?"

"Scouting. If you had any experience on how to organize men, you'd do the same. Maybe you could keep your men from being shot at."

"Maybe I'll just walk in and take a look for myself." Will took two steps toward the man. Pin reached for his handgun. In one simple smooth motion Will whipped up his Winchester jacking a cartridge into the chamber as he grabbed the front stock with his left hand and leveled the gun at Pin.

"That gun clears leather and you'll be plugging holes in your chest."

As Will could see the demeanor of the man change in an instant, he knew he'd beaten his play with time to spare. The man's face now carried a look of question combined with anger."

"You shoot me and there'll be five men come to my aid."

"Then they'll get the next five shots. Magazine holds plenty for that group."

Neither man moved. Neither man gave any ground. It was Paris who next spoke.

"We only want to speak to the man with the long rifle."

"He ain't here," said Pin. His hand still hovered over the grip of is sidearm. "Besides, this is not your land. It belongs to Mr. von Schmidt. I'd be in my rights to shoot anyone entering uninvited."

Paris looked behind them to make sure no one approached from the rear.

"Will, he might be right about the land ownership. Even if we get to talk to the man with the gun, I doubt old three corners here is going to let him open up to us."

Without taking his eyes off Pin, he nodded. Then he addressed tri-corn.

"I understand your name is Pin. Well Pin, you'd best be careful who you're dealing with when you go to pull your gun."

"And you'd best be careful whose land and whose camp you intend to invade."

Paris turned to head upriver. Will could sense his movement behind him. He began to back up keeping his gun aimed at Pin the entire time.

"Might be back."

"I'll be waiting."

When they got a hundred yards or so upstream, Will turned his back to the camp and followed Paris's lead. He turned several times to make sure no one in the camp came out with something more than a handgun.

"You're right, there is definitely something about that man that rubs you the wrong way."

Paris laughed, "What was your first clue? His friendly attitude?"

Will mused, "Wonder why he's so confrontational. It's like he has something to hide. Could he be the one who's been ordering the shots taken? What's in it for him?"

Paris shrugged, "Don't know. I just know that every time I talk to the man, he does his best to pick a fight."

*****

Two small single man tents opposed a simple temporary fire pit. The canvas on each displayed the colors of long term use. What had once been a vibrant tan was now a mild brown dotted with evidence of the droppings from the many forests they had visited. Light and easily foldable, each was propped up with branches from the immediate area, a portable abode that could be carried in the simplest of packs. There was no fire at the moment. The air was warm this time of the day, even at this altitude. Brilliant white clouds billowed sporadically above. A silence of biblical tranquility pervaded.

The camp sat high on the crest of the Sierra's about a mile upslope from the Truckee dam. Silas Drummond sat on a log writing in a small journal. He looked up from his composition. He marveled that from his position, a man could see east all the way across Tahoe and west almost down to the town of Placerville. Trees were sparse. Not because of logging. They were too far away from the river to make cutting timber worthwhile in this area. The lack of trees was due to the altitude. Little grew up here beyond scrub. But a small creek ran close to the camp. The quiet movement of fluid was lined at its borders with spring and summer alpine flowers. Purple-blue sky pilot sprouted from the rockiest of soil. Alpine daisies grew here and even at higher elevations. The low standing flora fluttered in the easy breeze that cupped over the crest. Drummond felt more at peace here in the heights more than any other spot on earth.

"Silas, you look to be daydreaming."

John Muir strode into the camp. He grabbed the single shoulder strap of his ever present carry sack lifting it over his head in what undoubtedly was a very familiar motion. Muir then set the homemade rucksack down carefully.

"Nothing wrong daydreaming here in one of God's special places."

Muir smiled, "You're probably right." He stood looking west at the horizon. "God did do a remarkable job when he made this didn't he?"

"There is a pot of stew sitting on the coals. Not sure it is still warm as I made it this morning. But it has some greens, prairie potatoes and a smattering of rabbit meat."

"Why, thank you Silas. I am a bit hungry."

Muir grabbed a simple tin bowl and scooped out a portion of the liquid brew. He then sat.

"Lots going on down in Tahoe City."

Silas did not answer or ask to pursue. Muir continued in between bites.

"A man was shot on the Truckee River dam. Don't know if he'll survive, but folks in town are quite upset. Met with Mr. Harriman, Mr. Bliss and a rancher named Toal. All were interested in seeing the flow of water increased even if it meant that the dam had to be destroyed."

"Will Toal?"

"Yes, do you know him?"

Silas set down his journal and looked downward at the earth between his boots before raising his head up to respond. "I was in Carson City when Toal helped Duane Bliss find the person who was trying to burn out his logging operation in Glenbrook."

"It was quite obvious he knew Bliss, but he never mentioned the nature of their acquaintance."

"Back then I was making speeches in town trying to get people to rise up and put a stop to the logging. Toal confronted one of our marches. From what little contact I had, he seemed to be a straightforward man. Too bad he supported Bliss."

"He did appear to be a person of direct and sincere purpose. It seems the men hired by the railroad arrested someone named Dale Paris for the shootings. But Bliss and Toal were adamant that they had the wrong person."

"Dale Paris is in Tahoe City?"

"Yes, well he's out at the dam looking into the shooting of the original superintendent. Paris was also hired by the railroad according to Harriman."

"I've run across Paris too." Drummond shook his head as he looked off into the vista.

Muir watched Silas's reaction with interest. "I think we've arrived at an agreement with the railroad to create a protected area around Tahoe. Bliss will build his railroad spur to carry tourists up the hill and carry the railroad's logs downhill. Everyone will help with our efforts in Washington."

"Sounds like everything worked out quite well. Are you not happy? You seem tired," said Drummond.

Muir sighed. "The beginnings are set. But there is a long way to go before we get the government to take control of Tahoe and Yosemite. It's never been done before. But with the railroad's help, maybe we can finally establish the first protected lands here in the U.S."

There was a period of comfortable silence between the two men used to long solitary times in the mountains. Then Drummond uttered, "Toal and Paris are both in Tahoe City. Interesting. I wouldn't count on their help in our efforts though."

## Chapter Twenty-Nine

*Early September 1877*
*Sacramento, CA*

The sound of hard leather soles striking polished marble echoed in the large empty hallway. Leland Stanford listened to the rhythmic click of his shoes on the dense stone floor. He liked the sound. There was a sort of power to it. Stanford was alone, as if he owned this place—he practically did.

Stanford was most familiar with the state capital building of California and had spent many hours over the last two decades in this building. He had once been the state's governor and knew how the process of governance worked in these halls. The day's objective had been achieved thanks to the final vote in the state senate, the chamber he had just left. Stanford had traveled to personally watch the final vote of the State Legislature on a motion of his own creation. The motion ostensibly reaffirmed the rights of the Donner Boom and Lumber Company established seven years earlier to control the flow of the Truckee River. The motion had carried. He had won. It had taken money, influence and favors called in, but this was his world. It was a world in which he was used to winning.

Stanford had pushed the legislative motion with one single purpose: to clarify beyond any argument that Donner Boom had legal control over the flow of the Truckee. The strategy was to leapfrog any local attempts by the City of San Francisco to create confusion on that issue in their recent dealings with von Schmidt. It was if he had stepped up to a higher power above the authority of a local city. He was dealing here at the state level. He had upped the ante in the political poker game. Today, he felt like he had dropped a pair of aces in the face of Von Schmidt's pair of kings. Now all he had to do was to collect the pot.

"Stanford!"

A door closed behind him. Stanford turned to see Von Schmidt stride up, following his path through the hall. The man cut a fine figure. Possessed of handsome features brandished below a full head of hair, his aquiline face was framed by ample sideburns. Dressed impeccably with high collar and extravagant cravat, his well-trimmed figure moved with agility in his suit.

Stanford had always been subtly soft, overweight. He had never attained the look of an athlete even as a young man. Years of high living on rich foods and leisurely activity had only worked to expand his figure, not slim it. But Stanford felt comfortable in his own skin. Standing five-feet-ten-inches with ample girth, Stanford felt a personal sense of power in dealing with most men.

"Allexey, you decided to come watch the proceedings for yourself, did you?"

"Nothing's changed, Stanford." Von Schmidt's Prussian roots influenced his English, especially when he was excited as here.

Leland allowed a smug smile to spread across his face. He could immediately tell Von Schmidt was upset.

"You're right. Nothing has changed. Donner Boom controls the flow of water from Tahoe down the Truckee. Just like in 1870, the Legislature has confirmed our rights."

"You have the right to the *flow*. That is the right to deal with whatever water is left in the river, but you don't *own* the water." Von Schmidt highlighted the two key words, *flow* and *own* as he spoke.

"You have the right to let water flow out of Tahoe, but there is nothing in today's proceedings that will prevent my company from taking water out of the river and send it down to San Francisco."

Stanford now turned to fully face Von Schmidt.

"Allexey, I would be careful what you say and do. Lawyers could use the comments and actions to your detriment." There was a sarcastic hint in Stanford's delivery.

"Stanford, you have no ownership rights to the water itself. You get only what's left. If anyone has riparian rights arising from ownership of land adjacent to a river, they have every right to take water from that river. I own property on both sides of that waterway. Nothing in today's proceedings changed that. I have ownership rights to the water itself. You only have rights to a *flow*." Again, the word *flow* was issued emphatically.

There was no secret to the decree issued in the Water Act of 1870. Stanford knew the Act governed only the flow and provided no indication as to actual ownership of the water itself. But no one other than Von Schmidt came close to disputing what Stanford and his company felt was an unfettered ability to control the Truckee. Outside of the weather and the current draught, von Schmidt was the only thorn in the side of Donner Boom's ongoing logging enterprise.

"That flow cannot be interrupted or diminished Von Schmidt. If you take any steps to do so, then the lawyers will grind you to dust."

Stanford now displayed his own level of rising emotion. He knew the issue of water ownership was fuzzy at best. Because of the vulnerability, he had to stay on the offensive and display no weakness. The railroad's fuel source depended on it.

"I'll bet you thought your legislators did a good job of protecting your backside. But Stanford, they stopped short of saying you owned the water. They couldn't, same as back in 1870. Nothing's changed."

"We will float logs down the Truckee at our pleasure. Those logs are fuel for the rail lines and needed to support the entire economy of California. The Legislators know that and will take whatever steps necessary to protect it. You try to interfere Allexey at your own peril."

"I have the right to take water, to build another dam and I will. You may have taken control of my first dam, but there is nothing to prevent me from building another spanning the river from property I own on both sides."

"Von Schmidt, your fantasy of channeling water from Tahoe to San Francisco is a pipe dream, literally."

"We shall see Stanford. My men are at the river now surveying for the construction of a new dam, below yours."

"Are those the same men who are shooting at my employees?" Stanford now did nothing to hide his escalating anger at the direction of the conversation.

"Never. My men are not doing any shooting. You have enemies in many corners Stanford. Any one of them might be out to make your life difficult."

The reply came with a turnabout. The smugness had now moved to Von Schmidt.

"A second man was shot two days ago. Another of my employees might not survive. Von Schmidt, if you've had anything to do with either of those shootings, not only will I own your business, but you will spend the rest of your days in jail. Be careful where you take this as we will return any overt attack in kind."

The tail end of his comment had slipped out. Stanford realized he might have overstepped his advantage.

"That sounds like a threat Stanford."

Stanford knew he had opened a door and, in keeping with his strategy to show no weakness, he could not back down now. They were still alone. There were no witnesses.

"Von Schmidt, we will fight fire with fire. We have rights to float our logs and we will make sure those rights are not interrupted. If you seek to impact those rights adversely, you do so at your own risk."

"Stanford, I have the right to take water. San Francisco needs that water. I intend to protect my rights."

Von Schmidt grinned, turned and walked further down the hallway to the exit from the Capital. Stanford watched him without moving. He would have to tell Hopkins and Huntington; this was heading to trouble.

## Chapter Thirty

*Early September 1877*
*Along the Truckee, NV*

Silence dangled in the confined space like an uncomfortable mistake. A fire flickered at one end of the room. Wood crackled as the logs reduced themselves to orange yellow coals. It was the only source of noise.

But the fire was not the only source of heat. Four anxious men in thick coats stood side by side just inside the door. Heat came from both their collective bodies, and the emotion gripping the room. A question, a demand had been made. The four men hesitated with their answer.

Finally, Bob McCollum, one of the four asked, "Are you sure you want to do this Angus?"

"You bet I do," came Ferguson's reply. His Scottish brogue warped the last word into something sounding more like "dew".

Angus flashed a foreboding face at the foursome standing across the room shoulder to shoulder as if in a military review.

"I told ye what we're to do. Did ye not say you wanted that dam gone? Did ye not say you'd join and bring men?"

Another silence blanketed the room like smoke from the chimney blaze.

Finally, one of the men, Carter McKinnon, looked to his side beyond Bob McCollum at the row of additional fellow guests. Sensing the temerity of the others, he decided to answer.

"Yes, Angus. We told you we'd come and we have."

"And did ye bring your men?"

"We did, they are outside trying to stay warm in your bunkhouse along with your men."

"That dam needs to go. We all know it."

Ferguson assumed a steadfast stance between the other ranch owners and his hearth. With the only source of light being the fire, he must have looked like a haunted silhouette to the men before him. Ferguson counted on the image. He had planned it.

McKinnon continued. "Angus, we heard that a suit has been filed by the State of Nevada to stop California from taking Tahoe's water. Maybe that will be enough. Maybe we don't need to take this ride."

"Ah, politicians. They're useless. Nothing but a bunch of blowhards looking to protect and serve only themselves. They don't have our interests at heart. Each of us came to this country with nothing. We've each created thriving ranches with our own sweat and breaking our own backs. But they've taken our water. It'll ruin us and we all know it."

McCollum then asked, "How do you intend to destroy the dam, Angus?"

"Blow it up."

"Blow it up with what?"

"We'll get the dynamite near the depot in Truckee. There's a general store there that sells the stuff to all the miners here in the mountains. We can stay overnight in Truckee and head up to Tahoe City early tomorrow morning."

McKinnon then interjected, "You got this all figured out, don't you Angus?"

"I've been thinking about this for some time. All we need to do is break a hole in one piece of the dam so the water can flow."

McKinnon responded quickly, "I've heard the people who own the dam have hired men to protect it."

Angus scoffed, "That's why we're bringing our own men. We need some simple cover fire while we ride on to the dam and drop the dynamite. The plan is simple. There is no need to over think this."

Just then the door opened. Henry Dangberg walked in and surveyed the scene. He moved around the wall of men standing to take a spot between them and Ferguson. All five watched Dangberg.

"Good morning gentlemen. A bit cold this early."

Dangberg looked back and forth between the opposing forces. Ferguson knew he had to collect his supporters and get going soon. Based on earlier conversations, he did not think he could count on Dangberg helping.

"Henry, we are about to leave."

A crease furrowed across Dangberg's brow. "You're headed up to the lake? You are not still thinking of destroying that dam, are you?"

Again, a silence descended on the room. This time, Ferguson was included in the group hesitating to respond. Dangberg looked back and forth at both sides. Hearing nothing, he continued.

"Will Toal is up there right now trying to convince the people who control that dam to let more water flow. He knows men who are working with the owners. The man he is going to talk to has a plan to be a part of a project that involves railroads, land preservation, tourists and regulation of the Truckee's flow."

"Tourists!" Ferguson's raised voice bounced off the walls and penetrated ears. "Just what we need. More people invading. Eventually, they will want to split up all our land holdings. We don't need tourists."

Dangberg flung both arms in the air in derisive disgust. "Angus, if it means a few people travel up to Tahoe to watch the waves in return for a constant flow from the Truckee, what do you care?"

Carter McKinnon, now spoke up. "I'm not much in favor of having a bunch of tourists wandering around either."

Ferguson tried to suppress a sigh of relief. McKinnon's comments could not have come at a better time. Angus knew he had to get the group on the move and quick. He could not let his faltering little army wither away before they even started the march.

"Men, we have to take control of our own futures. No one else is going to do it for us. Let's ride."

Ferguson strode out of the room wedging himself between the middle of the four men who had been standing just inside the door. The quartet of ranch owners began to follow. Angus pushed open the front door and turned to face Dangberg.

"Henry, you're welcome to join us. We ride to the town of Truckee and stay there tonight and then we'll move on to the dam tomorrow. You can come now or meet us in Truckee. Do as you will. But we are riding."

"I'll stay Angus. I've no mind to push the limits of the law as you intend."

"Suit yourself."

*****

Dangberg moved outside the Ferguson home. He watched as ten to twelve riders started west. He assumed they would ride up the edges of the river until they got to the city of Truckee. Then they would turn south and head up the mountain taking the same road over the pass toward Tahoe City that the stage used. That way the group would follow the Truckee River to the point where they came across the dam.

Henry knew he had to get word to Will. But how? He also knew he had to speak to the Carson Valley ranchers to keep them from following Ferguson. He walked up to his horse, formulating a plan as he covered the ground. He would ride to tell Beth about what was happening first.

Maybe she could get one of her hands to ride up and find Will. That might take some time. Without knowing exactly where he was, it might take some luck to get word to him before the ranchers arrived. But Will had to be warned.

Dangberg intuitively knew he would be the best one to keep control of the Carson Valley ranchers. All of them could see the devastation the lack of water caused their stock. Some might just agree that blowing up the dam was at least something they could do to try and save their herds. But dynamite and gun play was not the answer. Some of those men might not come back. Dangberg remembered only too well what happened when he and a collection of ranchers got caught in a crossfire with experienced gunmen hired by the railroad to foreclose on their ranches. Some of the ranchers did not come home. He had to do what he could to avoid that happening again.

Dangberg pulled his reins from the hitching rail. He mounted and spun his horse around. He would ride west too, but he would take a different road to the Toal camp on what they called the Purcell Ranch. Timing was becoming critical.

# Chapter Thirty-One

*Early September 1877*
*Purcell Ranch, along the Truckee*

"Ma, a rider's coming in."

Beth shook some dust off her hands and wiped them on her apron. She looked up at Luke's announcement and moved to the opening of their oversized tent home to get a wider view. Following the direction of Luke's focus, she could see someone approaching. It was a rider but she did not recognize either the man or his horse.

"Ma, I'll get my rifle." It was Sean. Will had told the boys that at least one of them should have a rifle in hand if they ever saw an approaching rider they did not recognize. Beth smiled at how they were growing up. She hoped they would never have to use a gun to shoot at anyone, but she knew their father's advice and training was the right thing here in the wilderness.

"Hello ahead. I come with a message for Will Toal from attorney Sam Grande."

The announcement caused Beth to waive her hand at Sean. "Don't worry about the gun, it's only a messenger."

"Dad said it didn't matter who it was. If we didn't know them, either Luke or me should have a rifle until we knew exactly what they wanted."

"Alright, but don't point it at the man, at least not yet."

Sean spun and hurried around the side of the family tent to grab his gun.

The rider came into the clearing at a walk. He kept an eye on Luke who was the farthest from the abode and nearest to the rider's approach. The rider stopped as he came up to Luke.

"I have a message for Will Toal. Do you know where he is?"

"Pa is not here. He should be back shortly. You can give the message to my mother. That's her over there." Luke waved in the direction of Beth now standing just outside the tent.

The rider stayed in his saddle. He moved his mount slowly closer to the temporary dwelling and handed an envelope to Beth who had walked out to meet him.

"Ma'am, I was told by Sam Grande to deliver this to Will Toal as soon as possible. He said it was mighty important. He also said I was to hand it to Will Toal personal or his wife."

Beth smiled. Sam Grande was probably the only man who would consider her on a par with her husband. She could hear him giving that instruction.

"I am Elizabeth Toal, wife of Will. I can take the message. You can tell Sam that you handed it to me."

"Much obliged. Mr. Grande told me I'd better get it done right as he would be talking to you soon and making sure I delivered it to the correct people. I had to ask around the other ranches to find out where you might be."

"Well, you tell Sam that you found Beth Toal and that I'm glad he saw fit to consider a woman worthy to accept his message. See if that gets a smile on his face."

Beth looked at the simple handwriting on the envelope. All is said was "Will Toal". She turned the thin packet over and was about to rip the seal when Luke called out again.

"We got another rider coming. It looks like Mr. Dangberg."

The messenger turned his horse. "I'd best be going. I've gotta try to get back to Carson City tonight. I'll tell Mr. Grande what you said."

Beth smiled up at the young man, "You ride safe now and give my thanks to Sam."

Beth looked out in the direction of the approaching Dangberg. Even though Henry appeared to be pushing his horse, he was still a couple of minutes away so she opened the letter. It was difficult to read in Grande's handwritten sloppy male script, but she struggled through it. Direct and simple it accurately reflected the tenor of its author:

Will,

I have filed the motion in Federal Court requesting an emergency injunction as we discussed. There will be a hearing in fifteen days. The court will hear and rule on the considerations of all parties. I have served both states and all relevant corporate interests. With this message, consider yourself also served. You will have to be in Carson City in fifteen days along with anyone necessary to represent the ranch owners as they are all interested parties too.

Keep those people from starting a war until the motion is heard.

Sam Grande

Beth took a moment to read the note again. Never one to shy away from a courtroom fight, she figured that when Sam Grande said he had served all relevant parties, that would include Donner Boom, von Schmidt, the ranchers and maybe even Duane Bliss. If a war had not broken out before the hearing, a collection of those folks in one courtroom might be volatile enough to create one all by itself.

"What's it say Ma?" Sean always had the first question on anything new.

"It's a message for your dad. It has to do with his trip to Tahoe City."

Beth began to think out how she could get the message delivered to Will.

"Sean, get your horse and ride over to where the ranch hands are staying and ask both Juan and Maria to come here as soon as they can. Tell them to bring some clothes for a couple of days."

The chance to be relieved of daily chores around the house and be able to ride generated a broad smile across the boy's face.

"I'll get going right now."

Beth watched as Sean ran off to the corral. She turned back to the approaching Dangberg.

"Hello Beth."

"Henry, you and your horse both look tired. Come sit and rest."

"I'd be happy to do just that, but I can only stay a short while. Things are happening and I have to talk to the Carson Valley ranch owners as soon as I can."

Beth led the way to the circle of logs outside the tent that served as the only chairs here in the mountains. Dangberg followed. He landed on the widest log a little extra hard. Beth could see some emotional aspect to the body movement.

"What's wrong Henry? Why do you have to go speak to the other ranchers?"

Dangberg did not try to suppress a sigh. "Ferguson and the local ranchers have ridden up to Tahoe City. They intend to blow up the dam. They left about an hour ago."

"How did you find out about this?"

"I was invited to a meeting this morning. Angus collected the other Nevada ranchers and some of their hands. I believe Angus thought he could convince me to go with him. If I agreed, then Angus probably figured I'd bring in the rest of the Carson Valley ranchers to ride with him. I just left that meeting."

"Are they going straight up to the dam?"

"No, they said they were going to ride up to the Truckee and stay there tonight. I suspect they intend to stop in Truckee to buy some dynamite later today. They're heading up to Tahoe City and the dam first thing tomorrow morning."

Beth handed Grande's letter to Dangberg. "Take a look at this."

Dangberg read. His shoulders lifted ever so slightly as if buoyed by some good news.

"This is a great step."

Beth shook her head. "Maybe, but it's only a court hearing. The judge could decide for California, or not decide anything at all and just kick the can down the road."

Dangberg did not seem inclined to pass it off so lightly.

"Any event to collect all these crazy different interests together before an impartial decision maker has to be a step in the right direction. No judge can ignore the needs not only of the ranchers along the Truckee but all the folks in Nevada who depend on that water."

Still unimpressed, Beth sat down more heavily than usual, herself. "It's only a hearing Henry."

"Back when we drove the herd through Carson City, Eric Pasin and a group of Nevada legislators told me they were going to file suit. They said it was going to be huge. They were going to include all the big interests, as well as the railroad and the city of San Francisco. They must've done it."

"I don't hold out as much hope as you do, Henry, but no matter. Either way we must get word to Will. He must know the hearing is set. Based on what you just found out, he also needs to know Ferguson is coming."

"Can you get one of the hands to ride up and tell Will? Maybe Juan?"

Beth shook her head.

"No, without Will Juan needs to stay here and keep watch over the herd and ranch hands. But I did just send Sean out to get both Juan and Maria."

Henry leaned forward, "What have you got in mind my dear? I have come to know you fairly well and by the look on your face I gather you have a plan."

"I'll make sure Juan knows to keep track of the men and stock and have Maria watch the kids."

"And what are you going to do?"

"I haven't fully figured that out yet, but I'm thinkin' on it."

# Chapter Thirty-Two

*Early September 1877*
*City of Truckee, CA*

A lone rider walked his horse over the dirt road at the center of town. Puffs of dust rose like feathered cushions around the horse's hooves as each landed on the soft earthen street. The drought had reached even here high in the mountains bleeding the town's main avenue of all moisture. It was early and quiet but for the movement of the single horse.

The city of Truckee lay pressed into a small alpine valley near the crest of the Sierras. Green forested ridges softened the horizon's transition from earth to sky. The town provided a respite to those who had scaled the western slopes of the coast's largest mountain range. Whether one traveled up the slope on horseback, stage, teamster wagon or the Central Pacific's transcontinental railroad, Truckee was a welcome stop for all. It had started as nothing more than a train depot, Coburn Station. But the traffic the railroad later brought made the small station grow into a full, vibrant junction, a city.

Angus Ferguson stood, arms crossed as he watched the lone rider pass in front of him. Once rider and horse passed, he scanned the skyline from his location on the wooden walkway in front of the Truckee Hotel as he pondered thoughts of the day to come. He and the four ranch owners had spent the night at the hotel in the comfort of warm beds. The hands had all spent the night in the livery stable, undoubtedly not as comfortable.

"Chilly in the morning up here in the mountains."

The comment came from Carter McKinnon.

Without moving his feet, Ferguson turned at the waist to look over his shoulder at McKinnon. He returned his gaze to the horizon before speaking.

"Aye, feels brisk indeed. Makes one feel like setting to work on what needs to be done. The heat will come soon enough. Look at how dry the road is under that horse."

McKinnon looked away from the horse and rider. "You can see why the railroad set their depot here. A fair size valley with good flat ground and Donner Lake nearby to provide water. Strange though, a place like this."

"What makes you say that?"

McKinnon paused as if to collect his thoughts.

"We seem to be at the bottom of a bowl. Sure, the mountains look fine enough, even impressive. But in this little valley we're surrounded by forest and slopes. There is no view of the horizon. I like the wide open space of our ranch back home. I feel almost confined here."

Ferguson looked again at McKinnon. This time assessing the man's comments as he could.

"Some folks might feel protected down here in this bowl as you call it."

"Maybe, I just think it was the flattest spot for miles so the railroad decided to stop and catch its breath."

Angus nodded. "Probably started as a staging area for the railroad construction. I'll bet they felt real good about getting their track laid up the slope and needed to take a break."

McKinnon had moved forward out of the hotel adjacent to Ferguson. Hands stuffed down far into his coat pockets; he now did his own study of the terrain. "Once they finished the Summit Tunnel, heading east must have felt like heading downhill. I heard it took them almost two years to dig that shaft."

"Well, the railroad wanted this to be a crossroads too. There on the other side of those buildings across the street is the Truckee River. The railroad needed this town and its sawmills to split up the logs for their locomotives. That's what's given us the dam. That's the job we must see to today Carter. The dam must go," Ferguson commented.

"You are set on doing this?"

"Aye, I am."

McKinnon did not turn to look at Ferguson. "You got the dynamite?"

"I do."

"Have you been thinkin' on how we're going to accomplish this?"

"As I said before back at my ranch, we need to keep this simple. I say we ride up the stage road until we get close to the dam. The road is on the east side of the river, so, when we get close, we then cross the river to the west side. It's low, so that shouldn't be a problem."

"Why do we need to cross?"

"I sent my son, Dirk, up here some months ago to check out the dam. He tells me that there is a set of gates on the west side. That's the spot we need to attack. I have the dynamite in my saddle bags. We'll collect after we cross the river. That will be a good time for the men to check their guns. I'll light two sticks and ride at the dam. All I'll need you and the men to do is to give me some cover fire."

"You just going to throw the dynamite at the dam."

"Exactly. The closer I can get, the more damage I'll be able to do."

"Sounds simple enough."

Ferguson now turned to face McKinnon. "Are the men fed?"

"They all got a good meal. There was some grumbling about the lodgings last night, but they're in a better mood after their meal."

Ferguson scoffed, "Grumbling. I spent the first two years while building my ranch sleeping out in the open on my own range. One night in a cover building and they grumble. Men are going soft."

"They'll give you the support you need today though Angus."

"They'd better." Though the volume of his voice did not rise, the last comment was delivered with enough emphasis to make a vertical vein stand out on Ferguson's forehead.

McKinnon hesitated to respond.

Ferguson turned to head back inside. "Let's get these grumblers moving. The sooner we get up the hill, the sooner our beef will get water."

*****

Will glanced at the horse Paris rode. It's short brown legs were working overtime to keep up with the long stride of Powder's canter. A smaller horse possessed of stout solid bones like the animal next to him could be counted on for soundness on long rides. But the limited length of the legs made for a choppy gait. That translated to a constant bounce for the horse's rider, in this case Paris. Will counted his blessings at sitting atop his tall gray gelding and his smooth flowing gaits.

"It's gettin' hot again today. Wonder when this heat spell will break."

Will smiled, "Well we could have headed out of town a little earlier to beat the worst of it. But someone dallied a bit."

"Dallied? I had to speak to Hopkins's man who brought the wounded superintendent into town."

Will let his grin spread even wider, "Sure, after you slept in 'till nine o'clock. Easy money this investigation stuff. Short workin' day."

Paris rose to the bait, "You didn't seem to complain a whole lot to sleep in a hotel bed here in Tahoe City on my expense account with the railroad."

Will nodded, "Bed was nice, won't say I'm not grateful. But I was up before the sun rose just like home. Checked the horses, got something to eat and stopped to talk with Duane Bliss before you even trudged downstairs."

"You never know when you might be up two or three nights in a row. Need to catch up on your sleep when you can in this business. And I've been shot at twice in twenty-four hours. How many times you been shot at out on your ranch?"

"As a matter of fact, my ranch has seen far too much shooting."

Knowing he had little defense to his late morning arrival, Paris decided to try and change the topic.

"Did Bliss say whether he was able to strike a deal with the railroad?"

"He did not go into any details, but he said he had a handshake agreement to build his railroad spur. Lawyers and paperwork would now start. Ultimately, the devil will be in the details, always is."

Just then a shot rang out ahead. Then another.

Paris looked at Will, "That's up by the dam."

His look still fixed on the road ahead, Will said, "We've got about a mile to go. Best make it quick."

Spurs hit the flanks of both horses. The slow walk was now a full gallop.

*****

Will and Paris pulled up still within the cover of the forest.

"Those men downriver are shootin' at the superintendent shed."

Will looked back and forth between the shed and the camp downriver as each shot was fired. "Wonder what started all this."

Paris reached out and touched Will's shoulder. "It doesn't matter who started it, we have to get to the shed and help Miles and Houston. They only have two guns against what sounds like a lot more in that camp. They'll blow holes all through that thin walled shack in no time."

Will kept looking back and forth as the gunfire continued.

"We have one serious problem. How are we going to get across the river?"

Paris offered, "We can ride down into the riverbed in front of the dam. The gates are closed and there's only a trickle running. We'd be out of range while we're down in the riverbed."

"No, we won't; anyone sitting in the front of that camp would still have a direct shot."

"The only other way is to ride over the top of the dam. We'll be sitting ducks up there."

Will shook his head from side to side. "Neither one looks good to me. How about we cross upriver behind the dam. We'll have to swim it with the horses but they can't shoot us behind the dam."

"I like it. One problem."

"That is?"

"Never swum my horse."

"Just follow me and Powder. Powder will swim and if we head out there fast enough your horse will just follow. As soon as the water rises to the saddle level slide off the back and hold onto the horn. If you can, pull your rifle out and hold it up overhead with your other hand."

"What happens when we get to the far side?"

"We'll mount up while still below the level of the dam, then ride like crazy to the back of the shed."

Will would normally slide back into his saddle as Powder exited the water, but he was not sure Paris could do the same. It took some practice. So, he opted to keep things simple and just plan on remounting once they crossed.

Paris did not speak. He stared at the dam and the pool of water behind it. Will could see the apprehension written at the crease of his brow.

"Don't think about it. Just follow."

Paris sat back in his saddle. "Let's go."

Will pushed Powder forward. Paris followed just behind. Both horses raced over the opening between the forest edge and the short sandy beach. Powder thundered into the water splashing with elongated strides as he reached for solid footing. Finally realizing that it only got deeper, he settled into an instinctive subsurface stride that formed the equine swimming motion. With only his head now above water, Powder made steady progress across the liquid gap. Paris and his horse splashed right behind and sank down to a similar level and began the swim across.

Will looked behind. He was happy to see Paris had pulled his rifle from his scabbard and was holding it above his head. Guiding a horse swimming in water is not easy. Normal reining does not work. But Powder had crossed many rivers with Will. He knew he just had to get to the other side. Paris's horse seemed content to follow.

Upon reaching the far bank, Will slid off to the side and stood as Powder started to shake the outer layer of water off. The motion started at the head and proceeded with almost a serpentine motion along the length of his body until it ended with his tail. Will helped grab Paris's horse who climbed out of the water a bit spooked. He was obviously not used to a midday swim.

Will made sure Paris had a good hold of his horse before he let go himself.

"Let's get mounted and then ride up the riverbank and across the short opening to the back of the shed. Then we can find out what is going on."

"Agreed."

Both got into their saddles and dug in spurs. Powder leaped up the riverbank in three powerful strides lifting Will out of his saddle and back again with each thrust. Up on flat ground, Will leaned low and looked behind to make sure Paris made it up too. A gunshot whizzed by.

"Don't need this. It's like being back in the war."

Paris imitated Will and leaned low and forward on the left side of his horse away from the direction of the oncoming bullets. "That's exactly what this looks like, a war."

They reached the back of the shed. Both dismounted and tied up to a bush.

Will yelled out, "Miles, Houston, it's Will Toal and Paris. We're coming in the door."

"We saw you across the river. Come on in. Can use the help."

Both men were prone on the floor. Will and Paris got down flat too.

"What the hell's going on?"

Will saw Paris's face flowered in a bright red as he spoke.

Miles answered, "I have no idea what started this. Heard a shot, don't know where it came from and all of a sudden everyone in that camp downriver started shooting."

Will crawled to the wall facing downriver. He took off his hat and sat up quickly to look out the window. He sat down as fast as he had risen. He looked at Paris.

"That face doesn't look good. What do you see?"

"I cannot believe I'm gonna say this. I thought I'd left this forever after the war."

"What?" Paris was now more than anxious.

"I think they are going to charge."

# Chapter Thirty-Three

*Early September 1877*
*Truckee River Dam, CA*

"Charge, What ya mean charge? Are you sure you are not just having a bad war dream?"

Will looked across the room to Paris lying face down on the floor. Another fuselage of bullets ripped through the Superintendent's shed. Will slid down from his position leaning against the wooden wall as it was obviously not stopping too many bullets. He did not like Paris's tone. It brought up memories, not only of the battles he had been in, but he could see the deep apprehension now building in men being attacked. It had been a familiar scene not that long ago during his time as a teenager with Johnson's army when tasked to stop Sherman from getting to the sea. They had failed. He had seen looks of fear on the faces of soldiers much like the looks he now saw on the countenances of Paris and the others in the room. He was not looking forward to failing here. He knew he had to come up with a plan and soon.

"It's not a dream. Though I've had many of those since the war, this is no dream. It's real."

Paris still questioned. "What makes you think they are going to charge?"

"I saw them collecting near the road next to their camp. Tricorn waved his men toward the forest on the edge of the road. It only took a second but I've seen motion commands like that before. My guess is that they will come up the road as fast as they can, staying inside the tree line. When they get close, they will send out cover fire as others try to cross the dam."

Will then inched his back up against the wall again and popped up to look through the window for a moment and then slumped back down.

"Yep, they're coming. They seem to have more men too."

Miles now answered, "About four or five more men arrived yesterday."

"That gives them about ten, right?"

Miles nodded his agreement.

"I saw about six running along the road on the east side of the Truckee. That leaves four in their camp. Okay, here's what we're gonna do. Houston, you man the window facing west over the river. Start shooting at anything you can get. Miles, you stay here at the window facing downriver. My guess is that the fire from their camp will diminish. I'll bet some of those left in camp are now heading uphill on the west side, the high side of the river. Their plan would be to have us in a collective crossfire from both sides of the river."

Paris looked back and forth between Miles and Houston then back to Will.

"What are you and I going to do?"

Will smiled, "You and I are going to head uphill and move down river just a bit."

"Why are we going out there?"

Will motioned Paris to move in the direction of the door. After Paris started, Will followed. As they crawled toward the door, he answered Paris's question.

"Two reasons. First, we can take positions to have open shots across the dam. Essentially, we keep that group from crossing here to the shed. Second, we will keep moving upriver on the west side. The idea would be to stop anyone coming at us from that angle and instead flank them just as they are trying to flank us but doing it on the opposite side of the river."

The gunfire increased. Miles and Houston crawled to their respective windows.

"That fire is cover for their men on the move. Miles and Houston, are you ready? When you start shooting give it the most you can. With your fire, Paris and I will run out uphill into the trees. Then we will give those across the river some additional excitement to think about. Ready?"

Both men nodded, rose, and started firing from their repeater rifles as quickly as they could squeeze the trigger, jack another round into the firing chamber and pull again. The sound in the small wooden room was deafening.

Will nudged Paris who opened the door, stood, and started running for the forest. Will followed. One bullet hit the ground right between Wills feet as he ran uphill. When they got to the forest line, Will moved several feet towards Tricorn's camp then stopped behind a tree.

"Look, they are going to try and cross the dam. You get the first guy out of the trees; I can see two others still taking cover."

Paris aimed and hit the man running toward the dam. Another man had started out after the lead attacker but he stopped and turned once he saw the spearhead go down.

Now bent down on his knee to brace his elbow, Will aimed his Winchester at the man who had turned back for cover. He did not miss. Two down.

Will then focused on two men leaning around trees on the east side trying for better shots at the shed. From his angle now straight across the expanse of the river, Will had an open shot at both. He aimed and hit the man closest to the shed immediately dropping him. He took quick aim at the second who seemed surprised and stunned at his comrade's falling. He should have instinctively moved away from a new line of fire. He didn't. He must have thought the earlier men crossing the dam were hit by fire from the shed, not this new angle. Will hit him with the second shot.

"That evens the odds a bit. There are now only two left out there across the river in the woods. Miles and Houston should be able to handle those."

Paris pulled off a second shot just missing another man, one of only two left from the original charge. The fire from across the river died down considerably.

Will rose and touched Paris on the shoulder.

"Don't let up. Keep them pinned in the woods. I'm going to head downriver and see if I can start shooting into their camp and disrupt things."

Paris tried unsuccessfully to grab Will.

"I'm going with you."

"No, you have to stay here and provide protection for the men in the shed. Keep those other guys from crossing the dam."

"If anyone tries to run across the top of the dam, they'd be wide open targets from this spot."

Will turned and began to run downriver hugging the tree line at the river's western edge.

*****

"Those idiots!" Pin had uttered the words with a distinct burn of anger.

Greerson looked up from his position, then skulked back deep down behind some barrels. He was unarmed. Pin had just looked up and over the barrels himself and had now returned behind the barrier.

"I told them to stay in the woods until we started the cover fire and then charge across the dam."

"What happened?" asked Greerson.

"They got stopped on the road across from the shed. They never made it over the dam. Now it looks like at least three of them are shot and the rest are pinned down. Someone is shooting from across the river to help those in the shed."

"Who could be doing that?"

The man called Sniper provided the answer.

"Two men ran out of the shed just before our side started heading across the dam. I think they are the ones who took out the men trying to cross."

"You think they are on the uphill side?"

"That's where they are, alright."

Pin told Sniper, "Keep firing at that shed. I'm heading uphill and I'll try to eliminate the two you saw moving uphill. Maybe we can get this done yet. Greerson, here take my rifle. I won't be needing it in the woods. I'll get close enough to use my handgun."

"I can't shoot."

"Learn, and quick. It may save your life."

*****

Angus Ferguson raised his arm. The ranch owners and hands came to a stop behind him.

Carter McKinnon moved his horse up next to Angus.

"That's a whole lot of gunfire."

Angus squinted up ahead. "This might just work out fine. I don't know who is shooting at who, but we can use it as a distraction while I ride up and toss the dynamite."

"But Angus, I thought the idea was surprise. You've' got people firing guns all over the place."

"Exactly. They're firing at each other, not me. I'll cross the river from the road here on the east side and then ride along the west side just like we planned. I'll head for the dam's gates which are up on that side of the river. They'll be so focused on each other they won't see me coming. All you and the boys will need to do is ride up within range but not too close and cover my escape."

"Sounds risky to me."

"There was always going to be some risk. But I think this will work just fine. The authorities will never know we were involved. The two parties shooting will blame each other and not be able to identify any of us. It's perfect."

Dirk Ferguson now rode up next to the two men in front.

"Pa, let me ride up with the dynamite."

"No, I'm the one who set this all in motion, I'll do it."

"Pa, I'm a better rider, got a faster horse, and can throw the sticks of dynamite farther. Plus, you would be better guiding the men with the cover fire and getting them all back down to Truckee before anyone figures out who we are."

Angus did not respond immediately.

"You know I'm better suited. I've seen the gates. I know exactly where to throw the dynamite."

Still Angus hesitated.

"The boy might be right Angus," added McKinnon.

After another silent pause, Angus finally looked directly at Dirk. "Okay, you can make the ride. But you drive hard in there, throw the sticks and get out of there pronto. Got it? No stopping to do any shooting. You ride in, throw, and ride out."

Dirk smiled, "I'll do just as you say Pa."

Angus then turned his horse to face the men behind him.

"Here's what we're gonna do. We ride across the river. Dirk is going to take the dynamite ahead riding fast. We'll pull up behind their camp, but not too close. As soon as Dirk throws the dynamite, we shoot over the heads of those in that camp to keep them low. Dirk rides out and we head home. Any questions?"

None of the riders raised any queries.

Angus leaned back to open his saddlebags. "Good, Dirk, here are two sticks. Light the fuses once we are across the river and take off. We'll be close behind you.

*****

Will stopped. He listened. He had moved downriver and was now directly uphill from the Von Schmidt camp.

"Hold it there cowboy."

Will started to turn.

"Nope. Don't move. You're gonna drop that rifle right now. If you don't drop it easily, you're a dead man. So, do it now."

Will heard the distinctive sound of a hammer being pulled back. Will dropped the Winchester.

"Now you can turn."

Will spun slowly on his heel. Before him was Pin sporting the distinctive tricorn hat. He stood uphill from Will. His six gun was leveled at Will's chest. Pin held it quite steady.

"Well now cowboy, still feel like giving instructions on how to handle guns?"

Will's mind raced for some solution while he forced himself to appear calm.

"Still have my own six gun here at my side."

"You're welcome to make a move for it. Doubt you live to touch it."

"Might be quicker than you think."

"No one is quicker than someone pulling the trigger of a cocked gun."

Will also knew that it had not been long since his sidearm had been dunked in the river as he and Powder crossed. The gunpowder was probably still good and wet. No telling if any of his cartridges would fire even if by some miracle he pulled fast enough to beat Pin under the circumstances.

At that moment, a rider yelled at the top of his lungs. He and his horse were riding hard up the gap between the Truckee's western border and the tree line just beyond. He held two sticks of what looked like dynamite.

Will and Pin both turned to see not only that rider but several others coming up the river. All had their guns drawn.

Sniper rose from his protected position, took aim, and fired at the rider with the dynamite. Dirk Ferguson fell from his horse just as he started his arm motion to throw both sticks in his hand. The dynamite lofted high into the air but landed up the riverbank and away from the river. Dirk did not move. The dynamite was not far from where he landed.

Then came the explosion. It rocked everything and everyone near. Both Pin and Will stumbled and struggled to hold their balance. Pushed by instinct at the barest of opportunities brought on in the blast and confusion, Will pushed off with his downhill foot lunging at Pin and hit him full force with his shoulder. Pin's aim had waivered in the blast just enough for Will to punch his hand with his fist knocking the gun out of his grasp. The pair tumbled to the ground clutching each other rolling downhill in the dust and pine needles. They separated after multiple turns and came up both bent at the waist but balanced looking for the next advantage. The look in each man's eyes was pure hatred. They circled.

Will could see Pin's anger rising to the surface. Watching his plan disintegrate appeared to lift his emotional level from cool confidence to rage. Maybe Will could use the change to his advantage. An overly emotional man might just make mistakes.

Pin sneered, "Sniper knew we were to retake that dam. He saw that dynamite and had to take the shot. I figure you and your rancher friends are here to blow it up."

"Not me nor mine. That's Angus Ferguson and his group," replied Will.

"I don't believe a word from your mouth cowboy."

The quiet in the canyon was broken by a man's shriek. Based on the direction and words that followed, Will knew it was Angus Ferguson. "They shot Dirk! They shot my son. Kill 'em."

The riders behind Ferguson then charged into the Von Schmidt camp. Sniper had shot Dirk Ferguson with his Remington rifle. It was a single load firearm. He did not have enough time to open his breach and insert a new cartridge before the ranchers descended on the camp. Both Sniper and Greerson were shot multiple times.

"Looks like your little army is no longer." Will issued this jab with no small amount of satisfaction.

"This is your doing cowboy, I know it." Pin's scowl became primal.

Pin then drew his belaying pin from the leather holster at his side. To Will it looked like a hard black club. Will rushed forward lowering his head even further as he lunged. The move was a simple attempt to knock his adversary over. But Pin was ready and landed a hard blow on Will's back just off the center of his spine into the abutting hard muscle. Will did hit Pin and both initially went down. But air rushed out of Will's lungs. Pain surged outward and down from the site of the blow. His body went numb. Nothing responded. Pin rose unsteadily but coming into control of his balance. Will lay prone at his feet.

"Now you're gonna feel the real pain cowboy. I've already killed a man with this pin, you're gonna be number two."

Pin lifted his hand held weapon high above his head setting the arc for the next blow.

A shot rang out. Pin's body spasmed momentarily. He caught himself and set his feet to complete the blow to Will's head. Another shot screamed throughout the canyon. This time Pin simply collapsed next to Will.

Will rolled over, the only movement his body allowed. Tentacles of pain still shot down his back into his legs. He looked up. The smell of gunpowder drew his attention to the shooter.

# Chapter Thirty-Four

*Early September 1877*
*Truckee River Dam, CA*

"Beth? Is that you? I can't believe it's you. What are you doing here?"

"I came to warn you that the Nevada ranchers were coming. Are you hurt bad?"

Beth knelt close to Will. He tried to rise but winced and fell back.

"I'll be alright."

"Doesn't look like you are feeling alright to me."

"I'd have been feeling a lot worse if you had not come along when you did."

Will exhaled. The tension of the last few hours streamed from his chest almost as much as the air from his lungs. He tried to push his thoughts from the pain in his back. It didn't work. Another wince crossed his face. Beth watched every move and took in every reaction. He tried to divert her focus. He didn't want her to worry.

"Teaching you to shoot with that Pocket Navy five-shooter has come in handy."

Beth smiled, "That's the second time I've had to shoot someone who was about to kill you. I think I may be leading the competition between us. Maybe I should start carving notches in my gun handle."

"You would do that just to keep reminding me. But I think between the bell tower in Virginia City where the kidnapper had you and with the ride down Bliss's V-flume, I've saved your very pretty little behind more than you have saved mine."

"You must be feeling better to start commenting on my figure."

Will remained flat on his back. He felt no urge to move, but he grinned. She wore her riding outfit of hand-me down clothes and secondhand hat. "Can't really say much about your outfit of old pants and raggedy hat. It's a good thing I know what's inside that getup. I do have a high opinion of the figure under the outfit."

"You now must be faking and looking for sympathy. Your mind is drifting to places that I would not normally associate with someone in pain."

Will sensed some progress with his diversion despite the bolts of agony in the rear of his ribcage.

"I'll be up in a minute. How did you know the ranchers were coming? By the way, your timing was not all that great. You arrive with the news after the shooting starts."

"Got here as quick as I could. Cut across Donner Pass to beat them up the hill. Stayed off the road as I didn't want them to see me up ahead. That's how I ended up on this side of the river only to come across my husband in dire straits."

"I must say I'm glad you arrived when you did. But it would have been nice had you given a guy a little bit more notice."

Beth reached out to touch Will at the side of his face. The motion carried so much more than a simple touch. It stood as a measure of the closeness between the two. She leaned down to kiss him.

A blast rang out. Beth's hat flew off her head. Her blonde trusses flopped across Will's face as her head hit his chest. Then he felt the blood.

"Beth! Beth!" His voice carried pure panic.

She had gone limp. She didn't move. Will tried to feel the outer reaches of her head. It all felt intact, but blood flowed from the opposite side out of his line of sight. He gently gripped both sides of her head to try and turn to see the source of the bleeding. Will was initially afraid to touch her fearing he might cause more damage. But after more than a minute passed, he decided he had to find the source of the bleeding. In addition, there was a shooter out there. They had to move. He lifted her head off his chest. As he rolled her head backwards, Beth's eyes opened and reached up to Will's stricken face.

"What happened?"

"Somebody shot you."

"I did the shooting. Had she not leaned down she'd be gone. You would have lost your friend and partner just as you took mine."

Will turned to see Silas Drummond standing with a long barreled rifle. He opened the breach and started to insert another cartridge.

"I missed that time, but I won't miss again."

He rammed his fist on the bolt action with emphasis. The weapon was again loaded.

"Silas, what are you talking about?"

"You took Ida Murray from me!"

The words came as almost a scream.

Will tried to block his own discomfort as well as his panic for Beth and process what he now heard. Beth was alive, but bleeding. He had to get her to a doctor. But Silas now stood as a clear impediment to any notion of leaving right away. Will's thoughts ran at a speedy clip. Silas seemed to have claimed he had a relationship with a lady, Ida Murray, who had tried her best to kill Will almost a year ago. Surprised at this information, Will did not have any idea Silas Drummond even knew Ida. His only interaction with Silas had been when the two had exchanged heated words during a demonstration Silas led in Carson City. Will had agreed to help Duane Bliss find the person responsible for blowing up his sawmill in Glenbrook Nevada mainly because that same person had caused injury to Beth in the blast. Silas had led his protest group to Bliss's office door at a time when he and Will had been talking. In the end, while Ida Murray had not been the one who set the first explosion that destroyed one of the sawmills, she approved of the act and was going to kill Will and Paris to make sure another bomb would destroy a second of Bliss's sawmills. The original blast had caused a severe injury to Beth's shoulder necessitating the ride down a very cold V-flume on a large cut timber. Both Will and Beth had almost drowned in the process.

"Ida Murray was going to blow up Bliss's sawmill."

"She wouldn't," came Silas's immediate reply.

"She admitted it to both Paris and me just before she was going to kill us both."

"You are a liar. You will have to answer before our maker when you meet him real soon."

"Silas, that is the absolute truth. She was going to kill both Paris and me. We had no choice."

"You always had a choice. You didn't need to hunt her down."

"She hunted us. She also admitted taking shots at me and killing Joe Ascona."

"You speak with the Devil's tongue. Ida would never do anything like that. You will pay through eternity."

"Ask Paris, he'll confirm what she said just before the shooting. She admitted to it all. She said she was committed to saving the forest."

"Ida would never take those kinds of steps. Only I could have done something like that."

Stunned, Will could not hide his confused look. Then it hit.

"You're the one who has been shooting the dam employees."

The truth now out, Silas did not seem constrained to dispute.

"Yes, and I started the shooting today too. Those trigger happy thugs in Von Schmidt's camp didn't know where the first shots came from. But they were only too happy to start the war they had been itching for. As for me, I know what my fate will be. But I think I've now raised enough focus to finally protect Tahoe as one of God's greatest gifts. I'm headed for hell, but I'm taking you with me."

Silas slid his left hand down the length of the elongated barrel of his large rifle. He started to raise it to aim at Will with Beth still on his chest.

Then again, the silence of the forest was broken with the sound of a gunshot. Silas dropped his rifle and clutched his chest. He waivered, then his legs buckled and he landed on his knees. Staring at Will he fell face first in the dirt.

"I don't feel good about shooting someone in the back, but if he had lifted his rifle any further to aim at you both, he might have still pulled the trigger even after being shot."

It was Dale Paris. He walked up to Will and looked down.

"This is getting to be a habit. You keep getting into difficult positions and I keep bailing you out."

"I'll thank you later. For now, help me with Beth. She needs a doctor."

"I don't need a doctor"

"But you are bleeding."

"My head really hurts, but I want you to take me home."

Will lifted up as best he could at the same time cradling Beth's head.

"Let me take a look. I need to see what's bleeding."

Paris then bent down, "Let me help. Maybe it would be good if you both could stand."

Paris cupped his hands around Beth's waist and firmly lifted her up until she was stable on her feet.

"I feel dizzy."

Paris kept his hands on her waist until she stopped wavering.

"That's better. I'm feeling more stable now."

At the same time, Will rolled onto his side looking away from the other two so that they could not see another wince. He swallowed a groan. Next on to his knees and to his feet. It hurt all through his chest each time he took a breath, but he now stood.

Beth turned and reached for her husband. Only too happy to oblige, Will clasped his wife in a complete embrace. After a moment he pushed her out to arm's length.

"Okay, turn around so I can see the back of your head."

Beth slowly spun around. Will kept his hands on her shoulders.

"Yep, you have a score across the back of your head. It's not deep. But the bullet probably gave you a pretty good wallop as it passed by. Another inch and you would have been a goner."

"It's weird. I know the bullet passed the back of my head, but it is the front that hurts."

Will took the scarf from around his neck and wrapped it low at the back of Beth's skull and lifted it forward to a knot above her forehead.

"There, that should hold until we can get you to Tahoe City. You think you can ride?"

"I can ride. What I'd like to do right now more than anything is to go home."

"Let's ride to Tahoe City first and see the doctor. Maybe we can ask Mr. Paris here to pay for another night in a hotel and we can head home tomorrow."

"I'd be glad to pay for another night. I think Mr. Hopkins and the CPRR would be most happy that we not only found the man who shot their employees, but we also stopped the effort to block their logging operations."

Beth shot Paris a thankful look, "You might be right, a night in a proper bed would be wonderful."

Then Beth turned back to face her husband.

"There was another reason I came here personally."

Will looked puzzled. "Another reason other than the ranchers coming to destroy the dam?"

"Yes. Sam Grande has filed some Federal Court motion in Carson City. He filed it two days ago. You must be in court in thirteen days. You're one of what he calls an interested party. So is the Carson Cattlemen's Association, the city of San Francisco, the railroad and everyone else with water rights down the Truckee. As an owner of property abutting the river, you have an interest. So, we have to go home back to the ranch soon."

"Sam has everyone coming to the same courtroom?"

"That's what the note said."

"Angus Ferguson just lost his son. The railroad is going to be real upset about this little gun battle. Von Schmidt is going to be upset he didn't get his dam back. And I have no idea what Duane Bliss and the others are going to think. But the collection of all those folks in one hearing is going to be more than interesting."

# Chapter Thirty-Five

*Late September 1877*
*Federal Court- Carson City, NV*

"Hear Yee, Hear Yee. All rise. Those having business before the court come to order. The Honorable Edgar Winters Hillyer presides."

The black robed elderly judge entered the courtroom using an entry door hidden from most views.

"Good morning to you all. Please be seated."

Samuel Grande sat alone at one of the two large tables arranged before the Judge for counsel representing parties. Other lawyers representing various interests in the Truckee River water flow sat in chairs rimmed around the courtroom just inside the bar. There were too many other lawyers attending to represent clients to sit at counsel table. Only Sam Grande sat there today. Sam looked straight ahead as he took his seat.

"Mr. Grande, I suppose it is left to you at this point."

"Good morning your honor."

"Counsel, I am interested to hear what you might have to say at this juncture. You elected to use an intriguing tactic when we started yesterday. You deferred your initial argument on your motion for an emergency injunction offering only your brief. I have seen that done in a trial setting, but not when it is a motion under consideration. A bold move."

Grande did not respond. He sensed the judge would continue. He did.

"Yesterday I listened to each and every one of the other parties interested in the water coming out of Lake Tahoe. Those interests ranged from the railroad to the city of San Francisco to sawmills in Nevada. You brought us all here with your motion, are you going to tell me what you think I should do?"

"Your honor, I deferred my initial comments, as I know from prior experience in this courtroom, you would have thoroughly read my motion and papers. I have laid out the circumstances the court faces there in writing. I saw no need to repeat a great deal of what I already said in those pages."

"I appreciate and welcome the lack of repetition. And yes, I did read your papers thoroughly. However, I would encourage you to elaborate on your conclusion. I found your approach different from all the other parties. In both their briefs and all the argument, I heard yesterday it seems to me that the other parties find it difficult to consider anything but their respective client's self-interest. While I might be mistaken, I understood your approach to be somewhat different."

Grande rose. He began to walk back and forth behind counsel table.

"Your honor, I stand here representing the Carson Valley Cattlemen's Association, a collection of men who own ranches in the Carson Valley. While the Truckee River is not a source of water for their resident properties further to the south, their herds are currently based on what is commonly called the Purcell Ranch owned by Will Toal. That ranch borders the Truckee River and Mr. Toal does have riparian rights to draw water from the Truckee. However, if the snow pack this year finally reaches normal limits, those ranchers and their herds will return south to the Carson Valley. In view of that circumstance, I felt my clients should offer a more objective and maybe a more comprehensive solution to the problem facing the Court."

"You certainly have provided a plan that appears to address a broader scope of action. But I need more detail from you counsel. Your papers begin to outline this plan, but you must elaborate."

"My plan is to keep things as simple as possible. The border between the states of California and Nevada split Lake Tahoe with about sixty-five percent of its surface water in California and thirty-five percent in Nevada. My plan starts out with the simple recommendation that this court order the flow out of the Truckee be parceled out on a pro rata basis according to that split in the surface."

"But Mr. Grande, while your split sounds wonderfully logical, what flow are we to split? Is it the remainder of water that would flow over the five foot of elevated reservoir now resting on the original level of the lake or is it something else?"

"My suggestion your honor is that the flow should be defined as the volume of water that exited down the Truckee before the dam was built. That amount would vary according to the season, but the current superintendents of the dam have kept records and we know what that seasonal flow is."

"And what about control of Mr. Von Schmidt's dam? Does he not have rights to take water?"

"He does your honor, but only for the reasonable use on the properties that actually abut the river. He does not have the right to supply the entire city of San Francisco!"

Grande let his very ample voice rise to a level that carried minor reverberations in the high-ceilinged courtroom. He continued.

"The city has no rights to the water whatsoever and Mr. Von Schmidt has rights only to that which could be reasonably used on his very small parcels."

In keeping with a common approach in Federal Court judges, Hillyer continued to ask pointed questions almost reverting back to the Socratic method of instruction used in most if not all law schools.

"But what if California wants to use some of their allotment under what I will call the Grande Plan to supply San Francisco?"

Grande knew questions could come from any corner of the issues under consideration. But he was prepared for this one.

"If California sees fit to use part of its sixty-five percent allotment to send to San Francisco, then so be it. But the California Legislature has ruled that the flow is to be controlled by the Donner Boom and Lumber Company, not Mr. Von Schmidt. If the legislature wanted to provide for part of that flow to be routed to San Francisco, they have had two chances to say so but have clearly stopped short."

Grande watched for a reaction. He detected a hint of bemusement on the Judge's face. He took that as a sign that the Judge agreed. Cutting out any flow to San Francisco was a critical part of Sam's strategy. That Judge Hillyer might want to protect local Nevada's rights seemed to fall in line with the same strategy.

Grande pressed the point home.

"Mr. Von Schmidt drawing such a volume for the city could conceivably invade Nevada's percentage of the flow. That is patently unreasonable. The properties he owns adjacent to the river itself are minuscule parcels. Any reasonable draw to supply those parcels would be minute in the overall assessment of what needs to be done here. Mr. Von Schmidt should be limited to a diminutive draw based solely on what is needed for those two small parcels."

"I would tend to agree on that point. I cannot see any basis for San Francisco to draw water above and beyond other interests along the river when they do not even own a basic riparian right."

"The key your honor is that thirty-five percent of Nevada's natural flow be left unaffected twenty-four hours a day. The Donner Boom people cannot block the entire flow to then let a rush of water down the river to carry their logs. Thirty-five percent must flow to Nevada at all times."

"But what if there is no water collected in the reservoir as you call it, the five foot elevated store above the natural water line?"

"Your honor, that extra five feet creates an immense amount of water on a body twenty-two miles long by eleven miles wide. If they let out the equivalent of the natural flow under my definition, the flow would last for years even without any further snow."

A silence followed. Judge Hillyer thumbed through pages deep in thought. Sam knew from experience that there were times you kept your mouth shut. He had the strong sense he was winning the battle. If you are winning, you keep quiet in a courtroom setting. If it looks like you will not prevail, you never stop talking. You have nothing to lose.

Judge Hillyer finally looked up from the documents on his elevated desk.

"Counsel, I am going to generally agree with your plan. I will be ordering a more detailed study as to what and how to define what you describe as the natural flow. But I will sign an order that the volume of water coming out of the Truckee River is to be split between the states on a sixty-five to thirty-five percent basis. Mr. Grande, I am going to ask you to draw up the order and I will sign it."

## Chapter Thirty-Six

*Early December 1877*
*Carson Valley, NV*

Thin winter clouds floated high in a depthless blue sky moving slowly as if unsure of their intended destination. Will leaned against the weather toned wooden pillar holding up the ramada at the corner of his ranch house. He looked west at the Sierras. The peaks were covered with snow so white the color pierced his eyes under the sun's reflection. For some reason, the normal winds had abated. Life stood momentarily still. The mountains offered a majestic peace, a certainty of existence. Those tall walls of stone had been here before him, and they would be there after he had gone. For Will, there was a strange sense of comfort in their continuity. He hoped his land and ranch could last beyond his years too. That would depend on Luke and Sean.

"Come sit."

Will turned. Beth sat on the bench at the center of the porch. She patted the open space on the simple bench big enough only for two. It had no back, but it rested next to the outer wall of the house beneath the extended roof over the porch. This same bench had been the site of several of the most significant conversations in their joint lives. The oversized stool was a remnant of Will's original shed built as he started the ranch. It looked out of place, an afterthought. But he and Beth always gravitated to this spot when the conversation meant something. Neither would ever suggest it be removed.

"Looking at the mountains again? You always seem to be fixated on those crests."

Will sat and placed his hand into Beth's lap. She grasped his leathered palm in between both of her hands and settled back for his answer.

"There is something about those mountains. Something special. They're solid, constant, there for all to see just as they are. But there's a magnificence about 'em. Having them at the border of our ranch is like hanging a great painting on the wall of our house."

The porch faced east, out of the path of the ever present winds that regularly blew down those same slopes. The Sierras were out of view as the pair sat under the roof.

Beth gazed across the flat horizon reaching out from the house and mused, "For me, the mountains protect our backs. They rise up so quick at the edge of the property it's like a natural fort wall back there. We don't have to worry much about what might come up from behind, only have to keep an eye out here to the east."

Will watched her head move spanning the view. He noticed the bun at the back of her head. The small scar from the bullet wound caused by Silas Drummond usually got lost in her gift of long thick hair. But ladies could be so hard on themselves when it came to looks. Beth collected her wavy lengths into a bun more often than not now to make sure the little bald spot was properly out of sight. He smiled at himself for being shrewd enough to keep this thought to himself.

"What are you smiling at?"

"Oh, nothing." He had to divert this quick or he might fail to avoid revealing his thoughts which while innocent at his end would be read by Beth as an unwanted focus on some glaring imperfection. For Will, she had no imperfections. So, he reverted to his reflections on the Sierras.

"I had been looking at the snow. Gave a little thanks for what looks like a heavy snowpack this year. Maybe the drought will finally end."

"That would be something to give thanks for. Appropriate here on a Sunday. The last couple of years have been so hard."

Will nodded his agreement.

"The decision to drive the herds north ended up working out well. Water got released from the dam. There was enough to keep the cattle going until we were able to sell the steers at the end of summer. The condition of the herds was not great, but all of the ranchers from Carson Valley made enough to get through the winter."

Beth did not move. Will could not tell if she was just resting or deep in thought. He looked out across the flat ground to the east.

"And we've had enough rain here in the valley this month to sustain the heifers we drove back from the north through the winter. Should be able to replenish the herds by next spring."

Beth leaned her head back against the wall and closed her eyes. She did so carefully so as to not irritate the wound at the back of her skull that was still healing. She then spoke as if she had reached some conclusion.

"Water is the key, isn't it?"

Will leaned back and rested his head just as Beth had done. He decided to finish the thought that had struck him as he admired the Sierras.

"That snow will ultimately melt and refill Tahoe. The Truckee will flow to our ranch in the north. The snow will also supply the Carson River and its flow to ranch here in the valley further south. We can get back to raising beef and horses and use either ranch as needed."

"So, is Bliss going to be able to build his little railroad spur?" Beth asked.

"Word is that he will. Deal has been struck with the railroad. I heard that their plan to make Tahoe a protected zone ran into trouble in Washington D.C. But I never got the idea that Bliss was too worried about that. His focus centered on getting his tourists up to Tahoe and then on to Glenbrook."

"How does he intend to get them from Tahoe City to Glenbrook?"

"He's going to build a boat. A big one. Fancy too. Fancy enough to get San Francisco's high society interested to travel all the way to the new hotel he's building. They're going to remove the sawmills from the harbor and put in some big new fancy place he says he'll call the Glenbrook Inn."

"Maybe it will be too fancy for him to let us come up and stay like he has the last couple of years."

"Not sure, but Duane is not someone to forget what I did for him. I think we will still be able to visit here and there."

"What about San Francisco? Are they going to get any of Tahoe's water."

"Bliss told me that Von Schmidt has basically given up. After the judge's ruling, he finally figured he was never going to get any water from Tahoe down to San Francisco."

"So, the railroad wins?"

"Not really, they will get their new lands to lumber, but eventually they will change to coal just like to railroad lines in the east.

"So, who wins?"

Will gave this a bit of thought.

"Tahoe wins."

Beth grinned. "What makes you say that?"

Will did not answer immediately. Reflecting again on his thoughts of the range and alpine lake that bordered his world he decided to go one step further.

"The Lady of the Lake should keep going just like the mountains surrounding her shores. The mountains and the water are the constants."

Beth now moved her head along the wall until it came to rest on Will's shoulder.

"I have my own constant."

Will now reached his arm around Beth's shoulders and pulled her close.

"I have mine too."

# Fact From Fiction

If you have read any of the other books in this series, you'll know I have always admired how author Steve Berry weaves wonderful tales around historical events. At the end of his books, he always includes a section acknowledging his fictional additions but also points out the often-surprising facts. So, here is my humble attempt to emulate Mr. Berry. Below I try to identify some of the facts and events in my story which are nonfiction.

**Prologue**
There are several sources that reflect on the unintentional result of setting the California State Boundary along a length stretch of the $120^{th}$ longitude which runs virtually down the middle of Lake Tahoe. For the background as to Freemont's initial exploration and involvement in the California State Constitutional Convention which did take place at the Colton Hall in Monterey, CA, I have drawn liberally from Professor Scott Lankford. See *Tahoe Beneath the Surface* by Scott Lankford. Sierra College Press. 2010. The story here of how the argument was made at the Convention to set the California border is purely mine. However, the history of how the Convention was deadlocked over California entering the Union as a slave or non-slave state was real as represented. The arguments about whether to enter with borders all the way to the Rockies or sliced in half were also made and heated arguments followed at the convention.

**Chapter 1**
A dam was constructed across the Truckee River. Work was supervised by Col. A.W. Von Schmidt between 1865 and 1870. Von Schmidt

was a European trained engineer who emigrated to California during the Gold Rush. Von Schmidt was involved in several large engineering projects in the nascent budding metropolis of San Francisco including the cable car system. But he came into real notoriety when he started working for the Spring Valley Water Company run by George Ensign. Von Schmidt was instrumental in creating the Pilarcitos Creek dam and diversion to the supply city's need for water. However, beginning about 1865 Von Schmidt tried to break the Spring Valley monopoly by bringing water west from Lake Tahoe. He obtained approval from the City Counsel of San Francisco to construct an elaborate system of tunnels and pipelines to bring water across the entire state. The water was to have originated from Lake Tahoe and diverted via a dam across the Truckee River.

Von Schmidt had two goals: 1.) to break the Spring Valley monopoly, and 2.) to provide a long term solution to the future water needs. San Francisco needed more and more water. The Pilarcitos project did not produce a sufficient amount for the projected growth. This state of affairs would come to haunt the city in 1906 following the famous earthquake. As devastating as the quake was, the damage from the fire which ran unchecked due to lack of sufficient water system was catastrophic.

Von Schmidt was funded with $20 million dollars in 1865 money (approximately $200 million at today's value). He actually built the dam across the Truckee. It took him five years to get it done. But Von Schmidt had numerous adversaries. Papers in the State of Nevada called the project "The Tunnel of Doom" as mentioned in the story. More importantly, as will be discussed further below, Von Schmidt ran right into a direct confrontation with the Big Four. See *Best of Tahoe, Looking Back* by Professor Scott Lankford 2013.

Von Schmidt's failure to break the Spring Valley Water Company's monopoly would leave San Francisco at the mercy of a company in which many of the city's wealthy elite invested reaped benefits from unchallenged prices for years. For a fascinating history of the politics of San Francisco's water supply, see *Spring Valley Water Company-Historical Essay* by Libby Ingalls in *Found SF Digital Archives*.

Stanford and the barons of the Central Pacific Railroad had extensive Federal grants to lumber the pine forests along the western slopes of Tahoe. But they needed to transport them to the mills down in the Donner Pass area. The CPRR was alarmed at the construction of the dam which could interrupt the Truckee as the channel they had come to use for that transportation. Stanford and Hopkins incorporated a company called the Donner Boom and Lumber Company to undertake management of the flow of waters down the Truckee. The 1870

California Water Act gave the Donner Boom company rights to build another dam to make sure they had control of the water's flow even if they had to build it right next to the dam Von Schmidt had built. The barons made used their extensive political connections to obtain a "franchise" for the use of the Truckee River's flow. The act was approved April 4, 1870.

Von Schmidt did lose his battle with the railroad barons shortly after 1870. Instead of building a second dam, the Donner Boom company took over control of Von Schmidt's. Von Schmidt undertook a contract to accurately survey the eastern border of California. I was not able to determine if his efforts on this survey had anything to do with an ongoing fight with CPRR, but it was definitely the result of his fixation on the division of Tahoe. He completed his survey in 1872. He constructed small 4-5 foot obelisk monuments intermittently along the border. Only a few survive today. However, later surveys done with more modern equipment showed Von Schmidt was off by as much as 1,200 feet as he reached California's border with Arizona. See *1872 Von Schmidt Survey*, Sierra College Press Journal Fall 2009 vol. 2 no. 2.

The political, legal and environmental battles lasted from 1865 to 1915 when the Federal Government finally stepped in to mediate the disparate interests involved. A fascinating detailed history of the Tahoe watershed and the legal battles was outlined at the direction of the Federal Government in 1909. The study virtually reprints key portions of the 1870 California Water Act to highlight the fundamental origin of the very complicated legal mess created by the various claims to the *ownership* of the Truckee's waters as opposed to the *flow*. The history, research and collection of water data was done as background for a huge Federal analysis in 1909 to assess whether Tahoe or any of the surrounding alpine lakes could be used as part of a reservoir project for San Francisco city water. See the *Report of the Possible Water-Power*

*Development of the Watershed of the Truckee River Above Clarks Station, NV* by O.C. Merrill for the United States Department of Agriculture pp. 7-11 (hereinafter referred to as *Truckee Watershed Report of 1909*).

**Chapter 2**

Rainfall records for the Tahoe-Truckee watershed extend back only as far as 1870. Based on data accumulated for the U.S. Department of Agriculture, the average annual rainfall in the mountains surrounding Lake Tahoe is 43 inches. In 1874 that number dropped to 19 inches. The years on either side of 1874 were not much better. See *Truckee Watershed Report 1909* p. 14. I have moved the timing of this drought to 1877 to fit the timeline of the story here. The flow undoubtedly did not drain out of Tahoe's rim into the Truckee that year. The lack of outflow has happened multiple times over the last 100 years the last of which occurred in the multi-year drought running through the year 2014. See *Drought Hits Lake Tahoe, Truckee River*. Article in the Reno Gazette Journal published Sept. 29, 2014.

**Chapter 3**

As discussed in this chapter, Von Schmidt did try to get the San Francisco city council to issue an additional ten million dollars in bonds, however, that occurred before 1871. See *Best of Tahoe, Looking Back* by Professor Scott Lankford 2013. With the passage of the California Water Act of 1870, Von Schmidt's efforts to build the water delivery system back to the coast had been scrapped. Any representation of Von Schmidt pushing for bond issuances in 1877 are pure fiction to fit the story.

A.J. Bryant was indeed the mayor of San Francisco in 1877. He presided over a very tough time for the city. As represented in the story,

San Francisco was experiencing a serious economic downturn in 1877. While there was no request for bond issuance from Mr. Von Schmidt, the city was not doing well.

As mentioned above in the section referenced to Chapter 1, the activities and influence of the Spring Valley Water Company was as represented. Von Schmidt did enter the world of San Francisco water systems as an engineer for this company in the early 1860's. He was a key figure in the planning and initial construction of the Pilarcitos Dam north of the city. Spring Valley was the most influential and at times sole supplier of water to the city from 1860 to 1920. One historian, acknowledging the influence of the robber barons, described the company's relationship with the city as "fraught with corruption, land speculation, favoritism towards the moneyed elite" all of which generated "widespread ill will from the general population." See *Spring Valley Water Company – Historical Essay* by Libby Ingalls in *Found SF Digital Archives*. The same article chronicles the financial odyssey of the company's ownership. That the company eventually ended up as an asset on the personal balance sheet of William Sharon as represented in the story is also accurate. For more on William Sharon and his business activity under the umbrella of the Bank of California, see my book *Silver City Reckoning*, the second novel in the Will Toal series.

Pilarcitos Dam during its circa 1866

**Chapter 4**

The Dangberg Ranch house still exists in the South Carson Valley. I have been to the house which was once headquarters for the thirty thousand acre ranch. It is now used to host local historical presentations out on its lawn. The Cottonwoods still provide shade. The breadth and scope of Henry Dangberg's operation are still visible. Even today one can see the scope of the ranch's organization. Along with the main house, the rotation of pastures, and the differentiation between crops, the ranch was a shining example of forethought. The house itself reflects the same approach. Its kitchen with special eating room adjacent in the back for the hands (looked like it could seat twenty employees easily), to the workshops and food processing room, all carried the mark of planning and execution. Dangberg's ranch was self-contained, self-sustained, and definitely "precise."

**Chapter 5**

Whether by reason of the barrage of legal fees imposed on their opponent Von Schmidt or by way of lawsuits pointing to the authority of the 1870 Water Act, Von Schmidt abandoned control of the dam he'd built and conceded its operation to the Donner Boom and Lumber Co. However, that took place shortly after the act in 1870 and not as per the time frame here. I have obviously changed that timeline to fit the story.

The Stanford Mansion in Sacramento still stands. Now the Leland Stanford Mansion State Historic Park, the house museum is also still used for rare formal California state social occasions. In 1987 the mansion was also declared a National Park. Built for merchant entrepreneur Shelton Fogus, the Stanford's bought it in 1861 for $8,000 at the onset of his term for governor. He kept it but allowed subsequent governors to use if for official entertainment functions after he left office in 1863.

For years subsequent governors used Stanford's office when he was not in residence. That was often as Stanford later spent most of his time in San Francisco. The mansion is where Stanford's only son, Leland Jr., was born. Leland Jr.'s death of typhoid in Florence, Italy sent both Stanford and his wife into a mental down spiral for several years. Their grief culminated in the donation of their Palo Alto estate which became Stanford University dedicated to the memory of their deceased son and only child.

Hopkins would leave this fictional meeting of August 1877 and head south as part of his duties for the Southern Pacific Railroad. He died on March 28, 1878, aboard one of his company's trains in Yuma, AZ. As indicated in the story, he was in fact on a long range inspection of the company rail lines when it happened. His own mansion on Knob Hill (see below) was not yet finished at the time of his death. He left an estate worth over $1B in today's dollars, to a single adopted son, and a wife, Mary. Mary would undertake completion of the monstrous mansion on Knob Hill soon to marry the developer of the project, Edward Searles, and disinherit their son. The probate suit filed by the adopted son, Timothy Hopkins, was one of the biggest probate wars in San Francisco Society history. The son lost.

Stanford's home on Knob Hill was over fifty thousand square feet in size (see picture below). The ostentatious elephantine nature of the homes of the railroad barons on Knob Hill only exacerbated the CPRR's unpopularity with the common man. See *Leland Stanford, The Double Life of a Railroad Tycoon,* issued by In60Learning, 2017 p. 16.

The comment about Stanford's lack of conversational talents is also true. As mentioned in the chapter, Leland Stanford was not the chatty type. The reference to visiting dignitaries finding him virtually non-communicative is also true. One British dignitary had been granted an "audience" after traveling across the Pacific from the Orient. He spent almost an hour in Stanford's office trying to generate a conversation. Stanford never responded to the man until he stood to leave. As the dignitary move to exit, Stanford said, "Nice visit, we should talk again." See *The Big Four* by Oscar Lewis. Alfred A. Knopf, Inc. 1939, pp. 3-5 Section 1 on Stanford.

Hopkins Mansion Knob Hill

Stanford Mansion Knob Hill

Crocker Mansion Knob Hill

Huntington Mansion Knob Hill
(Originally Built by Gen. D.D. Colton)

## Chapter 7

Duane Bliss along with partner Darius Ogden Mills were the main investors in the Carson Tahoe Lumber & Fluming Co. Historians have estimated they took over 750 million board feet of lumber out of the Tahoe Basin between 1870 and 1890. As hinted to in the book, when the Silver mines of Virginia City petered out, Bliss changed his business model to resorts and tourists. His Glenbrook Inn was nationally renowned. It drew the elite of San Francisco society. He would also build the Tahoe Tavern in Tahoe City. More importantly, he built the railroad spur from the Central Pacific RR main transcontinental line up along the Truckee River to Tahoe City. With this spur, even the not so wealthy could travel from San Francisco all the way to Tahoe's shores in a single day. The picture inside the cover of the book depicts the pier Bliss built which acted as the terminus of the spur. That same pier functioned as the dock on which tourists would pick up their passage on the S.S. Tahoe, Bliss's 165' luxury steamship. Passengers would simply exit the train and walk across the pier to board the luxury steamship. See Picture below.

Tahoe City Pier and depot. S.S. Tahoe to the left. Railroad spur to the right.

The 'unholy alliance' between Muir and Harriman needed Bliss to be involved. Bliss wanted his railroad spur. Ultimately, he agreed to carry logs down from Tahoe at a reduced rate in return for use of the CPRR's right of way along the Truckee which they dubiously claimed by way of rights under the 1870 Water Act. See *By Rail, By River, by Lake*-article by Jerry Blackwill as reprinted Moonshine Ink, Feb. 11, 2019.

E.H. Harriman did become involved with Tahoe and the western railroads. However, that did not occur until almost 1900. Harriman cut his teeth buying bankrupt small railroads in the east and turning them around. He became a director of the Union Pacific in 1897. He soon took control over the UP. Harriman became the president of the Southern Pacific Railroad in 1901. His dealings with John Muir took place between that time and 1903. As you can see, I have compressed the timeline radically to fit the story line here.

While the maneuverings of the famous personages did take place, Muir did not press Congress to make a National Forest out of Tahoe and Yosemite until 1889. Bliss did not complete his railroad spur until 1890. Harriman was not a true force within the CPRR until the 1890's. I have altered the timing of the factual political battles over Tahoe's forests purely to enrich the story so as to correspond with the political and legal battles of Tahoe's water which did take place beginning in the 1870's.

It should also be noted that Silas Drummond is fictional as was any meeting between Silas and John Muir of 1877.

## Chapter 8

Washoe Lake has dried up numerous times in history. It doesn't take much of a draught to rob it of its shallow depths. It has a maximum depth of 12 feet even in good years.

## Chapter 9

The character Dale Paris notes that Charles Crocker claimed Collis Huntington felt Mark Hopkins was the most honest man he had ever known. Huntington had said it many times. That a comment like that to come from a hard wizened businessman like Huntington is saying something.

As mentioned above, E.H. Harriman did not become involved with the Central Pacific Railroad until the late 1890's. By that time, the CPRR was securely held as a subsidiary of the Southern Pacific Railroad. Both Stanford and Hopkins would pass from life substantially before Harriman would become involved with their railroad. This is another example as to how I have compressed the timeline here in the interplay of personalities that did not happen in true history. But though the personalities did not all interact, some did. Harriman did work with Muir. Muir was at Tahoe in the late 1870's. Muir worked with Harriman to try to save Tahoe and he, along with Bliss and Baldwin, all played rolls in the drama surrounding the Lake.

**Chapter 12**

Elias Jackson Lucky" Baldwin is a true historical personage. About the time of this story, he had purchased timber rights to over 130,000 acres of old stand forest at the southern end of Lake Tahoe. While his intent might be the subject of some debate, historians have speculated that his aim was to start logging and sell to the railroad whose land under timber license was now cut.

Baldwin was a colorful character whose initial wealth came from stock plays in the Virginia City mines. He was married several times and even shot by two of his ex-wives, one of which shot him in court. But he survived. The fortunate origins of his initial wealth and surviving attacks by his ex-wives led to the legend of his name, "Lucky".

Lucky Baldwin would have been forty-nine years old in 1877. The story accurately reflects a brief synopsis of his early life. He started a dry goods store in Racine, Wisconsin before he was twenty. He moved his family west with three wagons of goods, stopping in Salt Lake City to sell tobacco and whiskey to the brother of Brigham Young reaping thousands of dollars in the deal. He bought a small hotel in San Francisco, turned it over and began speculating in real estate. Ultimately, he built the Baldwin Hotel and Theater which carried a national reputation for luxury. He did buy the Tallac House from Ephraim Clements, but not until 1879, two years after my story here. Tallac House came with over two thousand acres of old growth, but he wanted more. Baldwin wanted a license to lumber more extensive forests to the south. He approached Bliss to join his efforts to block Muir's attempt to create a National Forest. However, those efforts and events did not occur until later in the century. See *Tahoe Beneath the Surface* by Scott Langford p. 142, 151-156. I have moved up Muir's activities to fit the story. All the while, Mr. Baldwin was simultaneously working to develop a parcel of land in Southern California called Rancho Santa Anita. It would become the cities of Arcadia, San Marino, Sierra Madre, and Santa Anita. The later would boast a well know racetrack where Baldwin serviced his penchant for blooded Thoroughbred racehorses under the name of "Santa Anita Stables". He died in 1909 on his ranch in the city of Arcadia.

Lucky Baldwin's Tallac House

Duane Bliss's Tahoe Tavern

## Chapter 13

The Barbary Coast did exist. It was the roughest most unruly point of entry on America's west coast. Hundreds of sailors arrived each day and channeled to the streets of the Barbary. Most would find their hard-earned sea wages 'lifted' by gamblers, women, or thieves. Some thieves plied their trade individually, some plied it in conjunction with others. The Bella Union was one of the Barbary's centerpieces for decades. Below are some pictures of San Francisco Bay circa 1870 full of ships along with the Barbary Coast and Bella Union along with the girls who "inhabited" its confines.

San Francisco Bay circa 1870

The Barbary Coast

The Bella Union

Barbary Girls

The man called Pin claims he got his name from the sailing hardware more specifically called a "belaying pin." These shaped wooden dowels were used to tie down lanyards and ropes attached to sails on square rigged ships. They would be pushed into holes on a bulwark or a special rail made for them called pinrails. The riggings would then be draped over the pins in figure eight loops which when done correctly would lock down the lines yet could be easily undone. Belaying pins could be removed and reset to a desired or required position depending on the rig setting. However, they were sometimes used as weapons in skirmishes among sailors. A picture is below.

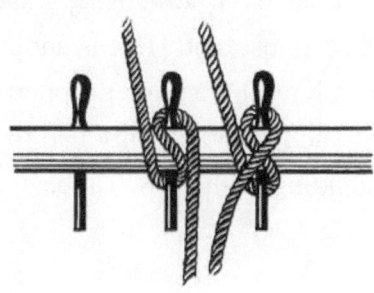

**Chapter 15**

By all accounts Leland Stanford, Jr. was an extraordinary young man. At a very early age, his father and mother included him in all manner of official engagements. By the time he was ten to twelve, his mother began having Leland, Jr. sit in on social and charity functions in place of his father as he did so much better in those settings than did his paternal namesake. In furtherance of his education, shortly before he reached the age of 16, his parents embarked on a European tour with their son. Unfortunately, Leland Jr. contracted typhoid fever in Greece. When the condition worsened, the family traveled to Naples, Rome, then Florence for the most advanced medical care they could find in southern Europe. However, the young man died March 31, 1884 in Florence never reaching the age of 16. Both parents were devastated with the loss of their only child who came to them late in life. Both struggled in extended periods of debilitating grief. After several years, Leland Sr. suggested they do something for "the children of California" and start a university in their son's name. The result: Stanford University was begun on the family's horse breeding farm in Palo Alto, California. See *Leland Stanford The Double Life of a Railroad Tycoon*. In60Learning eBook. 2017.

**Chapter 17**

Bliss had thoughts of building a pier out onto Tahoe to offload his well-heeled passengers in an environment separate from the rustic confines of Tahoe City. He did just that. Here is another picture of the pier Bliss built which shows how the engine dropped off its passengers at the depot 'on the lake' such that they only had to walk across the pier to step onto the ramp leading to the S.S. Tahoe.

Bliss Pier in Tahoe City.
Railroad depot to the left and S.S. Tahoe to the right.

Bliss did meet with John Muir. According to one historian, the two teamed up on a scheme quite similar to the one described in this chapter. Together they pursued having Tahoe designated as a National Park. The pair enlisted the assistance of E.H. Harriman to push the plan in Washington. As mentioned above regarding Chapter 12, this effort also involved Lucky Baldwin and his pursuit of logging licenses. With the combination of Muir's contacts in Congress by and through his relationship with Robert Underwood Johnson, the publisher of Century magazine, and with the influence Harriman could bring to bear on behalf of the CPRR, the plan almost made it out of committee in the House. However, just before the crucial vote for approval to send it to the floor and eventually to the Senate, a story broke exposing the CPRR's plan for a land swap to lumber further sections to the north. Several legislators expressed outrage. The proposal died just short of the necessary votes.

While the outline of this dynamic combination of personalities surrounding the waters and scenery of Lake Tahoe is historically true, most of the events did not take place until the late 1890's, not during the decade of the story. I have compressed the historical timeline not only to fit the story, but also to highlight the forces over the period of 1879 to 1900 that actually aimed to take control over the Tahoe watershed before the Federal Government stepped in. See *Tahoe Beneath the Surface* by Scott Langford p. 142, 151-156.

**Chapter 19**

The original dam across the Truckee River was a combination of rocks, logs, and earth. As Dale Paris comments in the story, it did not have a substantial look about it. The original dam was replaced by a concrete structure in 1915 and modernized to its present form in 1987. I looked high and low for a picture of the original dam but could find only one slide taken in 1907. As opposed to the drought in our story, that year was remarkable for the snow melt and water crested over the old dam. The unique rush of water must have been the reason for the picture. Unfortunately, you cannot see the simplicity of the structure as the flow completely covers it.

1907 Picture of water "going over crest of old [Truckee] dam"

Picture of the current Truckee Dam.

## Chapter 21

Three Croatian immigrants started the New World Coffee Saloon in 1849 serving sailors and ocean travelers coffee and grilled fish close to the wharves. In 1871 a sixteen year old Croatian transplant by the name of John Tadich was hired as a bartender. When the grill and saloon moved to the intersection of Commercial and Leidesdorff at the center of the city's main market section, he moved with the business. In 1887 he bought the establishment, giving it his name. Later moved to its current location at 220 California Street, The Tadich Grill continues as one of the most recognized restaurants in San Francisco today. It is the oldest continuous running eating establishment in California. *See the Tadich website for the grill's history.*

## Chapter 24

Most of the Sharps rifles manufactured during the Civil War came from the C. Sharps & Co. Christian Sharps and his master armorer Richard Lawrence were responsible for the design. Originally based in

Philadelphia, the company moved to Hartford and later to Bridgeport, Connecticut. As explained in the chapter, original versions used percussion caps. Towards the end of the war, the Union Army administration agreed to issue breech loading versions with rim fire cartridge ammunition. For some time, the army hierarchy resisted not only the breech loading cartridge versions but other multiple magazine rifles like the Spencer all on the basis a fear of 'over usage' by their troops. The worry was that their men would fire too frequently and run out of ammunition early in a battle. Logistics of the time were difficult and made supply a constant concern. But what a difference rapid fire weaponry would have made. The Sharps came in calibers of .52, .50, .45, .44, and .40. They had varied barrel lengths too. The heavier caliber and longer barreled versions were renowned for their accuracy and reliability. They were prized sniper weapons and made famous by the Union's unit called Berdan's Sharpshooters. See *From Musket to Metallic Cartridge: A Practical History of Black Powder Firearms* by Oyvind Flatnes. Crowood Press, Limited 2014. Pp 123-5. It is also true that Sharps ammunition was not usable in a Remington Rolling Block, also manufactured as a long barreled rifle used by snipers and buffalo hunters following the war. The reference mentioned in the story regarding the distinctive design of the hammers on the two guns is accurate.

**Chapter 25**

E.H. Harriman's amazing rise in life was as described in the chapter. Smallish, he was almost a self-taught banker-financier-corporate leader. He became interested in transportation after working on a railroad owned by his father in law, William Averell, who was a banker himself. After turning that small railroad around, he did it again on another rail system. This time Harriman personally organized the financing to buy this new railroad and turned it around for a handsome profit too. He was then asked to join the board of the then failing Union Pacific Railroad. Again, he organized financing of which he was a part of to actually buy the UP. Once involved, he became near obsessed with the details of all phases of the company and eventually became its president and CEO. He then moved to purchase the Southern Pacific Company joining the two largest rail systems in America. He was not yet fifty. See *The Life and Legend of E.H. Harriman* by Maury Klein, UNC Press, 2011. It was author Klein who notes that Harriman had been described as a 'bantam rooster' as mentioned in the story.

But as indicated above in Chapter 17, Harriman's involvement with the Southern Pacific RR (Central Pacific RR) did not take place until his consortium purchased it and the merger was approved on September 11, 1896. I have brought him into the story obviously again shortening the timelines involved.

Harriman did sponsor a trip to Alaska accompanied by John Muir. However, that trip would not take place until 1899.

At his death, Harriman owned the Union Pacific RR, the Southern Pacific RR, the Saint Joseph and Grand Island RR, the Illinois Central RR, the Georgia RR, the Pacific Mail Steamship Line, and the Wells Fargo Express Co. He and his wife had seven children, including William Averell Harriman of geopolitical fame before and after WWII.

During Harriman's stage ride up to Tahoe City he muses about being told how the dam would be closed, water levels and pressure then build up and then the gates would be opened to allow a shipment of logs to flow down the river. The description used in the book actually comes from personal observations noted in various accounts of the day. The idea was to create a wall of water that would carry the logs downstream without getting caught on the ever present rocks. It took a team of horses hitched to the gates on Von Schmidt's rudimentary dam to pull them open and start the flow. The dam had a set of "chutes" which were logs laying side by side abutting other logs set vertically into the ground. The inside faces were hewn smooth and greased with animal fat so that the gates would open with as little grind as possible in view of the pressure created by the backed up Tahoe water. Hooks were inserted on the riverbank side of the chutes and that is what the team of horses would be hitched to. Logs up to five feet in diameter and up to sixteen feet long weighing at least ten tons would be sent through the opening and down river as some described it "like a streak of lightning". Other logs would follow "like a drove of sheep". It must have been something to witness. See the historical accounts based on both personal observations and newspaper accounts in the case the Federal Energy Regulatory Commission decision entitled Pyramid *Lake Paiute Tribe of Indians v. Sierra Pacific Power Co.* under the heading of "Past Use and Suitability" at FERC P 61156 (F.E.R.C.) 1979 WL 31581.

The narrow easement along the Truckee River over which Duane Bliss would eventually build the spur from Tahoe City to Truckee

## Chapter 27

The first Federal Courthouse built in Nevada was not completed until 1891. It was and is located at 401 N. Carson Street, Carson City, NV. It originally contained not only the Federal Courthouse, but the Postal Office as well. All Federal operations were ultimately transferred to newer facilities in Reno by 1965. The building is now called the Paul Laxalt Building and houses the offices of Nevada Tourism. The first judge to actually sit in the Federal Building was Judge Thomas Porter Hawley. Again, I have compressed timelines to fit the story. A picture of the building is below. Judge Edgar Winters Hillyer was the presiding Federal Judge in Carson City as if 1877 as found in the story. His background and appointment by President Grant were as described in the story.

For any legal technicians who might have read the book and bear some skepticism as to the fact that any emergency injunction could be filed as represented in this chapter, I would invite them to look at the case of Nevada vs. Donner Boom and Lumber 6App 9th Cir, Appx R 8011(d)-1. Even in the days of the 1870's a filing such as this happened. Also see Federal Rule of Civil Procedure 65(B)(2).

I might also add that the real life Stephen Samuel Grande did meet and ultimately marry Sandra nee Goern under circumstances not altogether unlike the scene represented in this chapter.

## Chapter 28

John Muir and the fictional Silas Drummond assert in their conversation that 'there is a lot going on' revolving around Tahoe. This was essentially quite true.

John Muir did walk around Tahoe in late 1872 to 1873. He did send his letter to Jeanne Carr quoted at the beginning of the book in 1872. While the meeting here in the book between Muir, Harriman and Bliss earlier in Chapter 25 is fictional, Muir did participate in what previously would have appeared as an 'unholy' alliance with E.H. Harriman, Duane Bliss and the CPRR to establish a National Park that would have stretched from Yosemite to north of Tahoe. Hard to believe though it was, Muir knew about the proposed "land swap" which was part of the deal. The CPRR was going to get forested lands north of Tahoe in "replacement" for those bordering the lake that were already logged and played out. Had it not been for an investigative reporter who discovered that the CPRR was plying senators with cash to support the bill, it probably would have passed. It failed to get out of committee by one vote. See *Tahoe Beneath the Surface* by Scott Langford, pp. 142, 151-156.

## Chapter 29

I have found no evidence of any direct meeting between A.W. Von Schmidt and Leland Stanford. The meeting and conversation depicted in this chapter is complete fiction of my own making. However, I include the scene with literary license as a way of highlighting the actual debate that did take place in newspapers and legislative halls during the 1870's and beyond when it came to Von Schmidt's plan to take water from Tahoe. As mentioned earlier, Nevada newspapers called the plan the "Tunnel of Doom".

The Central Pacific Railroad had to be worried about their ability to float logs down a depleted river should Von Schmidt have been successful in his efforts. The city of San Francisco vacillated on Von Schmidt's plan too. They desperately needed additional water supplies, but the right to take water from the Truckee was not clear. The city alternately backed Von Schmidt and would later abandon him. On top of all that, there were draught years as I have indicated in this section above which made the "flow" of the Truckee anything but predictable.

But the most interesting aspect of the overall 'dispute' was the distinguishing argument between *flow* and *ownership* of the water itself. The Donner Boom and Lumber Co. never had ownership rights to the water, only rights controlling the flow. That distinction was clearly affirmed in research done by those involved in the Federal Study done by O.C. Merrill for the U.S. Department of Agriculture. See the *Truckee Watershed Report of 1909* cited in my comments re Chapter 1 in this section above. This distinction would become critical in later Federal Court Proceedings.

However, it needs to be made perfectly clear that A.W. Von Schmidt never hired any gun hands to retake the dam. That is fiction of my own making.

## Chapter 35

To clarify something from this chapter at the outset, there was no such thing as the Carson Valley Cattlemen's Association. That group as Sam Grande's clients, is of my own invention.

As for the ultimate resolution of the Truckee River flows, the seminal case deciding how Tahoe's water would be used did not occur until 1915. That case along with three other "decisions" now govern the flows from Tahoe. The four controlling decisions are as follows:

1. The case of <u>The United States of America, Plaintiff, v. The Truckee River General Electric Company, Defendant</u> 1915. That decision provided for defined flows of water to be released from the new concrete dam structure that replaced the original dam built by A.W. von Schmidt.
2. Newlands Project contract of 1926 between the United States and the Truckee-Carson Irrigation District, among others.
3. The Truckee River Agreement of 1935 again between the United States and the Truckee-Carson Irrigation District and others; and
4. Truckee River final decree entered on September 8, 1944, in the U.S. District Court in for the district of Nevada in the case of <u>United States of America, Plaintiff v. Orr Water Ditch Company, et al., Defendants</u>. In this case the court adjudicated over 700 claims to Tahoe's water flowing out of the Truckee River. The court followed the recommendations of a joint report by California and Nevada water engineers assessing the needs on both sides of the border.

While extraordinarily broad as to the parties affected, the court essentially followed an oversimplified assessment by the engineers who prepared the report. Just as represented in the story via the plan of Samuel Grande, the court in real life agreed with the engineer's recommendation that 65% of the water flow be used for California and 35% for

Nevada. *See the State of California State Water Rights Board Decision D 1056 Adopted Feb. 15, 1962.* The assessment comes strikingly close to awarding the rights of outflow volume based on the demarcations set on Tahoe's surface by the state line. If one looks at how the state line traverses the lake, about 65% of the surface is in California with the remainder in Nevada. Ultimately, it seems to this writer that the simple solution arrived at to finally end the decades of battles was to award water rights based on the original "Freemont error" in setting the border of California such that it split Tahoe almost down the middle.

But in splitting Tahoe with the border between the states, Tahoe did not become San Francisco's "Hetch Hetchy", the future dam of the Tuolumne River and reservoir that still serves as the main source of water for San Francisco and surrounding counties. John Muir once called the damming of the Tuolumne inside what had been a Federal Preserve of the Yosemite forest, an act by ". . . temple destroyers, devotees of ravaging commercialism . . . (who) seem to have a perfect contempt for Nature, and, instead of lifting their eyes to the God of the mountains, lift them to the Almighty Dollar." John Muir, "The Yosemite," Century, 1912, pp. 249-62. Though it took decades of battle, the destiny of Tahoe to become Federally protected ultimately became a reality. It did not become the source of San Francisco's water supply. The "Freemont error" might just have saved the Lady of the Lake as the jewel we now know.

# About the Author

**J.L. Crafts** was raised on the outskirts of a very large city in Southern California. Thankfully, back in those days the very distant outskirts of that city still included open spaces and small ranches. As a young boy he worked wrangling horses on one of those ranches learning to rope, ride and train one of the most magnificent animals our planet has to offer. Those early years created a lifelong connection with, not only horses, but with the west of the 1800's. College led to law school followed by over thirty years of trying cases to juries up and down the state of California. Speaking to juries in a simple directness, he did what he could to elicit facts and arguments wherever possible through stories of life in the saddle and open spaces. He now spends his days creating those stories on the page and enjoys every minute of it.

# *Coming Soon!*

## J.L. CRAFTS

## BREAK OUT
### WILL TOAL SERIES
#### BOOK SIX

A true breakout from the Carson State Prison occurred on September 17, 1871. This newest story in the Will Toal series finds that the escapees include a mix of true historical outlaws along with fictional prisoners holding a grudge against our leading Carson Valley rancher. They burn his home, steal his horse, and come close to murdering his family in their sleep. Will sets off with good friend, Dale Paris, determined to apprehend the escapees. The trail leads south through the badlands of Nevada to the mining fields of California. The historical chase ends in a gun battle on the watery shores of an alpine lake set at the base of Mt. Morrison deep within the Eastern Sierra crevasse called Diablo Canyon. The massive shootout would give its name to the waterway now known as Convict Lake. Will Toal won't stop until he brings those prisoners who threatened his world back to Carson City in chains following their . . . *BREAK OUT*.

**For more information**
**visit:** www.SpeakingVolumes.us

## *Now Available!*

## J.L. CRAFTS
### WILL TOAL SERIES

**For more information
visit: www.SpeakingVolumes.us**

## *Now Available!*

## R.G. YOHO'S
### ADVENTURE WESTERNS

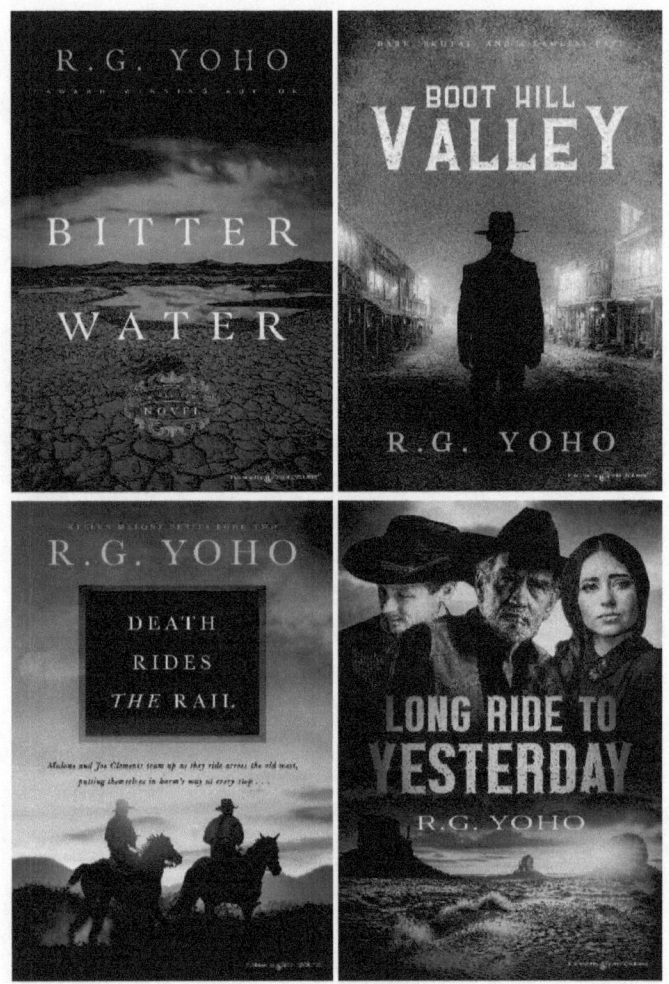

**For more information
visit: www.SpeakingVolumes.us**

www.ingramcontent.com/pod-product-compliance
Lightning Source LLC
LaVergne TN
LVHW041656060526
838201LV00043B/458